THE UNFAVORABLE HEROES

THE UNLIKELY DEFENDERS BOOK 2

LILY SKYY

First Edition: August 2022

ISBN 978-1-957989-06-8 (ebook)
ISBN 978-1-957989-85-3 (paperback)

Published by Books to Hook Publishing, LLC.
www.BooksToHook.com

CONTENTS

PROLOGUE

Charlie Rose was used to being alone. At home, where she was ignored by her parents, who always favored her older sister, as well as at school, St. Bernard High, where she often spent her lunch tending to the plants inside of the greenhouse in full solitude.

She never foresaw this changing—yet, in the span of three weeks, her entire life had turned upside down.

Part of her thought it was a good thing. Part of her liked that she belonged to something and that she was doing some good in the world. You know—saving the planet from aliens and all of that.

And another part of her was excited because she had a crush. A crush on somebody who she was pretty certain liked her back. Kire Hunter.

She had never kissed a boy before, and Kire Hunter had kissed her twice now.

But a lot of the time, she wasn't sure how she felt about her brand-new life. She knew she didn't work well with others and always felt like she could only count on herself to get a job done. Her new 'friends' weren't even the type of people she would've picked out to be friends with herself. Kaos and Trace were the meanest bullies in the school. Amberly was the most popular, but not because people liked her—it was because people feared her, including Charlie, on most days.

It was purely by chance that the five of them formed this group of theirs. The Unlikely Defenders. They all had just happened to be in a cave in the White Forest when the five egg-like structures had floated toward them and given them all a Quintet gift. Then the world suddenly counted on the five of them to protect it from an invasion—or from getting destroyed. So, whether Charlie—who preferred to go by her last name, Rose—wanted to or not, she was forced to spend time with Kire, Kaos, Trace, and Amberly. She had a whole new life and an entirely new way of thinking—especially since the gift she received that night in the cave had come with special... powers. Ones that she was still trying to figure out how to control and master.

First, the Jago creature attacked. Somehow, without the help of Amberly, the other four of the Quintets managed to destroy him. Then came Heno. That one had been a little tricky and resulted in Trace getting a broken leg, but in the end, they had all been able to defeat him, too.

Then their gifts, the only things that kept their group together, left them. It was troubling to Charlie, seeing as Kire's gift—a book called Halo—had given him a vision about Rezin, the toughest, vilest alien creature yet, finding the Quintets and preparing to kill them all. The vision hadn't come true yet, but Charlie wasn't certain how much time they had before it did.

Charlie Rose had never considered herself a fighter. She had never considered herself particularly brave. But when it came to being the defenders of the earth and using her gift, Charlie found that while she knew she couldn't always be braver and stronger, she at least wanted to try. She took her position on the team seriously—whether or not the rest of the Quintets did—and she wanted to be a part of saving the world.

Little did she know that with her band of gifted teenagers, there was going to be a lot more she had to learn before she could ever fully become her true self.

1

Charlie Rose felt jittery. She had changed her outfit three times already. However, it wasn't quite obvious what look she was trying to go for because each outfit she had put on was as equally eccentric—if not *more*—than the last. First, she wore green corduroy pants, a paisley-patterned mesh long sleeve top, pale pink chunky-soled combat boots, and she planned to accessorize it with tons of flower clips in her hair, small tree earrings, colorful bangles, a ring on each finger, and a fun belt that didn't match the outfit in the slightest.

The second outfit had been black tights, furry brown and white snow boots, a green floral print dress with long sleeves, and a furry scarf. She was going to accessorize that with her hair in pigtail braids that had vine-like accessories tucked in through the plaits of it. She was going to wear a large green suede coat over the dress as well.

Now, she was in a pair of army green flare jeans, white sneakers, a lighter green turtleneck sweater, and her hair was in two buns on top of her head. Normally when she wore her hair like this, people referred to them as her space buns. She put a couple of flower clips in her hair and a pretty bracelet on her wrist that she had made herself a couple of years ago.

Even still, she wasn't sure about this current outfit as she looked at herself in the mirror. She knew there was one accessory that would certainly complete the look—the Pendantix.

If only she still had it.

Forgetting about her outfit dilemma entirely, Charlie heaved a great sigh, walked over to her white iron-framed twin bed, and took a seat at the edge of it. She looked longingly at the climbing hydrangea plant peeking in through her cracked-open window—even though it was a cold, dreary day in the middle of winter in Montgomery.

She missed being able to talk to her plant friend dearly. Ramoni was wise, kind, and excellent at giving Charlie advice when she needed it. But ever since the Pendantix had disappeared after the battle against Heno had ended, the plant stopped speaking. The only sound coming from Ramoni now was his leaves rustling lightly in the wind.

"I wish I could get it back," Charlie whispered to herself.

That is when a solid *Thunk!* sounded from the inside of the girl's oak wardrobe across the room.

That's weird.

Cautiously, Charlie got to her feet and crept toward the closet, wondering where on earth the sound could have come from and whether she'd find herself in any trouble if she decided to open it and check.

Feeling nervous but knowing she wouldn't be able to think about anything else unless she opened the two magnetic doors of the wardrobe, Charlie persevered, and inside the wardrobe, lying at the very bottom of it among a pair of her sneakers and some crumbled up old homework, was the Pendantix.

It's back!

She snatched it up quickly, feeling warmth spreading through her body as she grinned at it. The Pendantix was the gift she had been given inside of a cave in the White Forest, a gold chain with a gold circular pendant that had a growing tree in the center of it. She had worn it all the time, except for in the shower because she wasn't sure if she was allowed to get it wet or not, and she had felt incomplete the past few weeks without it.

It wasn't fully clear yet what the Pendantix powers entailed. So far, Charlie had figured out that she could persuade plants and animals to act a certain way. Oh—and that she could talk to plants. As it turned out, most of them weren't very sociable. Ramoni was the only plant in her back garden that liked to peek in through the window and have a conversation with her. Charlie had no idea where his eyes, ears, or mouth were, and she had no idea if anybody else in the house could hear her talking to the plant or if it was just her, but Ramoni had started becoming a good friend of hers.

"I think this is the best outfit you've picked out yet."

Ramoni's voice came from above the small desk in front of the bedroom window.

Charlie turned and smiled at her climbing hydrangea plant.

"Do you think so?" she asked the plant before turning back to her mirror and putting the special pendant around her neck.

"I do," Ramoni replied. His voice was light and airy and always sounded friendly. "I'm so glad we can talk again, Rose. I wanted to point out that I've never seen you care so much about what to wear before."

"Oh. Well, it is the first day of the second semester," she reminded him.

"Are you sure there isn't a different reason?" Even though Charlie couldn't see his facial expression, she could gather that the plant was teasing her. She knew exactly what the other reason he was referring to was about.

Kire Hunter.

Even thinking his name made Charlie's stomach ache.

She focused on touching up the space buns on top of her mousy brunette head. She liked her space buns because they made her feel a little bit taller. Charlie had gotten her short, petite frame from both of her parents. While her mother was barely even five feet tall, her father was only five-foot-four.

"If you're trying to insinuate that I am trying to impress a boy, you are mistaken," Charlie informed her plant. Then a knock on her door startled her.

"Char? Who are you talking to in there?"

Charlie groaned and rolled her eyes. The mere sound of her sister's high-pitched girly voice made her want to hit something.

"No one, Ell. What do you want?"

Lexi Rose was visiting home from college during winter break. She still had another week until she went back to school, and Charlie had her freedom around the house back.

"I'm just making sure you are awake and getting ready for school!" Lexi called through the door. She tried turning the door handle to let herself in without asking first, but Charlie had learned quickly to start keeping her bedroom door locked.

"I'm changing now!" Charlie complained.

"Fine! I just thought maybe I could help you pick out something cute to wear for the first day back."

Of course, Lexi would want to pick out her clothes. Charlie's older sister did not understand her younger sister's eclectic, bohemian style. Lexi preferred to wear three colors—pink, white, and black. Nothing else. She always liked dresses and skirts, and Charlie hardly ever saw her in pants. She always looked fit to walk down a runway. It was only one of the many reasons why Charlie's parents probably preferred her over Charlie. Lexi was simply perfect. She was a type of perfection that Charlie would never be able to live up to, no matter how badly her parents wanted her to.

"I got it, thanks." Charlie didn't mean to sound harsh… or maybe she did.

When Charlie finally heard her older sister's footsteps retreating down the hall, she turned to her climbing hydrangea and growled. "You are so lucky you don't have to go to school."

"Come on, Charlie Rose. Learning is fulfilling."

"What do you know about learning?"

"I know a great deal, thank you very much."

"How?"

"My dear Rose. My knowledge is passed down from my ancestors. The plants that came before me. And from my own observations. What I learn in my lifetime, I will be passing on to the plant that springs from what I leave behind."

"Whoa," Charlie said. "You must know just about everything there is to know, then!"

"Pretty close."

"So, will you be able to help me do my homework, then?"

"Didn't I just finish telling you that you should want to learn on your own?"

Charlie crossed her arms and made a *Hmph*! noise.

Ramoni continued. "Come on, Rose. Why don't you try to just focus on your studies if you're feeling everything else going on in your life to be a little overwhelming?"

Charlie tapped a glossy neon yellow painted nail to her chin. Then she took a deep breath and tried to shake all of her nerves out. "You're right," she agreed. "Wish me luck."

"Good luck, Rose."

Charlie beamed at her plant friend and checked her appearance one last time, then she left her bedroom.

It didn't matter that Charlie Rose hadn't seen anyone from the Quintet group the entire winter break. It didn't matter that when she went to school today, more than likely, things were going to be just like they had been before she ever met them. And it definitely did not matter that Kire Hunter, the boy who had given Charlie her first kiss, the one who she had been hoping would ask her on a date, had spent a lot of his break hanging out with someone almost as bad as Amberly McHenry. Her name was Angela Altman, and she used to be the most popular girl in school until Amberly knocked her off her throne. She was a cheerleader, and apparently, ever since Kire helped lead the St. Bernard soccer team to the championship last semester, she had set her sights on him. It was practically a law around St. Bernard that important sports stars were supposed to date the cheerleaders.

But I don't even know if they're actually dating, Charlie thought to herself. She pulled out her cell phone to check for any new messages from the gang telling her they got their gifts back as well. The only one who had been able to keep theirs was Kire.

Charlie also almost sort of expected there to be a text from Kire telling her that he was looking forward to seeing her again.

Her heart fell when she saw that her screen was still blank.

Rose was surprised to see that breakfast had been prepared when she got downstairs. Timothy Rose and Beverly Rose were sitting at the breakfast table inside the kitchen of their old-but-slightly-renovated home.

Despite how she normally loathed her parents, she couldn't help but feel touched. The smell of cooked bacon and syrup wafted heavenly through her nostrils.

"You guys made breakfast for my first day back?"

Beverly looked at her daughter as if she had suddenly sprouted a third eyeball. "No, we didn't cook. Your sister did." Right after she said the words, Lexi breezed into the kitchen wearing an apron over her blush pink dress. She grabbed a rooster-themed pot holder—everything in the kitchen was rooster-themed—and pulled out a silver tray of bacon from the oven.

"I learned from a friend at school that it's better to cook bacon this way!" she told Charlie when she noticed her younger sister staring. "It prevents it from shrinking so much."

Most other kids would be happy that their sibling wanted to cook them breakfast. Not Charlie. She saw this as an act. As a way for Lexi to make sure she was still the favorite child even after she went back to college and wasn't around to help out around here.

"Oh, I'm actually not hungry," Charlie lied. She would've loved nothing more than to stuff one—or five—pieces of that bacon in her mouth right now. But she was being proud. She didn't need her sister's stupid cooked breakfast. She could grab something at school.

"Charlie Rose, don't be rude. Your sister made that for you," Beverly said in her snapping-turtle voice. She didn't even bother to look at her daughter as she spoke; Tim's and her eyes were glued to the television that was playing over in the living room. Charlie ignored her mother, grabbed the watering can by the sink, and began watering the plants littered around the house. It drove her parents insane to have so much greenery everywhere, but somehow, she had convinced them that it was incredibly good for their health to have, and she promised them that she would take good care of them. She loved her house plants. These ones down here didn't like to talk to her like Ramoni did, but it was probably better that way because if her family caught her talking to plants, she might end up tossed in a loony bin.

Charlie wasn't one to watch too much TV because she preferred to be outside or read books instead, but she couldn't help hearing bits and pieces of the news being broadcasted while she watered the plants in the living room.

The mayor was on the TV.

The mayor of Montgomery was short and stout and preferred to wear white suits that didn't fit him quite right, along with a white hat. He was roughly tanned and had a ridiculous dirty blonde handlebar mustache that made him slightly difficult to take seriously.

"I hope the students of St. Bernard High will feel safe as they go back to school this Monday morning," the mayor said in his surprisingly high-pitched voice. "Even though Andrew Longview, the suspect behind the kidnapping of the five freshman boys just weeks ago, has still not been located. I know search efforts have stalled a bit because of our frequent failed efforts to find him, but I assure you all that I won't be able to rest at night until I know the citizens of Montgomery are safe."

Fat chance of that happening, Charlie thought to herself.

"The five freshman boys who were taken from their homes in the middle of the night still have not been able to recollect anything about the incident, but we should all keep in our prayers that they get their memories back. If they do, it could help us a great deal when it comes to locating Andrew Longview."

Rose felt terrible about the five boys who had been kidnapped. But it didn't matter if they got their memories back or not.

Because Andrew Longview was never going to be found.

"Do we really want to do this?" Trace Henderson asked the four other members of the Quintets. They were all in an empty meadow in the middle of the White Forest. Charlie had sped up the growth of a tree so that there was one single one planted in the clearing. In it, they had carved the letters A L—right into the tree trunk.

"As long as we remember that we are honoring Andrew's memory. Not Heno's," Kire said. The five of them surround the tree. Amberly was dressed in all black with mesh netting over her ice-blue

eyes. Kaos stared at the tree with a stony expression, his hands deep in the front pocket of his jeans. Kire had his hands clasped together in front of him and was looking around at everyone to make sure they were all ready to be a part of this. To make sure they were all on the same page. Kire always seemed to be the one acting like the group's glue.

The tree served as Andrew Longview's grave marker.

Heno, an awful creature from another realm, had taken over Andrew's body and used it to fight against the five of them. Heno had lost the fight, and his body had melted into a strange purple goo. Albus then cleaned up that goo, along with any other sign of there ever having been a fight inside the White Forest at Kula Mountain at all. Andrew Longview was dead. And while the young kids had only wanted Heno destroyed, they hadn't realized that Andrew would never come back once they succeeded in doing so.

The guilt Charlie felt as she made an obnoxious amount of flowers grow around the tree with Andrew's initials on it was nearly crippling. She had never wanted Andrew to die. She hadn't known him that well, but he had always been a nice, quiet, decent guy. He never deserved to be dragged into this mess.

"I want to feel bad for what happened to Andrew, but every time I close my eyes, I see that horrible, hateful look that he carried in his eyes," Amberly said, not looking at anyone.

Her arms were crossed, and her blonde hair spilled around her shoulders in waves.

"Amberly, that wasn't Andrew. That was Heno." Kire gave her a reproachful look.

"I don't know," Trace added. "I'm kind of with her on this." And to show that he was, he matched Amberly's stance and crossed his arms while standing beside her. His bulging biceps nearly ripped through his long-sleeved T-shirt as he did so.

Kaos shook his head at them, his jaw clenched. "I think you guys are just trying to distract yourself from the fact that we killed somebody." His eyes fell on Kire. "Let's just do this thing."

Charlie swallowed. She tried to meet Kire's gaze, but he wouldn't look in her direction. Charlie did not understand why Kire kept acting this way. After they had killed Heno, Kire had kissed her passionately and held onto her like he never wanted to let go again. But now? He seemed like he didn't want to touch her with a ten-foot pole.

Kire cleared his throat and kept his head high as he stared at the tree trunk. "Andrew Longview was a good person. He was kind. Friendly. Great out on the soccer field. I didn't get to be his friend that long before Heno took him over. But I think if I had gotten the chance, Andrew and I would have been really close friends, and I'm really sorry for what happened to him."

"I hope that his parents are able to find closure in all of this some-how," Kaos added in. "I hope they don't spend their lives torturing themselves over what might have happened and where he might've gone."

That might have been what made Charlie feel the worst—thinking about Andrew's family. Thinking about how sad they had looked on TV when they asked the public to help them find their missing teenage son.

"I hope he rests in peace and does not come back and try to haunt me or whatever," Amberly said next. In front of others, Amberly hardly had any emotional range in her body. And she kept the walls around herself built up and strong at all times.

Trace spoke next. "He was a good guy, and even though it seems like he did a lot of bad stuff because there was someone—or some-thing—possessing his body—he still deserves to go to heaven. And if you're up there, Andrew, I hope they have a lot of soccer. The next goal I score will be for you." He kicked at the ground a little. It was clear that Trace was uncomfortable with this kind of thing, just like his girlfriend.

Now it was Charlie's turn. "Uh... I wish I had known you better, Andrew. And... I-I'm really sorry." Charlie wasn't much of a talker. She didn't know what else she could say.

"Let's... have a moment of silence?" Kire suggested. Everyone nodded their head in agreement.

Only then did Charlie think of something that would have been better to say. She didn't want to ruin the moment of silence, though, so instead, she stared at Andrew's initials on the tree trunk and said it in her head. I promise you, Andrew. I won't let your death be for nothing. And I won't let Yash burn the earth to a crisp. Whatever it takes.

"IT'S ALL RIGHT if you don't want to eat it, Char," Lexi replied when Charlie went back into the kitchen to set the watering can down, waving it off and smiling brightly. Her teeth were dazzling white and her pink dress somehow really brought out the green in her eyes. Charlie wished she had been born with green eyes. But no. She had poop-brown ones instead. Poop-brown eyes to go with her poop-brown hair.

However, Lexi was a good actress, acting unbothered at Charlie's rejection. Surely as soon as their parents were out of earshot, Lexi would be snapping at her sister about being ungrateful.

"Thanks anyhow," Charlie said. "I need to get to school early to... do a thing, anyway."

Charlie might have been dreading going to school, but she dreaded having to be stuck at home with these people a second longer or even more.

2

Charlie didn't like the bus. She didn't like sitting in a seat by herself with no one to talk to while everyone whispered about how much of a loner she was. So instead, she walked to school. It was cloudy in Montgomery. Rain was sprinkling down, unable to decide whether it wanted to be rain or if it wanted to be snow. Charlie kept her clear umbrella overhead, forcing herself to push thoughts of her annoying family out of her mind, and instead, she replaced them with thoughts of the Quintet group.

"I don't need them," she mumbled to herself. "I'll defeat Rezin all on my own if I have to." Wherever he may be. "I'm plenty used to being on my own. It's probably better this way, anyway." It didn't matter that Albus—the strange man who had created a hologram of himself to show up on Earth while he was back in his realm, which was also called Albus—and Kire's book, Halo, had told the Quintets that they needed to work as a team. Charlie thought she was strong enough. She also felt brave enough to handle it. The rest of the Quintet team could pretend like what happened at the end of last semester never occurred, but Charlie could hardly sleep at night knowing that

Rezin was still out there somewhere and that Earth was still in danger. Sure, Charlie and the others had successfully destroyed the Djigi—the portal from Yash's realm to Earth set up by two mirrors facing each other no matter how far of a distance away. Yash still had one of the mirrors, but Charlie and the others had destroyed the one here on Earth, making it impossible for him to get over—or so it was rumored to believe. Charlie knew that nothing was impossible, though. If there was another way for Yash to get to Earth, he was going to try and find it.

CHARLIE WENT to the greenhouse when she arrived on campus. It was deserted like usual, but she wondered if that was only simply because she had gotten here so early. She wondered if, in just a few minutes, the rest of the gang would show up like they had been doing in this spot frequently last semester.

While Charlie waited to find out, she decided to test out her magical ability from the Pendantix to see if she still had it. She focused on some plants grouped together in one of the corners, and right before her eyes, she made the wilting ones green again. Smiling because her gift truly had returned, she then made slow-growing plants get taller. Then she had a thick green vine snake its way off the wall and place a flower behind Charlie's ear. She had a tree branch's arms grow long and wide, and she made them pick up pots and gardening tools, twisting their branches tightly around the items to grip them. This was more like it. She couldn't mess around with the plants in her house like this with her family home all the time. It felt nice for Charlie to finally be somewhere where she could be alone with them.

Charlie thought everything was going great. But then something strange started happening. The branches suddenly dropped what they were holding; a couple of flowerpots fell to the ground with a loud shatter, and hand rakes and shovels clanged together as they, too, hit the ceramic flooring. The world around Charlie started swaying, and her body felt drained as if she were about to faint. She sank to her knees; that way, in case she did faint, she wouldn't be as in danger of hitting her head on her way down.

She dizzily looked around the greenhouse. All of the plants had returned to exactly the way they were before she started messing with them. Charlie found this infuriating. Sure, she had taken a little break from the Pendantix, but she should still be able to do all this stuff easily by now.

Fairly quickly, Charlie started to feel better, though. Another thing that came with being the owner of the Quintet Gifts was that she got super healing powers—immortality from disease and old age until the gifts had done what they needed to. Or until Charlie and the others perished. Before the five of them had received the gifts, many others had tried protecting the earth with them as well, but they had all ended up dying at the hands of Jago and Heno.

Once Charlie was no longer dizzy, she got back to her feet. Something dripped on the ground in front of her white sneakers. She looked down and realized it was a drop of blood. Quickly, she wiped underneath her nose with the back of her hand.

The blood was coming from her.

3

Charlie didn't want to admit it to herself, but she was incredibly nervous when her last class of the day, Botany, rolled around. It was the only class she had with Kire, and she hadn't talked to him yet. During lunch, she hadn't even bothered going into the cafeteria to see if Kire was going to want to sit with her or if any of the other Quintet gifted kids were going to be sitting together as well. Instead, she hung out on the bench in front of the greenhouse since the rain had finally let up. She had sat and appreciated the fresh air. It had been much needed to calm the anxious feeling inside of her.

But the fresh air could only help so much.

She sat at her table next to an empty rickety stool, a new plant in front of every seat that hadn't been there when Charlie had been inside the greenhouse earlier. Charlie could be a bit of a plant freak, so when she didn't recognize what this plant was, it bothered her slightly. It was incredibly strange-looking, sitting in a terra-cotta pot. It almost didn't even look real. On top of the soil, it looked as if somebody had dropped down several rocks. But when she timidly touched those rocks with her neon yellow painted fingernails as the class was filling in, she felt how soft and tender the rock-like nubs were—the rocks were the plant.

The uniqueness of the plant served as the temporary distraction that Charlie had been looking for. She didn't lift her head again until a shadow loomed over her.

Kire Hunter.

Her stomach lurched as he stood there smiling down at her. His brown eyes were dark but friendly. His hair looked as if he had gotten it cut over the break, yet it was still somehow messy and out of place at the same time. He was wearing a thick layered jacket that puffed out around him, and his black Converse sneakers were caked in mud from walking through puddles between the school and here. Kire was still handsome as ever. It filled Charlie with a sense of bitterness.

"Hi," Kire said innocently.

Charlie shot him a look. "Hello," she said coldly.

"I like your hair," he replied, not sensing her attitude toward him.

Charlie glanced down at the open stool at her table. The one that Kire wasn't taking a seat at. "Thanks."

When she looked back up at him, she saw him staring at her Pendantix.

"Did you..." he trailed off in a whisper, looking surprised.

"Yeah," she said. She didn't know why her gift had returned, but she had a feeling it meant something bad was coming. She didn't want to talk to Kire, but she also had so many questions. "Have you gotten anymore... information?"

He turned sharply and looked around. When he spoke again, he leaned in closer to her. "If you're talking about the book," he whispered, "then yes. But we can't talk about it here, okay?"

Charlie's heart had started picking up speed just by him being near her. But then a shrill, feminine voice interrupted the two of them, coming from toward the back of the greenhouse.

"Kire, come on!"

Charlie whipped her head around to see beautiful blue-eyed Angela sitting at a table with another open stool next to her, waving Kire down with a bright, pearly white smile.

Charlie's heart fell, but she didn't let Kire see it in her eyes as he glanced over at Angela before looking back at her again. "I'll see you later," he said. He stared at her a moment longer as if he was waiting for her to say something else. But Charlie refused.

Shrugging, Kire went to go sit next to Angela.

It was true, then. The two of them were an item. No wonder Kire hadn't asked Charlie to hang out at all during winter break. He had been too busy with somebody else. Apparently, the moments Kire and Charlie had shared together last semester meant nothing to him.

So be it.

Mr. Donnie breezed into the greenhouse moments later, looking slightly out of breath and sweaty even though it was freezing cold outside. You would've thought Mr. Donnie just left the sauna in his current state.

"Welcome back, class," he announced, bouncing on the balls of his feet. Mr. Donnie was an average middle-aged man with round glasses, medium height, and overgrown hair. He prided himself in being knowledgeable about plans, but he, to Charlie—and most of the other students at St. Bernard's—Mr. Donnie didn't actually know hardly anything about plants. Last semester, Kire's new beau, Angela, had nearly gotten her hand bit off by an Edax Animae. Mr. Donnie hadn't had a clue what to do, and Kire had been the one who came to the rescue, along with Charlie, who made sure he didn't kill the plant.

That was the first time Charlie ever really remembered interacting with Kire Hunter.

"I'm sure you noticed the plant sitting before you at your tables. There should be one for each of you," Mr. Donnie continued, gripping the red suspenders attached to his brown trousers. "That there is called a lithops plant. Or, in other words, a living stone plant—for obvious reasons, of course. It's a type of succulent native to southern Africa. Out in the wilderness, they're able to thrive well because of the stone-like appearance they have. Animals tend not to eat it since it blends in with surrounding rocks. I spent all winter break growing them in the greenhouse at my home, and for the rest of the school year, it will be your responsibility to keep it alive while only ever getting to tend to it here at school. No, I'm not going to give you any tips or advice on how to do this. Instead, I'm going to leave it fully up to you all to do your own research."

Already, Charlie was eager to get to the library and check out a book on exotic plants so that she could look up more information on the lithops plant. Maybe she would watch a video on YouTube about it as well.

"Mr. Donnie?"

Charlie turned to see who was speaking. It was Nathan Bury, a dimwitted foul-mouthed kid in her grade.

"Yes, my boy?" Mr. Donnie asked.

"Uh, if it's made of rocks, why would we have to take care of it?"

The class groaned in unison at his stupidity.

"You know what, Nathan? I'm going to let you figure that one out for yourself," Mr. Donnie replied.

"He can't be serious," Charlie heard Angela muttering to Kire. When Charlie peered over her shoulder at them again, she saw that they had their heads bent low together, giggling. Angela's dirty blonde hair had been longer last semester, but was cut to a short bob underneath her ears for a dramatic change for this semester, drawing attention to herself. Even Charlie could admit that the haircut looked good on her and brought out her angular, sharp, stunning features. Charlie might've even considered that Angela looked prettier than Amberly McHenry, the most popular girl in school.

And also the meanest.

An angry green-eyed monster swam around inside of Charlie's stomach. She didn't want to have this thought, but she couldn't stop it from forming in her mind.

That should be Kire and me sitting there with our heads nearly touching as we giggle together.

Angela caught Charlie staring and gave her a tiny wave, using only two of her fingers. She had a prissy expression on her face that only angered Charlie more. It was as if Angela knew that Charlie and Kire used to have feelings for each other and that Angela was proud of herself for stealing Kire away.

Charlie shot her a dirty look, but before she turned back around in her seat, she noticed the vines wrapped around the plants' misting system that hung down from the ceiling of the greenhouse. She discreetly gripped her Pendantix and thought hard about those vines since she couldn't make eye contact with them without it being obvious to Kire what she was trying to do.

Mr. Donnie resumed teaching, going over the course list they had for the remainder of the semester, but his lecture was interrupted by a crunching metal noise, followed by the sound of Angela crying out in alarm and astonishment.

Mr. Donnie stopped talking, and the entire class turned around to see what the commotion was. The mist system had broken open where two thin, white metal tubes connected with each other, and it was making water from the system pour out right on top of Angela's head. She had leaped out of the way quickly, but the damage had already been done, and her head, as well as most of her pretty blue blouse, had been drenched.

Kire had also backed off his stool, having been splattered slightly by the downpour as the class laughed hysterically. He glanced immediately over in Charlie's direction, but Charlie covered her mouth with her hand to hide the fact that she was laughing, too. All she had suggested to the vines was merely for them to constrict themselves around the metal tubes until they burst open on top of her Angela. She hadn't expected it to work so excellently.

4

____

Charlie somehow managed to get through the rest of the school day and back home without hardly talking to anyone. As far as first days back to school went, hers had been abysmal. It had seemed like any other day, minus the fact that she could make plants move and that her heart was hurting because of a stupid boy.

She hadn't even spoken with Trace, Kaos, or Amberly, despite the fact that they had all been lingering outside in the school parking lot as Charlie started her walk home after the bell of last period had rung. The three of them had acted like they hadn't even seen Charlie at all as she passed by them. Heck, maybe they hadn't.

From the outside, the Rose residence looked warm and cozy. Large, octagon-shaped windows faced the street and gave the exterior a stylish appearance. It was an L-shaped building with an extension added to the architecture years after the original house was built. The second floor of the home was bigger than the first, creating a dramatic overhang. The roof was low and triangular, layered with red ceramic tiles. The front lawn was surrounded by a modest garden covered in mostly grass with a few flower patches, and a mossy pond sat in the backyard. The house had an average-sized kitchen, two bathrooms, a comfortable living room, three bedrooms, a dining area, and a basement where the washer and dryer were kept along with miscellaneous storage of junk and Mr. Rose's workshop.

Charlie Rose liked the house she lived in, and the neighborhood was quiet and friendly, as well, but she often felt like an outsider. Everyone in suburbia seemed like carbon copies of each other with the same stylized outfits and haircuts and the fake friendly smiles plastered on their faces every time they ran into one another. Charlie didn't like to smile. She didn't like to be fake. She also didn't like dressing like everybody else. She prided herself in being unique, even if kids at school made fun of her for it. She couldn't wait until she was in college, where nobody knew her name and everyone had their own individuality.

Charlie paused outside the front door to her house and turned to the flowerbeds underneath the windows. Thinking hard, she tried to make them sway even though there wasn't even a breeze outside. A few of them budged, but most of them refused to move.

Charlie gave up, letting out the breath she had been holding in, getting herself dizzy. She went inside the house and found Lexi sitting in the living room having a video chat with her perfect college boyfriend, Lance Riley. The two were both going to school to get their marketing degrees.

Walking into the Rose residence, there was a step down into the living room and then a step back up again into the dining area before you turned right to the kitchen. Right past the front door to the living room, however, the couch's back lined the walkway, creating a path to the dining room. Lexi was sitting on the couch with her laptop on her lap, her face not visible to Charlie right away. Charlie could see Lance clearly on the screen of the computer, though. He was wearing a baby blue polo with a sweater tied around his shoulders. His dark brown hair was perfectly gelled back. His ice-blue eyes looked lovingly through the screen at his girlfriend.

"Barf," Charlie said as she passed by the two of them.

"Don't be like that, Char," Lexi said with a playful smile. "Come say hi to Lance!"

"No thanks," Charlie said, her tone flat. "And I go by Rose." She couldn't understand why her sister had this obsession with trying to get her to get to know Lance. If she had any idea, though, Charlie figured it was because she wanted to try and show him off.

But Lance wasn't Charlie's type.

Not that Charlie really even knew what her type was.

Charlie went to the kitchen, disappearing out of sight from her sister, and grabbed herself a granola bar out of the pantry. Her parents are both at work. Tim Rose owned a building contractor business, and Beverly Rose managed a large, fancy marketplace. They wouldn't be home until much later. More than likely, Charlie was going to have to fend for herself for dinner.

She opened the granola bar in the kitchen and nibbled on it, but when she could hear the baby talk coming from Lexi through the living room as she chatted with Lance—"Stop, you are the handsomest, bestest boyfriend a girl could ask for, babe!"—she decided to retreat up the L-shaped staircase into her room instead.

LATER IN THE EVENING, after Charlie finished working on her homework at her desk and fell into bed to watch some videos on the new stone plant they had been given in Botany, her phone dinged with a text message. The sound was almost foreign since she hardly ever got them.

She tapped on the icon on her phone—it was a text from the group chat between Kire, Trace, Kaos, Amberly, and her. It was the first time the group chat had been used in... a while.

Kire: *I think we should all meet up. Soon. Since you guys all have your gifts back.*

Charlie rolled her eyes. *Now they want to talk?*

But she was also slightly a bit worried, too. After all, Kire had mentioned that his gift, a worn leather-bound book called Halo, had given him more information about the evil entity, Rezin, one of the great and powerful Yash's minions. And apparently, Kire had talked to the others earlier today and discovered that their gifts had been returned to them, too.

She didn't want to be the first one to reply, so she sat there waiting until somebody else did.

Amberly: *Some of us have lives.*

Charlie could practically hear the attitude and Amberly's voice. That girl had been sentimental toward Kire when she confessed that she was the half-sister that Kire's father, Gerald Hunter, had abandoned before she was born when she thought Kire was possibly about to die while they had been fighting Heno a while back. Now, it seemed as if she was back to her Kire-hating self.

Kaos: *Why do we have to meet? Did something happen?*

Trace: *Dude. Kaos, I thought we agreed we weren't going to text him.*

Kire: *I'm still in this text thread. I can see what you're saying, Trace.*

Kaos: *I'm just making sure it's not an emergency. Sue me.*

Kire: *It sort of IS, though. Halo talked to me. Don't worry, we can meet somewhere secluded so that nobody sees us all together.*

Finally, Charlie chimed in.

Rose: *I'll be there. When and where?*

Trace: *Nah. I'm good.*

Kaos: *I'm there.*

Trace: *What?!*

Amberly: *It will give me an excuse to get out of work tomorrow. I suppose I will go too.*

Trace: *Traitors.*

Rose: *Trace, just come.*

Charlie thought it was important for the five of them to try and work together. She would do this without them if necessary, but she knew it would be easier if they wanted to be a team.

Kire: *My house after school?*

Amberly: *Absolutely not!!!*

Kire: *Fine. Then where do you guys suggest?*

Rose: *Aunt Marg's?*

Kaos: *Her back room is closed for a paint and sip session tomorrow.*

Kaos: *Don't ask me how I know that.*

Kire: *But how DO you know that?*

Trace: *You guys are the worst. But I'll come. The Challenge Shack. After school.*

Kire: *Whatever Trace wants, Trace gets.*

Kaos: *Kire. Don't start, dude.*

Amberly: *It's been decided, then. The Challenge Shack after school tomorrow. Now stop blowing up my phone!*

Charlie added in one last thumbs-up emoji text, but it was more to annoy Amberly than anything else.

5

Charlie, bundled up in an oversized mint green puffy jacket, dipped into the White Forest when the bell signaling the end of the school day rang that Tuesday. She decided she would just meet the others at the shack and not bother trying to see if they wanted to walk there together.

She did a little bit more practicing with her gift as she made her way over. She just did little things, such as making the plants move. She could hear whispers of the thick, dense greenery in the White Forest conversing with each other, but she did not want to try to focus on what they were saying, nor did she feel like trying to get them to talk to her. She didn't want to chance falling ill again right now, especially in front of the others. She hadn't missed being teased by Kire, Kaos, Trace, and Amberly.

The beautiful sequoia trees were still green and vibrant. The giant tree roots in the ground moved out of the way as Charlie followed the path to the old, abandoned cabin. She hadn't been to the White Forest in a while, but she had missed the smell of the forest rot and moisture that hung in the air.

She passed by the base of Kula Mountain. She certainly did not miss hiking up it.

She was the first one to arrive at the Challenge Shack. It was the place where those five freshman boys had been taken after Heno—who had been in Andrew's body—kidnapped them and drained their life source to gain more power for himself. The building wasn't as much a shack as it was a small cabin, and it was very wide-open inside. Every step Charlie took through the entrance—which was missing a door—creaked heavily under her feet, and she was actually quite light in weight.

Most people would be scared to be in a creepy place like this all alone. Not Charlie. The only things she was afraid of were the treacherous creatures that might have been lingering about, trying to sniff out their next meal. Even *not* so treacherous critters made Charlie uneasy.

"Hey."

Charlie jumped and turned around. All four of the others had arrived together—go figure—and we're ducking through the police tape to make their way inside next to Charlie.

Charlie crossed her arms and looked at Kire. "So, what is that you have to tell us?"

"*Someone's* eager," Kaos Miles jokes. As usual, he was dressed in all black. His turtleneck sweater was black. The denim jacket over it was black. His jeans were black. His designer shoes were black. He also had a pair of black sunglasses over his eyes even though they were all well shaded, not only in the canopy of the trees above them but in the cover of the Challenge Shack's ceiling as well. Kaos' freckles were not nearly as noticeable as they were in the summertime, but Charlie could still see them smattered across his nose. His auburn hair was slicked back stylishly, and as he leaned against one of the pillars that were keeping the roof from caving in on them, he had a way of looking effortlessly cool. Kaos was one of the most intelligent people Charlie had ever met, right next to Kire. But Kaos was also sly and cold. His favorite hobby seemed to be making people feel terrible about themselves.

"Not eager," Charlie corrected. "I just want to get this over with."

Kire sat his bag on the ground, and it thudded loudly from the weight of it. He must have had Halo inside.

"She's right," Kire agreed. "We should just get this over with. You guys might not like what I have to tell you."

"Oh, how superb," Amber said with a huge eye roll. "And here I thought we were going to be celebrating the fact that the gifts had nothing left for us to do, and they simply just returned to us because they wanted us to enjoy their use."

Charlie didn't want to give Amberly any indication that she knew she was even there, but it was hard *not* to look at her. Charlie was envious of Amberly's appearance, just like all the other girls at Saint Bernard High were. Amberly had long, thick blonde hair and doll-like—yet harsh—ice-blue eyes. She was the head cheerleader, and all the boys wanted her.

But she was also the devil.

"Sorry, Amberly," Kire said sheepishly.

"Don't address me directly," she hissed at him, her eyes turning venomous and her posture looking ready to strike.

"Babe, it's okay," Trace tried in his thick voice. He put one of his massive biceps around her in an attempt to comfort her, but she didn't relax.

Trace Henderson. The tyrant. The apex predator. The moron.

Even though he and Amberly were dating, they could almost pass for brother and sister. Like Amberly, Trace also had blond hair and blue eyes. He had a huge athletic build and towered over most of the other kids in the school. Trace ruled the school, and nobody else had a say in it. Kids ran away in fear in the hallways just at the mere *sight* of him. Sometimes,

Charlie was certain he didn't have a nice bone in his body. Other times, he did things—small things—that made her wonder if there really might be some kindness buried underneath his hard cruel exterior.

Kire cleared his throat. "Uh... so, anyway. Halo gave me a vision about Rezin. And I think that's why you guys all got your gifts back."

"What was this vision?" Kaos asked with a perfectly arched eyebrow as he listened intently.

"Isn't it obvious?" Charlie asked. "He's probably coming for us."

"Exactly," Kire said. "The vision said he is coming and that he is going to try to kill us all. And last night, it gave me the strangest dream. I had been with you guys at Kula Mountain. We had just killed Heno and... and Andrew. But right after we did that, when we were all high-fiving and telling each other how amazing we had just been, especially with Rose making that goat break the Djigi, Halo flew open and told me that Rezin was coming, and then when we looked up, there Rezin was in a tuxedo-like suit but still looking like an alien. He was shaking his head at the pile of purple glue that used to be Heno. Then he started stalking toward us. I still get the goosebumps every time I think about it."

"But it was just a dream," Trace clarified.

Kire snapped his head toward him, his jaw clamping shut. "No, duh," he barked.

"What did you just say to me?" Trace snapped, taking his arm off Amberly and moving aggressively toward Kire. "What makes you think you can talk to me like that, huh? Why have you been acting like such a spitwad to me lately? What did I ever do to you?"

Kire looked away. "It doesn't matter. I just wanted to let you all know that we need to start preparing."

"Should we do some practicing now?" Kaos asked, patting the pocket of his backpack. "I got my crown right in here."

Trace nodded his head toward the door frame, and Charlie saw his magical sword leaning against the wall next to it. "You know I got mine," he said.

"My stupid glove thing is in my backpack, too," Amberly huffed.

"*Gauntlet*," Kire corrected. Then he winced like he knew he shouldn't have said anything. Like it was merely a force of habit for him to correct others.

Amberly growled and balled her fists. "You're lucky we can't use our gifts on each other. I would *so* like to punch you so hard that you fly to the other side of the earth."

"Amberly, for the last time—"

"What?!" she bellowed. "Are you going to try and tell me that you finally told your father that you know about me? Because unless you're about to tell me that, I don't want you to speak to me. Ever!"

"It's not that simple, okay?" Kire snapped back.

"Yes, it is!" she screeched. "You go home, you walk up to your dad, you say, 'Hey, Pops! Just thought you should know that I found out about my long-lost sister Amberly McHenry— who you *abandoned*!"

"All right, all right," Kaos said, stuffing himself between the two of them. "Let's just all relax. We're supposed to be a team, remember?"

"We are a team," Trace said. Then he glanced at Charlie. "Well, for the most part."

Charlie glared at him and said nothing. Kaos looked in her direction.

"You know, Charlie—"

"*Rose*," she grumbled.

"Yeah, yeah, whatever—if you weren't so strange, we wouldn't care so much about being seen with you at school. My mom has tons of clothes she never wears in her closet. I can give you some, so you don't have to look so poor all the time."

"Excuse me?" Charlie asked, bewildered.

Now it was Charlie's turn to ball her fists and turn into a coiling snake. It wasn't like Charlie's family was poor—her fashion taste was just different from everyone else's, and she enjoyed getting her vintage looks from thrift stores.

To her dismay, Amberly let out a heinous laugh. This only angered Charlie more. She turned to the airheaded blonde.

"What's so funny, Amberly?" she asked. "Tell me, how is it even possible that you are the most popular girl in school, but you still don't have any friends?"

"Are you serious?" Amberly sneered. "I have *friends*. You're one to talk!"

"I never see with anyone besides Trace," Charlie pointed out. When she glanced at Kire, he was making a face that said something like 'she's got a point'.

"You're just jealous because I have a boyfriend, and you're going to be alone forever." Amberly smiled.

"I don't need a boyfriend," Charlie clarified. "I'm happy being alone."

"Is that why you and Kire aren't a thing anymore?" Kaos asked.

Charlie's stomach dipped violently. She didn't answer. Instead, she waited to see what Kire's reply was going to be.

Kire cleared his throat awkwardly. "I..."

"Kire's with *Angela* now," Amberly reminded everyone. "She's the best you'll ever get, *Brother*. Don't mess it up."

Charlie desperately wanted to leave. She had had enough of this. Out of all the people at Saint Bernard High, why did it have to be these four who ended up in the cave in the White Forest when the gifts had chosen them? Charlie had been in the cave already, working on her bioluminescence project—she would have been chosen regardless. The others never liked to go into that cave. It was by pure chance they ended up inside of it because Trace and Kaos wanted to fight Kire, and Amberly came too because she wanted to cheer Trace on since she hated Kire so much.

"Angela is hot," Kaos agreed. "Seems like you're getting cooler and cooler every day, Kire."

When Charlie glanced at Kire, she noticed his cheeks flushing pink. It made her hate him. It made her wish she could summon some thick vines hanging from the trees in the forest to wrap around his neck and choke the life out of him. How dare he give her her first kiss, make her think he cared about her, just to dump her without any explanation?

"You guys, I'm not finished," Kire said, clearly wanting to get the subject back on why they had met up here in the first place.

"Look at Rose's face," Amberly said, pointing at Charlie and ignoring Kire. "She's so upset that she got *dumped!*"

"I didn't get dumped!" Charlie snapped. "We were never together!"

"Guys!" Kire tried again as Trace and Kaos chuckled. Before Kire could get out what it was he wanted to say, there was a sudden, loud, whooshing noise.

Then Rose saw a flash of blue outside the broken windows of the Challenge Shack.

Then she felt the immense heat.

"What's happening?!" Amberly yelled, her voice rising in pitch.

"Who is doing this?" Trace demanded.

"It's none of us!" Kire called, looking around for the source of what suddenly made the entire shack become engulfed in a perimeter of bright blue flames.

"Who is it then?!" Trace asked, ducking and beginning to cough. Seeing it made Charlie start to cough, too. Smoke was billowing in through the openings of the crumbling cabin.

"Who do you think?" Charlie and Kaos said at the same time.

A booming deep voice sounded, filling the shack and nearly drowning out the sound of the flames.

Out of Yash's minions who were here on Earth, Jago had been killed. Heno had been defeated. There was only one other.

Rezin.

"Look at you foolish toddlers," Rezin's voice said. It sounded as if ten speakers had been placed inside the shack, and he was speaking through a microphone. "Wasting time arguing about petty, insignificant things moments before you're all about to perish."

Charlie wouldn't have that. Not if she could help it. She turned to the open window, trying to get eyes on any sort of plants she could use through the gaps in the flames to extinguish them or get her and the others out of here.

Was Rezin here? Outside the shack?

"Kire, what do we do?!" Amberly pleaded.

"I-I don't know!" He lunged for his backpack, probably to get Halo out, but Charlie didn't get to see what he did next-suddenly she was no longer in the shack. She was no longer surrounded by flames.

"What's going on?!" she cried out in fear. "Where am I?! Guys?!"

No one responded.

It looked as if she was standing in the middle of the aftermath of a bad forest fire. A fire that had burned everything, as far as the eye could see, to a crisp. The sky above her was dark and gray, covered in lingering smoke and smog.

Charlie coughed. "Kire? Guys?!"

"Look around you, Charlie Rose," Rezin's voice said, just as loud and clear as it had been moments ago back in the shack. "And look closely."

"Where did you take me?! Bring me back!" she demanded. Since there were no remaining plants around her and no animals, she might as well not have had any powers. She was helpless and defenseless here.

Rezin didn't answer—he just chuckled menacingly.

Her heart pounding, Charlie turned around and looked at the burned earth before her.

Only it wasn't just earth.

Lying before her, all lined up in a row, were her family and the Quintets. Timothy, Beverly, and Lexi. Kire, Kaos, Trace, and Amberly, too.

But yet, they weren't really there.

They were dead, their bodies just as charred as the rest of the world around them. Charlie could barely even recognize them.

She fell to her knees and reached out, but she knew there was nothing she could do. "No." She gasped at first. Then when the pain started *really* settling in, she started to wail. "NO!"

Rezin's voice continued laughing.

"What did you do?!" she sobbed. "What did you do to them?!"

"Isn't this what you wanted, Charlie?"

"No!!" she cried again. All she could think about was how much she wished it had been her instead of them.

"But you prefer to be alone, do you not? Isn't that the way you like to live your life? Never letting anyone in? Never getting loved by anyone and never feeling any love in return?"

"STOP!" she screamed at the top of her lungs. She didn't even recognize herself.

This has to be a dream. This has to be a dream!

6

Charlie kept screaming until she felt somebody shaking her shoulders. Was it Rezin? She didn't want to open her eyes to find out.

"Rose!"

That voice sounded familiar to Charlie. But it couldn't be true, because that person was dead. Dead because of her.

"ROSE!"

She started getting shaken more violently. So much so that it forced her eyes into opening, and she discovered herself back in the Challenge Shack, Kire's hands gripping both of her shoulders tightly. They were still surrounded by blue flames, and Charlie felt disoriented and confused.

"What happened?" Kire asked her.

Charlie opened her mouth to explain, but before she could, Amberly suddenly let out an earsplitting scream. She dropped down to her knees, her face contorted unattractively as she closed her eyes, covered her ears, and kept screaming.

"Amberly!" Trace shouted, rushing to her aid.

"What the heck is going on?!" Kaos asked, fishing his crown out of his bag and ungracefully tossing it on his head.

"You were all dead," Charlie answered, knowing her response wouldn't make any sense to Kire.

But apparently, it did make sense to Kire. "I think Rezin is getting into their heads!" he shouted over Amberly as she continued to screech. Her screeching sounded inhuman. What was it that Rezin was causing her to see?

Trace pulled out her gauntlet and slid it on her arm, probably hoping it would somehow be able to help her.

Kaos nodded quickly. "I'll try and stop him!" He squeezed his eyes shut right in concentration.

"AMBERLY!" Trace bellowed, looking heavily distressed at the sight of his girlfriend. It didn't seem like the gauntlet was doing anything. "Stay with me! It's okay! It's not real!"

"Kaos, hurry!" Kire shouted, then he started coughing heavily.

"I'm... trying!" Kaos replied in a strained voice.

Then out of nowhere, the walls of the shack creaked and groaned violently, and then all four walls around them burst wide-open, and the ceiling flew into the sky, away from them all.

"How is that happening?!" Kire asked. Charlie was unable to speak because she was trapped inside of her fear.

"I-I think it's Amberly," Trace called over. But if Amberly was the one doing this, she seemed to have no idea, for her eyes were still shut tight, and she was still emitting a bloodcurdling scream.

Then it became clear that it wasn't Rezin who had done it. The flames separated and cleared a pathway for Charlie and the others to get to safety.

"Come on!" Kaos demanded, waving the others to follow his lead as he jumped through the opened flames and landed on the other side in a roll.

"Rose, you go," Kire instructed.

Charlie stood frozen still. So then Kire took her hand and

pulled her along, and the two then jumped out of the flames together.

"Trace!" Kaos called. "Amberly! Come on!"

Rose dusted herself off, coughed the last bit of smoke out of her lungs, and waited for Trace and Amberly to emerge from the flames, feeling nervous that they weren't going to come. Then thankfully, Trace carried a ghostly Amberly through the opening in the flames.

As The Unlikely Defenders stood outside the circle of blue flames around the shack that had burst open as if a tornado had run through it, Charlie strained to hear Rezin's voice again because she felt certain he hadn't left their presence yet. As long as there were still blue flames, she thought that surely meant he had to be nearby.

So then, where was he?

"Amberly, I can't believe you saved us," Kaos said to the trembling cheerleader as Trace gently set her back on her feet. She looked wearily at the gauntlet on her arm and then back at the flames.

"Where is he?" she asked in a shallow, shaky voice.

"What did you see?" Kire asked.

Amberly ignored him, so he looked to Charlie for the answer.

"I saw the world, and everything in it burned to a crisp," she said shortly.

Trace was looking rather tense as he stood there as part of the circle they had all formed in front of the shack.

"Trace?" Charlie asked in a careful voice. Something was up with him.

"I—I can't believe I wasn't able to do more to save Amberly," he muttered, not making eye contact with anyone. "I can't believe I couldn't do more to fight against him. He—he wasn't even..."

"He wasn't even there," Kire finished for him. "I don't know how he did whatever that was, but Rezin is nothing like the last two. He's going to be much tougher to defeat."

"How can we even expect to defeat him if we can't see him?" Kaos asked.

Trace stepped closer to his girlfriend and put a comforting arm around her as the others all stayed silent. Charlie was certain none of them had the slightest clue.

"I haven't even finished telling you guys everything," Kire told them. Slowly, the flames began dying away, and Charlie felt less worried that Rezin's presence was still lingering. She did not long to be ever brought back to whatever strange, horrible place Rezin had brought her.

"Great, there's *more*?" Trace asked, using a deep, whiny voice.

"I don't know how much more I can stand to listen to today," Amberly whispered.

"Amberly, are you sure you're okay?" Kaos asked. "Do you want to talk about it?"

Charlie felt hurt that no one seemed to be checking on *her* to make sure she was okay, too. Maybe she hadn't been screaming as much as Amberly had been. Maybe she didn't look as sickly as Amberly did, so everyone else thought she was fine.

Or maybe they just didn't care.

"I'm not talking about it," she hissed. Kaos raised his hands in surrender.

"You guys..." Kire trailed off before he began explaining the rest of what Halo had shown him. "Yash found another way to get to Earth."

"What do you mean he *'found another way'*?" Charlie asked.

"He is planning great destruction."

"Just great," Trace complained.

Kire nodded. "She said we have to search for something quickly to ensure that Yash isn't able to cross over."

"So, we have to look for and destroy another Djigi while we avoid being slaughtered by the alien jerkwad all over again?" Kaos asked.

"Apparently." Kire shook his head. "I don't know if I can do this all over again."

"Hah," Amberly barked out sarcastically. "For once, I agree with you about something."

"We have to," Charlie chimed in, talking louder than she normally did. "We are much more capable of finding whatever it is we are supposed to find if we work together."

"She's right," Trace agreed. "And I need another chance to prove myself that I am a fighter. I want to stab Rezin with my flaming sword and watch the life leave his eyes!"

"Of course you'd agree with her," Kire muttered.

"What's that supposed to mean?" Trace and Charlie said at the same time. Kire simply shook his head and looked away from everyone.

"Well, I'm in," Kaos said simply. He still had the crown on his head, and it made him look like the ruler of all of them. The one in charge who had the final say of what it was they were all supposed to do.

"Same," Charlie agreed, in case it wasn't already obvious to the others.

They all stared back-and-forth between Kire and Amberly, who still looked very hesitant.

"Fine," Kire eventually mumbled, looking at his feet.

"Amberly?" Trace asked, rubbing her back in slow, comforting circles.

"I guess I don't really have a choice."

"Great, then," Kaos said. "It's been decided. We're all going to work together again to stop Yash from ending life on Earth."

"I should make us superhero suits," Trace mused, eliciting a heavy sigh from Charlie.

8

As the Quintet group made their way back out of the forest, a whirring noise behind them startled them all, and they stopped walking. Charlie was too afraid to even look behind her to see what it was this time. Would Rezin try to attack them again so soon? Were they all destined not to make it out of the White Forest alive?

Luckily, Trace seemed to be the brave one in this instance. "Oh, it's you," he said, looking at something behind him. Since he didn't seem the slightest bit afraid, Charlie and the others turned around to see whom he was referring.

A misty vision of Albus was forming right before their eyes. It was his hologram, only instead of it being a scientific one, it was a magical one that his engineer cooked up for him back in the Albus Realm—the magical realm.

"Hello, you all," Albus Bridge said in his majestic, booming voice. Only his head and torso were visible—everything past that point on his body seemed to dissolve into a blue, foggy mist. Albus' milky all-white eyes stared around at them, his coiled, curly white hair hanging down to the middle of his stomach. His long and narrow nose seemed more pointed than

Rose remembered, and he didn't appear to have his usual chipper attitude this time.

"Hi, Albus," Kire said.

"I see you five just had an incident with Rezin's mind powers."

"So *that's* what that was?" Kaos asked. "He used only mind powers to attack us?"

"Is he even nearby?" Charlie asked.

"He is closer than you might think," Albus answered. "But that is not why I have come here to talk to you, I'm afraid. And I don't have long, so you all must hold your questions until I am through telling you what I must. Am I understood?"

"Yes," the five teens replied.

"Good." Albus clasped his hands together in front of himself, and it appeared as if he was going to be the bearer of bad news about something. "Kire, I know you were shown a vision from Halo about Rezin attacking and about Yash and how he found another way to get to your human realm. This is true. He found another way to get to Earth, and that way is through a magical portal. One of the portals is in your world, and the other one is in the Albus Realm. What I do believe this means is that Yash is going to come here to the Albus Realm to find our portal and use it to get to Earth. I believe he will stop at nothing to get to it. So likely, he will be attacking the Albus Realm. There will be a great war between us here and him. I am beginning to prepare for it as we speak."

Charlie felt sadness developing swiftly inside her. She didn't like the thought of Albuses being under attack by the evil Yash and whatever other minions he had on his ship. Albuses were kind, friendly, and peaceful.

"We do have some luck on our side, however," Albus continued. "It is going to take some time for Yash to get to the portal, even if he destroys the Albus Realm entirely. Not only does he not know where the portal is located in our world, but he doesn't know how to activate it once he finds it. He probably *did*, however, talk to Rezin and tell him to stop at nothing to prevent you five from finding and destroying the other portal so that he cannot get here to Earth. So not only is Rezin going to be trying to end all of your lives, but he is also going to be trying to thwart any efforts and plans you make to try and locate and destroy the portal."

"When you say *try* and locate...?" Trace trailed off.

Kaos swatted at him. "Dude, he said to hold our questions until the end!"

"It's quite all right, my dear boy. I know how Trace is so used to being able to say and do as he pleases," Albus said. Then he heaved a sigh before continuing. "By *try*, I mean that I do not know where the portal in your realm is. It will be up to you five to locate it and up to you five to destroy it. And you must do it quickly. We do have some time before Yash finds his way there, but not an infinite amount."

The others waited after Albus stopped speaking to make sure he was completely done with telling them everything he wanted. When the silence lingered on for a little bit too long, Charlie decided to speak up.

"Do you know how we can destroy it, at least?" she asked Albus.

"Or what it looks like?" Kire added.

"When you need the help, I am sure it will come to you," Albus told them. Then he looked over his shoulder—whether it was at something in their realm or something in his realm, Charlie had no idea. "I see I have some cleaning up I have to do back there. We can't have anyone seeing the destruction that was done to your beloved Challenge Shack."

"Albus, don't go," Kire said, taking a step forward. "We need your help. How are we supposed to do this? What's going to happen to you on your side?"

"I'm afraid I must go, Kire Hunter. I want to help you all as much as possible, but while preparing for this horrific battle in my realm, I am sorry to say that I simply will not have the time to do so. I know you all can do this, though. I have the utmost faith in your abilities. As long as you all work together, I really do think you can fix this. You five have given me the greatest hope in all my years." His hologram drifted closer to Amberly as he looked at her. "You must open up your heart, Amberly. It is a cold and dreadful place in there. And that coldness could be your downfall." Then he swayed over to Trace next. "Use your words, Trace."

"What do you mean? I know how to talk!"

Albus chuckled. "You also know how to throw a mean punch. Why do you harbor so much anger, Trace? Don't you think there might be another outlet? Maybe an outlet that will let you continue to fight while also doing some *good*?"

Trace scratched his head as Albus gave him a bemused smile and moved over to Kaos next.

"Kaos, I know you feel you are struggling to get a grasp on your powers. You must search inside yourself to find why that is. With the crown, you could have such greatness. But knowing what to do with that greatness will be your biggest life lesson to date."

Kaos' eyes clouded over darkly. Albus merely shrugged at the expression and moved on to Kire next.

"Kire, you mustn't doubt yourself."

He squinted. "Well, I try not to, but..."

"Ah," Albus replied. "See what I mean?"

Kire fell silent.

Charlie knew that her turn was coming next.

"Rose," Albus said when he floated in front of her. "Be careful with your abilities. You are fragile. More fragile than you realize. If you continue to go full force with the Pendantix when you haven't opened yourself up to the idea of letting others in, the cost will be greater than you could ever imagine."

Letting others in? But Charlie tried that already, and all it got her was hurt by Kire!

Still, she didn't want to say this to Albus, especially with all of the others listening in.

"How do you know all of this stuff about us anyway?" Amberly asked, crossing her arms.

He looked over at her. "Sweet girl." His mist started fading away and blending in with the background of the forest behind him. "I know everything."

"Albus, wait!" Kire tried.

"You know what must be done." Albus' hologram began going haywire, ricocheting around the forest as if it was a confused gnat. And then, as if he had never been there at all, Albus was gone.

9

The Unlikely Defenders all moaned and groaned after Albus cleaned up their mess and left them in the White Forest.

"So, we're looking for a portal of some sort?" Kaos asked.

"On top of trying not to get killed by Rezin," Charlie added, swallowing audibly.

"*And* before Yash destroys Albus' realm and then finds his way here to destroy our realm," Kire added. Already, Charlie thought the boy looked quite tired at the mere *thought* of what was to come.

"Stop being such babies," Trace said. "So it's going to take a little bit more work than we thought it would." He pulled his sword out of his scabbard and held it in his hand, the blade immediately bursting into flames which became a part of him. "As long as I get to fight some bad guys, I'm ready for it."

Charlie felt more nervous than she had before after hearing the warning Albus gave her. What did he mean when he told her she was more fragile than she realized? Was that part of the reason she got the bloody nose when she had been practicing her gift inside of the greenhouse before? Wasn't she supposed to be impervious to that kind of thing now that she was a Quintet?

"I'm not afraid," Kaos was quick to say. "That thing Albus said about me was bogus anyway. Let's do this thing."

The others all mumbled something about how what Albus told them wasn't true either, and then an awkward silence fell over them, so Charlie decided to start walking again, and the others followed suit. They didn't get very far, however, before in front of them, right in their pathway, a medium-sized cat appeared. It was slender and quiet, sitting and staring almost frivolously at them. Half of its body was black, and the other half of it was as orange as a carrot, the two colors creating a dividing line right down the center of its face.

Charlie stopped dead in her tracks.

"A cat," Trace pointed out, seeming almost excited about it. Amberly stepped forward with an arm outstretched, wanting to pet it, but as soon as she got too close, the cat simply turned around and started walking down the path away from them.

Amberly looked over her shoulder at Charlie and sneered. "Scared of a sweet little cat, Rose?"

"No," Charlie lied. But it wasn't just the fact that it was a cat that made her uneasy. There was something strange about the animal. Something... off. Was she being ridiculous, or did it seem as if the cat had somewhat humanistic characteristics? The way it kept looking over its shoulder at them as it continued walking along the trail ahead of them. The way it didn't run off or seem skittish or afraid of them.

Charlie eventually started walking again, not wanting to fall too far behind the rest of the group. As she did, she thought about her gift. How she had made the goat destroy the Djigi on Kula Mountain. It was the only time she had ever managed to control an animal before. She concentrated on the cat, trying to will it to leave them alone.

However, she had no such luck.

"So, this portal," Kire started as they reached the edge of the forest together. "It hasn't been found for hundreds of years..."

"Ask Halo," Kaos said. "I'm sure she'll tell you."

"It's not like she knows everything," Kire snapped. "Honestly, why did *I* have to be the one that got stuck with the book? I mean—I *like* Halo and all, but it seems like all of the answers to our questions and all of the information and responsibilities seem to fall on me. You're the one with the crown, Kaos. Why don't *you* tell us what we should do?"

"Fine," he said with a simple shrug. "I am no longer asking you to ask Halo about the portal. I am *telling* you."

Trace snickered, and even Amberly joined in, some of the color coming back into her cheeks. Charlie was not pleased to see it.

"Whatever," Kire grumbled, glancing over his shoulder at Charlie, who was still considerably far back from the rest of the group. Not only did she not want to be by the cat, but she didn't want to walk with the other four, either. She didn't feel like she was a part of the team. They didn't want her, so she didn't want them.

"Why are you all the way back there?" Kire asked. At his question, the others turned to glance back at her, too.

"Yo, Rose. Come on," Trace said with an eye roll. "It's just a cat. Look—it's harmless. It doesn't even want to come over to us."

"I can't believe she's scared of a harmless cat," Kaos said, talking as if Charlie wasn't even there.

"She's probably scared of cute little bunny rabbits and newborn puppies, too," Amberly said. Charlie wished she had the willpower inside of herself to ignore them, but she simply didn't.

"Why can't you all just leave me alone?!" she shouted at them as they exited the forest, the cat still up ahead of them, looking over its shoulder again.

Trace cleared his throat. "Chill out, Rose. We were just messing around."

But Charlie didn't find it very funny, and hearing Trace telling her to "chill out" only seemed to be making her angrier. "I don't care! I am a part of this team, whether you like it or not. You're not my ideal teammates either, you know!"

Amberly crossed her arms. "Yeah, because you'd rather have no one. wouldn't you?"

"Shut up, Amberly!"

Finally, Kire piped up. "Guys, just knock it off."

But Charlie shook her head quickly and pointed a finger at him.

"Don't even try to pretend like you're any better than they are, Kire Hunter!"

He looked offended. "Wait. You're mad at *me*?"

Charlie became so enraged that she almost felt slightly crazy. It made her laugh because she didn't know what else to do with herself—his comment had been entirely too absurd.

"I'm *especially* mad at you!" she snapped. "You're all jerks!"

"But Ro—" Kire tried, but Charlie wouldn't let him finish.

"Don't bother!" she told him, turning sharply on her heel and storming off. The cat stared at her with its beady green eyes as she walked a large distance around it on her way back to her house.

It wasn't necessarily Charlie's fault that she oftentimes found herself alone. Her mother and father had cast her aside because they favored Lexi. Lexi cast her aside, too, because Charlie hadn't turned out to be as cool as she was growing up. Now, when Charlie was finally a part of a group at school, she was cast aside even by them.

During her lousy walk home, Charlie was certain she hadn't felt more alone in her entire life.

10

When Charlie arrived home in the darkness after an eventful, awful afternoon in the White Forest, she worried her parents would be angry with her for staying out so late without letting them know what she had been doing. She walked through the front door and noticed right away that no one was in the living room. When she entered the kitchen, however, her family was all sitting at the table, eating dinner together.

"I'm home," Charlie said to them. They all looked up at her at the same time, then they turned and looked at each other. Beverly Rose, a woman with graying hair and a permanently sour look on her face, wiped her mouth on a napkin before speaking.

"Char—*Rose*. I didn't even realize you had gone anywhere!" She laughed shortly, and Timothy and Lexi Rose chimed in.

"What do you mean?" Charlie asked. "You're sitting at the table having dinner together. Didn't you call for me to tell me to come down to eat?"

"Well, we didn't think you'd want to have dinner with us," Timothy said. His cleft chin had a spot of tomato sauce on it, and his protruding beer belly also had a few stains from how sloppily he had been eating.

"Why wouldn't I want to have dinner with you?" Charlie asked.

It was Lexi who spoke next. "Because you haven't exactly seemed like you've wanted to spend time around us lately."

Charlie found her shoulders tensing. "Oh yeah, Lexi? Or is that just a lie *you* fed to Mom and Dad so that you can continue to have them all to yourself?"

"Charlie!" Beverly snapped. "You know your sister wouldn't do that to you! She loves you!"

Lexi looked overly offended. Maybe it was a trick of the light, but it even seemed as if she had somehow forced real tears at the waterlines of her eyes.

Dang, she was good.

"Yeah, *Rose*. Come on," Lexi said.

Charlie couldn't take any more of anyone else's atrocious behavior today. "Whatever," she snapped at her family, rolling her eyes and stomping her way up the stairs to her bedroom. Once she was fully inside of it, she slammed the door and locked it behind her.

"Someone's having a rough day," a pleasant, happy voice rang out from inside her bedroom.

"Tell me about it," Charlie replied, turning to Ramoni, her only friend in the whole world.

"Would you like to talk about it?" he asked her.

She sat down on the edge of her twin-sized bed with a huff and kicked her shoes off. "I don't know. I'm just feeling... overwhelmed. Like you said. I *would* focus on my studies and try not to worry about the rest of it, but it's just so hard to when the other stuff going on seems significantly more important than stupid high school."

"What would be more important than learning and growing up?" Ramoni asked.

Charlie laughed sarcastically. "The world ending, probably."

"I see."

"And I have to be one of the ones to prevent it from happening."

"Because of your gift?"

Charlie sighed. It was nice that Ramoni seemed genuinely interested in knowing what had happened and why she seemed to be having such a hard time, and she knew him to be very helpful, so she launched into the lengthy explanation of everything that had happened in the White Forest. She only had to pause a few times during the story when she heard the sound of her parents or Lexi coming up the stairs. She didn't want them to catch her talking to her plant—or worse—they'd think she was talking to *herself* since plants aren't supposed to be able to talk!

When Charlie finally finished filling Ramoni in, he immediately seemed to know exactly what to say.

"I think I might be able to be of some assistance."

"Really?" Charlie asked. She was suddenly leaning much more forward in her seat, in danger of falling off the edge of it, for hopefulness had just filled her heart.

"My ancestors *have* been around for a long, long time, remember?" he reminded her.

"Right, okay. What do you have for me?" She knew talking to Ramoni about this would be a good idea!

"Well, by word of mouth, I have learned about others with the Quintet gifts who had tried and failed before to defeat this Yash being and his minions."

"Yeah?"

"There is a small old library not too far out of town with a journal in it that has entries from one of the previous fighter's experiences."

"Are you referring to the Norduke Library?" she asked. "What is in the journal? Are you sure it's still there?"

"Correct. Norduke Library. And I believe it is still there. It was the last I heard, but I suppose that *was* several years ago... Nevertheless—no one else can make sense of the journal. Many think the man who wrote it, James Winterfell, was just a kooky old man who wrote the diary as a work of fiction. But to the Quintets, it might offer useful information."

"Might?" Charlie's hope dissipated slightly. She didn't want to be banking on "might." They needed to know where to find that portal, and they needed to know how to destroy it before their realm was demolished. Before the horrible, terrible vision Rezin had forced her to see back in that cabin became Charlie's reality.

"I have never read the journal, nor have any of my ancestors," Ramoni said. "I am sorry about that. But its' still worth looking into, wouldn't you say?"

She shrugged. "I guess we have to start somewhere."

"You're very brave, Rose. Did you know that?"

Charlie smiled fondly at him, but she was sure he was only saying that to be nice. If she *was* brave, she wouldn't be so scared of silly, helpless, harmless animals like the cat she had seen in the woods.

"Thanks," she muttered anyway.

When she got into bed after completing her seemingly never-ending homework for the night, Charlie felt a little better about how impossible the mission Albus had given her, and how the others seemed. At least they had somewhere they could look for potential clues about the portal's location. This James Winterfell person, even though he had inevitably been killed by either Jago or Heno at some point, might have known of a way he could help the new Quintets.

Hopefully, the book was still at the Norduke Library.

11

Charlie Rose had found herself back where she desperately never wanted to be again. She was alone, on an earth burned to a crisp. It was charred and dead. There was no sign of the sky around her because the smoke in the air was still so thick and black.

As terrified as she was, her stomach constricting violently, she looked down again. Thankfully, this time, her family and the rest of the Quintets were not lying before her, dead. Burned alive like everything else.

"Thank goodness," she said, putting a hand on her heart. She tried to swallow, but her mouth felt incredibly dry. How had she ended up here again? Was she back at the Challenge Shack? Was this the doings of Rezin's horribly incredible mind powers again?

"Hello!?" she called into the nothingness around her. She coughed, choking on the air. Her voice echoed for miles and miles, seeming like it was going to circle all the way around the earth and come right back to her.

I have to get out of here, she thought, closing her eyes for a moment so she could try and think of a way how. She became too afraid to open them again in fear of seeing Rezin standing before her, ready to kill her—the last human alive in the entire realm.

"Hello, Charlie," a voice said, sounding like it was being spoken into the world's largest and loudest microphone. The sound of it vibrated in her chest. She knew right away that it was Rezin's voice. It couldn't be anyone else's.

"Leave me alone!" she demanded; her eyes still shut tight.

Rezin chuckled darkly, but the sound of it slowly faded as if he was getting further and further away from her. When she could no longer hear him at all, she braced herself and opened her eyes.

She screamed, but Rezin was not the thing in front of her.

It was Kire, Trace, Kaos, and Amberly. They looked dead, but they weren't. Before her they stood, their bodies all badly burned, charred, and bloody. They were so covered in soot that she could barely even see the whites of their eyes. And yet, somehow, they were all alive, getting closer and closer to her with every step. So close, she could feel them breathing on her.

"No!" she pleaded. This couldn't be real.

"Why would you let this happen to us?" Kire asked.

"This is your fault," Trace said.

"Of course, it is," Amberly spoke.

Charlie suddenly bolted upright in her bed, covered in sweat and trembling all over.

It had only been a dream.

12

"Are you all right, Rose?" Ramoni asked as Charlie continued to pant in her bed, still feeling terrified over the nightmare she had just woken from.

"Yeah," she gasped out. "I think so."

"Well, not to alarm you further, but you have a visitor."

Charlie's stomach almost flew out of her butt at his words. A visitor? Now? In her home when it was so early in the morning?!

Slowly, Charlie turned her head. Her blood ran cold when she caught sight of a cat sitting on her desk, right next to where the climbing hydrangea was poking in through Charlie's open bedroom window. It was the very cat who had been in the White Forest with Charlie and the others the day before.

"What are you doing here?" she asked it, backing up into her headboard to get as far away from it as possible. But just as she had been assuming, the cat did not reply to her. It sat there, still as a statue apart from the menacingly slow waving of its tail.

I made the goat knock that mirror over on Kula

Mountain, Charlie thought to herself. If she had controlled an animal once, then who was to say she couldn't do it again?

She tried focusing harder, clutching her Pendantix with one hand. She stared at the cat and willed it to either tell her who he was or get out of her house. But after several minutes of trying and feeling like she was running out of breath, the cat did neither of those things.

"Dang it!" she grumbled. "What do you want?!" Was the cat really Rezin in disguise? Had he used his mind powers on her to make her have that dream last night? Was he going to hurt her now?

To her relief, the cat eventually turned and crawled back out the window, seemingly on its own accord. However, right before it did so, Charlie could have sworn she saw it give her a disappointed shake of its head.

13

When Charlie went to school the next day, as much as she wasn't looking forward to it, she knew she had to tell the others about what Ramoni had told her last night. They needed to search for James Winterfell's journal at that library just outside of town so they could check it to see if there were any clues as to where the portal to the magical realm was inside. She figured maybe they could take Kaos' car and go together when school got out, and that they could stay in the library all night researching if they had to.

She readied herself and entered St. Bernard High's cafeteria at lunch. It was just as horrible inside as she remembered. Grumpy old ladies in hairnets served questionably prepared food in front of lines full of dozens and dozens of starving, sweaty, immature teenagers. The cafeteria's high ceilings, vinyl flooring, and thin walls made the echoes of everyone's obnoxious voices even more aggravating than it was when Charlie had to endure it in the hallways in between classes. The place also smelled like dirty mop water and week-old chicken salad.

The worst part about Charlie going inside the cafeteria wasn't any of that, though. No—the worst part was seeing that

Kire Hunter was sitting at the same table as Trace, Kaos, and Amberly as if he was officially one of the most popular boys in the whole school. And even worse than that? Angela Altman was at their table as well, seated right next to Kire and giggling at whatever—surely stupid and moronic—thing he was telling her.

They hadn't spotted Charlie yet—something she was immensely grateful for.

She dashed quickly behind the crowd of the long lunch line, clutching her aching stomach. Why did it have to hurt so badly every time she saw Kire with Angela?

I came here to tell them the news about the journal, and that is all, she tried to tell herself. She could do this.

She took a few steps toward the table, coming out of her hiding spot behind the lunch line. She'd just ask to speak to them in private, tell them what Ramoni told her, keep it short and sweet, and then she'd be back to the greenhouse taking care of her lithops plant in no time.

But as Charlie made the trek across the squeaky flooring of the cafeteria, a thought seemed to nag at her, somewhere that started in the back of her mind but somehow made its way quickly to the front. Charlie had told Kire he was a jerk last night, and he had seemed completely confused as to why. *And* he hadn't even chased after her after she had walked away, nor had he tried to offer her any sort of explanation or apology over a text or a phone call to her later.

No. Apparently, Kire was more than fine with Charlie being mad at him. Apparently, he didn't think Charlie was worth an explanation or apology, no matter how simple it might have been.

These thoughts poisoned her mind and made her stop walking yet again. This time, she turned sharply on her heel and took off at a run, desperate to get away from Kire and the others as quickly as she possibly could.

CHARLIE DREADED GOING to Botany last period, even though it was her favorite class. She knew she'd again have to bear watching Kire and Angela flirting with each other at their table in the back. She kept her fingers crossed and hoped over and over again in her mind that the rest of the Quintets hadn't seen her running out of the cafeteria earlier. She was already embarrassed about it enough as it was.

She was already seated at her table—again with no one sitting next to her—when Kire and Amberly entered the greenhouse together. Kire walked ahead of her down the aisle in between the two columns of tables, and Charlie was almost positive he wasn't even going to cast a glance in her direction, let alone stop at her table to talk.

However, he came to a halt right in front of her, gripping the edge of her table with both of his hands and rocking back on his feet. "Hi, Rose."

"What do you want?" Charlie muttered, glancing at his girl-friend—or whatever she was—and feeling uncomfortable about her listening in on their conversation. Especially since Angela looked extra pretty today in her green floral dress. Charlie loved the dress and hated that she felt that way about it.

"Uh, I saw you at lunch today," he pointed out, making the tips of Charlie's ears turn bright red.

"So?"

"Kind of a weird place for a jog," Angela teased, reminding Charlie all too much of Amberly. Was it a requirement during the cheerleading tryouts that everyone had to show what a bully they could be?

Kire ignored Angela and continued looking at Charlie. "I guess I just wanted to know if everything is okay."

"It's fine."

"Come *on*, Kire. Let's go," Angela whined in an annoying voice that made Charlie want to plug her ears. "I want to tell you about these new shoes I'm thinking about getting this weekend so you can tell me if you think they will look good on me or not."

"Rose?" Kire tried. But Charlie faced straight ahead and pretended as if she could no longer hear or see him. So, with a small sigh and a nudge from Miss Bossy, Kire continued to his table in the back.

14

Charlie couldn't help but wonder if it would be the worst thing in the world for her to just... not tell the rest of the Quintets what Ramoni had told her about James Winterfell's journal. She could just take the bus to Norduke Library and find the journal herself. She didn't need the others.

And they didn't need her.

"Hi, Char," Lexi greeted Charlie when she got home from school later. She was standing there in the doorway, wearing a pink plaid skirt with a matching blazer, her hair in soft curls around her shoulders. Immediately, Charlie found it suspicious.

"Uh... hi?" she questioned, gritting her teeth. Her sister simply waved a dismissive hand at her.

"Don't be like that. I just wanted to check in and see how the first week of your second semester is going! Any boys you're talking to? Crushes?"

Charlie feared she was going to be sick. She never talked to her older sister about boys. Not only because it had never been something Charlie wanted to do, but also because until just that moment, it had never been something Lexi seemed interested in doing.

"Crushes?" Charlie asked, a slight edge to her voice. "No. I don't have time for boys. I need to focus on my studies and on getting into college."

Lexi made a face at her as if Charlie had just told her she had made the decision to drop out of school and become homeless. "But Char—"

"Rose."

"It feels weird to call you by my last name!"

"I don't care," Charlie snapped.

Lexi rolled her eyes. "Fine. *Rose.* Come on. I'm in college, aren't I?"

"Yeah, and?"

"And *I* still had time for boys while getting perfect grades. If I can do it, then so can you!"

"You're delusional," Charlie said, trying to get past her sister so she could go and get a snack from the kitchen before heading back upstairs to talk to her plant and work on her homework. However, Lexi put a hand out to stop her from going anywhere.

"I bet you'd be so much happier if you had a boyfriend like Lance. He is the sweetest guy on the planet! If you'd just let me help you with your horrendously weird wardrobe and add some highlights in your hair..."

Charlie bugged her eyes out at her sister so that she'd see just how much she would rather do *anything* else. "I like what I wear," she told Lexi for what felt like the hundredth time in her life. "And I like my hair like this! I don't need to change myself into you in order to get a guy to like me!" After all, Kire had liked her, even if only briefly, and she hadn't needed to change a thing about her.

"But I leave in a few days, and I just wanted to—"

"You just wanted to make me feel like garbage about myself.

I get it! Nice try, Sis. But it's not going to work. Now get out of my way." Charlie slammed her shoulder hard into her sister's as she made her way past her. Now she was so aggravated that she didn't even want a snack. She just marched right up to her room and locked the door behind her again.

AFTER CHARLIE SPENT what felt like a lifetime working on her English Lit paper for Mrs. Goody, which was due tomorrow, her cell phone suddenly began vibrating on her desk. She picked it up and saw Kire's name on the screen, and right away, her heart sank. It was only him texting her in the group chat with the other Quintets. Charlie didn't want to even bother opening the messages as they started rolling in, but she knew she should.

Kire: *Have you guys all been working on perfecting your gifts at all lately?*

Trace: *Kinda hard to prance around with a flaming sword in my backyard without drawing suspicion from my mother.*

Kaos: *Maybe a little. Why? Have you gotten any information out of Halo yet?*

Amberly: *It's not like we have all day, Kire. We need Halo to tell us what she knows so we can find this portal and close it up for good.*

Kire: *Halo might not be the only thing that can help us figure out where that portal is. That's why I asked you all if you've been practicing. The more you use your gifts, the better you will get with them.*

Kaos: *Unless you're Rose.*

Amberly: *BURN!*

Kaos: *What? No, it's not a burn, Amberly. I was being serious. Don't you remember what Albus told her?*

Amberly: *Why would I pay attention to anything that has to do with Rose?*

Trace: *Because we're all supposed to be on one team, babe.*

Kire: *Guys! Leave Rose out of this. You need to stop ganging up on her!*

This was when Charlie decided it was time for her to chime in.

Rose: *I don't need you to protect me, Kire!*

Trace: *Ha! Now THAT's a burn!*

Amberly: *Good thing he has Angela to protect then, huh? (;*

Kire: *I'm just trying to help. But fine, I'll stop. You guys need to work on your powers. That's all I'm saying. I'll keep trying with Halo. In the meantime, let me know if you find out any information!*

Charlie tossed her phone carelessly on her bed and stood up from her desk chair.

"Ramoni?" she called, looking at her plant. It was freezing in her bedroom, and she knew she could solve that problem by shutting her cracked-open window, but she didn't want to shut Ramoni out in case he had something important he wanted to tell her.

"Good evening, Rose!" Ramoni replied.

It was time for Charlie to work on her powers like Kire had suggested. "Is it okay if I manipulate you into helping me escape out of my bedroom window down to the sidewalk outside?"

"Are you sure that's wise this time of night?" he asked. Hearing him ask the question touched Charlie; Ramoni had sounded more like a father to her just now than her real father ever had before.

"I'll be careful," she explained, throwing her coat and gloves on. "I just want to head to the forest to do a little Pendantix work."

"All right. Thanks for asking first. You may proceed."

Charlie put the fingers of both of her hands to her temples and focused on the beautiful plant. The leaves of it started moving and rearranging. It started growing thicker, and the branches and stems tied around each other tightly. After a few minutes of work, Charlie had managed to make a sort of ladder out of the plant, and she crawled down it through her window with complete ease.

"Thank you," she told Ramoni, doing a little bow once she was safely on the sidewalk. Then she continued focusing and using her magic until Ramoni was back to just the way he had been before.

"I think I'm getting better at this!" she cried excitedly.

"Be safe, and don't stay out too late," Ramoni reminded her. She flashed him her dazzling smile and then made her way to the White Forest—her own personal garden.

It felt good to be able to use her gift so well out here. After several minutes of practice moving vines and branches and stimulating plant growth and decay of various species of plants in the forest, she couldn't understand why Albus had even said to her what he had before. She felt fine. She was doing fine. She wasn't fragile. She had her gift totally under control.

Until suddenly, she didn't.

The plants started retreating back to how they had been before Charlie had started manipulating them, even though she had been right in the middle of trying to create a perfect floral meadow. She held on as long as she could, but the more she did, the more the plants seemed to do the opposite of what she wanted. It appeared as if they were even starting to die. Not wanting to harm any of them, Rose eventually gave up, and when she did, she felt that familiar rush of dizziness consuming her.

Not again, she thought miserably. She sniffed, thinking maybe she had started crying, and wiped her nose on the back of her hand.

Only, when she pulled her hand away, it wasn't snot. It was blood again.

A rustle in the bushes beside her made her jump. The half-black and orange cat had emerged out of the shrubbery, back to stare creepily at Charlie again.

She backed away quickly.

"Don't you ever go bug any of the others?!" she asked it. The cat said nothing. Just as it had the two other times before, it merely sat there and stared at her while slowly swaying its tail.

Charlie began her walk back home.

"Not today, Rezin," she called over her shoulder to the cat as she went.

15

Charlie was nervous as she walked into Economics class. She had to tell the others about what Ramoni said, but she wasn't sure how they would take it. If they would want to believe anything a "stupid plant" would have to say when it came to finding the portal to the magical realm. When she had told Kire—the least judgmental of the group—about Ramoni and the fact that she talked to him and considered him a friend, even *he* had seemed freaked by it. Who knew how the others were going to react? Who knew if they even wanted to listen to a single word Charlie had to say to them? Why should they listen to her when they considered her to be nothing special?

Kire, Kaos, and Trace were all there inside Ms. Wright's classroom when Charlie arrived a couple of minutes before the bell rang. Amberly was the only one out of the Quintets that didn't have this class during the sixth period. She was off in Yearbook with Mr. Hartley.

"Hey, guys," Kire said, motioning for Charlie, Trace, and Kaos to gather around him at his desk in a huddle before class started. "I have to talk to you about something really quick."

Trace glanced up from his phone, seeming like he wasn't interested in paying attention to Kire. "What is it?" he asked, sounding immensely bored as his phone beeped and played some sort of video game music through its tiny speakers.

Charlie felt off, like she wasn't supposed to be a part of this pre-bell huddle. She was surprised that Kire even wanted her to be a part of it at all. And what would their peers think, seeing the coolest guys in school wanting to talk to... her?

For whatever reason, Kire, Trace, and Kaos didn't seem to care too much about it, however.

Kire made sure no one was listening in on them, then he spoke in a hushed tone. "Halo told me something about the you-know-what that Albus wants us to find and close off."

"Okay, what was it?" Kaos asked, using the same quiet voice. "Please tell me she told you where it is."

"Uh, not quite," Kire replied. "But she did give... a hint, I guess. She seems to think the portal to the magical realm is somewhere in our town. She suggested that we all need to start meeting up as often as we can to look for it."

"Of *course*," Kaos said sarcastically. "Did she give you any hints as to *where* we are supposed to look, at least?"

"Yeah," Trace joined in, seeming a little more interested in their conversation now. Either that, or he lost whatever game it was that he had been playing on his phone just now. "Knowing it's in our town narrows it down a *little*, but Montgomery is still a huge place! It would take us months to search every inch of it."

Charlie knew they were right, but she also knew that they *had* to find the portal. If they didn't, who knew what would happen? Perhaps it would be just like Charlie saw in her dreams.

"We'll just have to start looking," she said resolutely. "It's our only option." She trusted whatever it was Halo suggested they do. She was a gift from the *magic realm*, after all, so she probably knew better than anything else did in this human realm of theirs.

Kaos and Trace looked at only each other for a long while, as if they were having some sort of mind-reading conversation with each other that Kire and Charlie weren't allowed to be a part of. Then they nodded their heads and looked back at Kire and Charlie. "You're right, Rose," Trace said. "We'll do what Halo recommends. When should we meet up first?"

And just then, the bell rang, forcing them to pause their conversation.

Charlie took her seat next to Kaos at her usual Economics class desk, her mind racing with all the possibilities of where the portal could be hidden. She was so lost in thought that she didn't even hear Ms. Wright call her name for attendance. All she noticed was how everyone suddenly seemed to be staring at her.

"Oh," she said, clearing her throat and feeling her cheeks turn red from embarrassment as she realized *why* all eyes were on her. "Um, here." She sank lower in her seat, wanting to disappear. Ms. Wright, a woman with skinny legs and a round belly, just shook her head and continued on with the roll call. As soon as she was done, she launched right into her lecture for the day.

"Okay, class," she said in a tight, shrill voice. She held a wooden pointing stick in her hand and slapped it against the whiteboard loudly. "Today, we begin our next module in the textbook. *The basics of supply and demand curves.* Everyone open your books up, and I'll start reading while you follow along."

Charlie didn't open her book like everyone else was doing. It was because she wasn't paying attention. Her mind was still racing. With thoughts about what Kire had told her. With thoughts *about* Kire. And with thoughts about what Ramoni had told her.

Kaos tapped her on the shoulder, getting her attention.

"Hey," he whispered. "Are you all right? You seem really out of it today."

Charlie shook her head, trying to clear her thoughts. "Yeah, I'm fine," she lied. "Just a little tired, that's all." Besides, why did he care? He and the others hated Charlie. They probably wished it was Angela who was the fifth Quintet. Not her. And what if people saw him talking to her in her "weird" outfits? What would they think of him? Why would Kaos be willing to take that risk? He hated the way she dressed.

"Okay..." Kaos trailed off. It was clear he didn't believe Charlie for a second.

Whatever.

"Kaos. Rose. Please pay attention," Ms. Wright snapped, narrowing her eyes at them. "Rose. I said to open your textbook to the next module. Goodness, someone's head is in the clouds today."

"Sorry, Ms. Wright," Charlie replied sheepishly. She peeked at what page Kaos had opened his book to, then she did the same.

She knew she couldn't keep the information about James Winterfell to herself for long. She had to tell the others about what Ramoni had told her. They needed to know that there was a possibility that James Winterfell's journal in the Norduke Library could give them a clue as to where the portal was hidden. Even if it was just a slim chance, it was worth investigating. After all, they had nothing else to go on at the moment.

Kire turned around in his seat during Ms. Wright's horrendously boring read-aloud and mouthed, "We should meet up after the soccer meet tomorrow."

Charlie and others nodded in agreement before turning back to their textbooks. Trace looked as if he was about to fall asleep any second. Kaos was already four pages ahead of Ms. Wright, reading to himself intently. Charlie went back to doodling flowers inside the margins of the book. She knew the textbook was just a rental that she'd have to return at the end of the semester, but she didn't much care about the condition it would be in when she did so.

She ended up finding herself drawing Ramoni without even really thinking about it. She had to tell them. Whether she wanted to or not.

She sighed and resolved to just get it over with. After the soccer meet tomorrow, she would tell them everything that Ramoni had said. What the team would do with that information once they received it, Charlie had absolutely no idea.

Charlie had never been to a St. Bernard High soccer meet before, but she went because she had to meet up with Kire and the others afterward, and sitting in the bleachers, in the freezing cold, watching the game and the ridiculous cheerleaders doing their inappropriate dance moves in their inappropriately short skirts still seemed like a better plan than having to go home to deal with Lexi annoying her or her parents ignoring her.

Shivering, Charlie scoured the field in search of Kire, the school's new best player—apparently. It was easy to find him on the field. He was the one with the untidy brown hair flying behind him as he ran. Even though she didn't know the technical rules behind soccer, she could tell he was doing a decent job playing based on how he was dribbling the soccer ball down the field more than anyone else on his team—including Trace and Kaos—was.

She was surprised by how big the crowd was and how excited everyone seemed. She supposed she wouldn't have guessed that so many people at her high school were as into their school's soccer team as they actually were. It seemed almost as if everyone from school was there watching, no matter what temperature it was outside. Rain or shine, the school still had its fans. Several of them had made posters with Kire's name on them and were shouting his name eagerly.

It was still early in the game at that point, however.

As the game went on, Charlie started nibbling on her fingernails, feeling anxious and nervous. The game itself was turning out to be very interesting to watch, even though she didn't really understand it. What she *did* understand was that the team had started to do really badly. They were losing...by a lot, to Maple Ridge Academy. The other team's players looked mean and triumphant whenever they scored another goal. Charlie felt terrible for her school's team, but she also secretly felt glad that Trace, Kaos, and Kire were all getting their butts handed to them.

They deserve to be beaten and knocked off their high horses, she thought.

She could see the new coach from the sidelines. Coach Fletcher was a tall man with dark hair and an angry expression. He was shouting at his players and waving his arms around wildly. Everyone on the team looked scared of him, even Kire. Charlie didn't blame them. She could see that he was a very scary person.

No wonder they were playing so terribly. How could anyone do well with a coach like him?

As the game got deep into the second half, it became clear that St. Bernard High was not going to win. They were still losing badly, and Coach Fletcher was getting angrier and angrier at them. But Kire persevered. It seemed as if Fletcher's wrath only fueled Kire's determination. But ultimately, in the end, St. Bernard High lost the match.

Coach Fletcher was so enraged that he threw his clipboard on the ground and stormed off. The players all hung their heads in shame as they walked off the field. Charlie surprised herself because she found that she truly felt sorry for them.

It must be really hard to lose like that, she thought. Especially when they had been playing so well when they had Coach Turner in charge of the team. Why did he have to leave them to go back to his family in Barcelona at the end of last semester? This new coach was going to ruin all of their chances of making it to the end-of-year championship.

Charlie stood up from the bleachers. She supposed it was time. Time for her to go meet up with the others so they could start searching for the portal and so she could talk to them about what Ramoni had told her.

However, as she started down the clunky metal steps, she couldn't help but feel a little curious when she saw Trace disappear under the bleachers after the game instead of letting Amberly and the other cheerleaders crowd around him to try and cheer him up.

Where could he be going? she wondered, trying to keep her eyes trained on him through the immense throng of people leaving the stands to go support the losing players. It was too peculiar for Trace to be acting in such a manner.

She decided to follow him and see what he was up to.

Making sure nobody was paying any attention to her, she ducked out of sight and crept around the side of the bleachers so that she could sneak under them, too, and go to a place where she was well hidden and could not be seen by Trace. However, she had a *clear* view of him and what he was up to. She watched in astonishment as he met up with another person from their high school, Billy Michaelson—a good-for-nothing bad boy who was a year above them. The two were looking around each other as if they were afraid somebody was going to see them. Then they stood close to each other, and Charlie could clearly see Billy handing him a wad of cash. Trace quickly put it inside the pocket of his soccer shorts, then he looked around himself again to make sure nobody saw the transaction. What he didn't realize, was that *Charlie* had seen it. She had seen the whole thing.

Her stomach sank. She stayed there, not knowing what to do as the other two separated quickly.

What had that been all about? Why had Billy Michaelson been giving Trace money?

She had her suspicions about what the mysterious meet-up had been about. About what it was Trace had earned money doing. Was he about to get into a fight with somebody else? Had Trace done something to get the money? Something he shouldn't have?

Or could it be something else? Their team never played horribly. The whole game, Charlie thought it was because of their new coach. But what if that wasn't it?

Even though Charlie didn't have the whole story, one thing was clear about what she had witnessed.

Trace Henderson was up to no good.

17

Charlie decided to purposely wait a little while before she came back out from underneath the bleachers. She didn't want Trace to see that she had been hiding out under there and get any suspicions that she might have seen what he just did.

When she crawled out into the sunlight, shivering from the cold winter air, she could see that the group was huddled near a tree off in the greenfield. She could see stupid Amberly in her cheerleading outfit. She could see Trace, Kire, and Kaos sweating in their soccer uniforms despite the temperature. Thankfully, Angela wasn't with them this time. Hopefully, they told her that this gathering wasn't meant for her, and hopefully, it hurt her feelings when they did so. For whatever reason, Charlie *wanted* Angela to feel pain. Pain like *she* had felt.

Dragging her feet while she walked, she joined the group. The closer she got to them, the more clearly she could hear Amberly complaining.

"Why do we always have to do what Kire wants? What if I don't want to go search for the stupid portal?"

"Amberly, don't be like that," Trace tried. "I know it's a weird adjustment for Kire to suddenly be cool now and everything, but we've been... forced to do this, I guess. We're the ones that came across those gifts. And because we did that, we were selected. We have an obligation now. It's not like it's Kire making all the decisions. It's the gifts, really. Do you have any better ideas on how we should go about finding a portal if you don't want to listen to Kire?"

"Trace is right," Kaos said. "You don't have to like Kire. But we do have a job to do, Amberly. You throwing a girly hissy-fit isn't going to help anything."

"Hey, Rose," Kire said when Charlie arrived at the group. She nodded her head slightly to acknowledge him, but she didn't feel like speaking to him. Nor did she feel like listening to Amberly's whining and complaining. It was as if that was all Amberly knew how to do.

Amberly crossed her arms and jutted out one of her hips. "Trace, I can't believe you're not taking my side."

"You know I always have your side, babe," he tried. "But like I just said—"

"How about you guys talk about your disagreements later on?" Kaos asked. "Now that we're all here, we really should get started."

"If he would just tell his dad—*our* dad—about me, then I'd feel differently!" Amberly continued, not listening to anyone. This was so typical of her. Making everything about her. The world revolved around her. At least, in *her* eyes it did.

"Amberly," Kire tried. He looked helpless. Exhausted. First, he lost the game, and now, he had to listen to this?

Amberly gave Kire the dirtiest look Charlie had ever seen her give a person. "Why won't you just tell him that you know about me, Kire?! I don't get it! Why?!"

"This isn't the place or the time," Charlie finally decided to say. She wasn't here to listen to this. She didn't want to be around the other four if she didn't have to be.

"No one cares about what you have to say, Charlie," Amberly hissed at her. Then she started backing away from the circle. "You know what? I'm not going. Trace, come on."

Suddenly, Trace's face went slightly red. He balled his fists. Instead of going with Amberly, he marched right up to Kire, getting close to his face.

"Look." His tone was angry. It reminded Charlie very much of how Trace used to treat Kire before they all joined forces last semester. "You need to talk to your old man. Got it? If you don't, there's a chance your face might accidentally run into my fist. Okay?"

Kire said nothing. Instead, he just stared at Trace. Trace eventually backed off, then went to go follow after Amberly. As he walked, he looked at Kire over his shoulder. "Besides. Once you do it, there's a chance Amberly will stop acting so horribly toward you. Just think about it. Decisions are yours."

"Come on!" Amberly continued shouting, a few feet up ahead of Trace still.

"Kaos, are you coming?" Trace asked. He stopped walking toward Amberly to see if his friend was going to follow with him or not.

Kaos looked between Kire and Trace. Conflicted.

"Dude," he complained. "I want to find the portal. You know, so we can just get this over with. The faster we get the stuff done, the quicker we can be done with all of this."

"Kaos, are you serious?" Trace asked, looking disappointed. Usually, Kaos and Trace were always on the same team. They were practically inseparable.

"Why can't you guys just listen to Kire?" Kaos asked, sounding resigned.

"Because he sucks!" Amberly called over her shoulder as she continued to walk away. This got a little chuckle out of Charlie, as much as she usually didn't care for anything Amberly had to say. When Kaos and Kire both looked at her, she put a hand over her mouth and turned away so they wouldn't see it.

"Man, whatever," Trace said, waving a dismissive hand and shaking his head at Kaos before turning around to go join his girlfriend.

"Fine then," Kire said. "Looks like it's just the three of us."

Just great, Charlie thought. *Just. Great.*

18

"Okay, then," Kaos said as the three of them stood around the greenfield by the school together. It seemed it would just be Kire, Charlie, and him searching for the portal today. "Where should we check first?"

At the same time, all three of their heads turned toward the White Forest.

"Of course, it would be in there," Kaos said.

"It's as good a place as ever to start looking," Kire said.

"Besides. You really expect it to be behind a Supermart or something like that?" Charlie added.

"*Psh*, no," Kaos said, trying to look cool. "Course not."

Kaos took off first, taking the lead. Charlie had it in her head that he just wanted to prove how brave he was and that he didn't care about having to go search inside the woods. Kire snickered at him from behind and tried to catch Charlie's eye, but Charlie avoided him at all costs.

"How do we know what we're looking for?" Charlie asked. They had entered the forest and were looking around themselves in all directions, going off the normal trails. "Is it like an obvious structure? Is it made of plants? Is it like a black hole in the ground or something?"

"Unfortunately, I have no idea," Kire replied. "Halo really didn't give me that much information to go off."

Hmph.

Sighing, Charlie decided it was time to finally let the guys know what she had heard from Ramoni.

"So, I was talking to my climbing hydrangea recently," she slowly started to say. Kaos looked over his shoulder at her with a weirded-out expression.

"Ramoni. The plant outside my house that talks to me. Remember?" she asked.

"Whatever," he replied.

"Anyway," Charlie continued, "Ramoni did give me some insight. About something that might help us figure out where the portal is."

Kire completely stopped walking and spun toward her. His eyes were incredulous as he held his hand up and said, "Why wouldn't you tell us sooner?!"

Charlie rolled her eyes. "Relax. I'm telling you *now*, aren't I?"

"Okay, go on, then," Kaos said, pausing in his step too. Charlie did the same.

She filled him in on everything Ramoni had told her about James Winterfell and his journal in the Norduke Library.

"So, your plant thinks we should go to some dumb old library and search through books all day long?" Kaos asked at the end, not sounding at all excited about the news Charlie had to give.

"It could be worthwhile, don't you think?" she tried. "I mean, what if it's written there plain as day in the journal where the portal is? But the reason nobody else ever understood it was because they didn't know what we know?"

"Yeah... you're not going to catch *me* at a library," Kaos said. "Especially not during the weekend. Sorry, not sorry."

"You know what?" Rose snapped. "I don't *want* you to come with anyway. I'll go alone. I'm just telling you guys what I learned from Ramoni."

"Come on, now," Kire interjected. "Kaos might be too afraid of looking like a loser inside of the library, but I'll go with you, Rose. I think Ramoni has a good idea. A good starting place, at least."

Charlie resumed walking. She wanted to pretend as if she hadn't even heard him, but she knew it was too obvious that she had. "I'm good, thanks," she said to Kire. "Going alone will be best."

"You know that's not true," Kire said, running to catch up with her. He tripped over a tree root on his way and flew face forward, knocking into Charlie and nearly sending her tumbling to the ground.

"Ow, what the heck, Kire?" Charlie asked, spinning around to shoot him an offended expression. In the back of them, Kaos was cracking up.

"I'm sorry!" Kire whined. "I just tripped!"

Huffing, Charlie turned back around and continued looking around for the portal. "Anyway," she resumed. "If we don't find the portal today—which I doubt we will—I'll head to the library tomorrow and try to find that journal."

"Same," Kire joined in.

Kaos snickered. "You two have fun with that."

Charlie knew it was going to be pointless to continue arguing with Kire. He wasn't going to take no for an answer—he was pretty horrible at doing that.

"Fine. Whatever," she said. "Kaos, you tell Trace and Amberly the plan, and then tomorrow, Kire and I will meet up and search for James Winterfell's journal. I'll keep you guys updated on our findings after that."

Despite the awkward day she was dreading having with Kire tomorrow, Charlie felt good as they continued their search through the White Forest for any signs of a portal. She felt as if she had made a decision for the group. And even though the majority of them wouldn't be coming with her, they had agreed that her plan was a good one. She might not have needed the Quintets, but she felt like maybe they did need her after all.

19

As the sun started to set while the three young teenagers wandered through the White Forest, it became clear to Charlie that their efforts to find the portal today were going to be futile.

"How are we going to even know which part of the woods we already searched when we come back next time?" Charlie asked, feeling as if this was all hopeless.

"Uh..." Kire trailed off, thinking. "I guess I didn't really consider that."

"Me neither," Kaos said. "The next time, we'll remember to bring colorful string so we can mark the areas by tying some around a tree trunk or something. That should help."

Charlie nodded and pursed her lips. "I think we should give up soon. Things get weird in here when it gets dark."

"Like what?" Kire asked.

"You know... like... creatures. Things that go bump in the night. Animals that want to eat us for dinner."

"*There* you go again," Kaos said, rolling his eyes. "Always so concerned about getting eaten or attacked by animals. You can't even handle something as small as a cat."

Instantly, Charlie thought about the black and orange cat that had seemed to be following Charlie around lately. "You know, *you'd* be unsettled too if it was following you around everywhere," she pointed out. "And besides. What if the cat was disguised? What if it was really Rezin underneath all that fur? Rezin could disguise himself as anything. Any*one*. We never know when he's going to attack again. What he's going to try next." Even thinking about it, Charlie was getting the chills.

It seemed like it was getting darker and darker by the second, and she was eager to get out of these woods. Normally, she loved the White Forest. She loved going into the caves and doing her bioluminescence project. Being at one with the plants and nature around her. And she had been brave enough to go into the White Forest alone to practice with her powers, but that had been before she noticed that creepy cat just staring her down in the shadows. Even now, she looked around herself every so often for a sign of it. A flash of that bright orange fur or a swinging black tail.

Just then, Charlie spotted something besides the cat—a plant that she admired and became thrilled about every time she saw it. The Dwarf Lake Iris. Or in Latin, *Iris Lacustris*. It had thick green leaves underneath a pretty bluish-purple flower with yellow buds that hummingbirds loved to suckle on. She knelt down to admire it closely, pulling her phone out and snapping a photo of it. She hadn't even noticed that Kaos and Kire hadn't realized she had fallen behind. When she finally stood up and was ready to continue on with this ridiculous portal search, only then did she discover that the others were out of sight.

Uh oh.

"Guys?" she called.

No answer.

She nibbled on her fingernail, chipping the nail polish off it but not really caring. It was still getting darker out.

But then, suddenly, it was pitch black. Charlie had no idea how it happened. The sun never set that quickly. And it wasn't as if there were clouds in the sky. From what she was seeing underneath the canopy of trees above her, it was a clear, starry night. How had it become so dark, then?

As she slowly turned about herself, she realized that the forest no longer looked familiar. She had no idea which way was which. The Dwarf Lake Iris was no longer beside her. In fact, nothing pretty or lively was. All the plants were now a dull green color. And all of the tree trunks, soil, and dirt on the ground were black.

"What's happening?" she asked out loud. "Where am I?"

If she knew one thing for certain, it was that she was no longer in the White Forest. She didn't know why, and she didn't know how, but all she knew was that she was in trouble.

"Kire!" she called, her heartbeat picking up speed as fear coursed through her veins. *How am I supposed to get out of here?*

She started walking, even though there was no longer a trail nearby to walk on. Everywhere she went, it sounded like there were twigs snapping and branches cracking behind her. Every time she whirled around, her stomach dropped to nearly the floor.

"Guys, help!" she tried again, but she knew it was useless. It seemed as if she had been the only one transported to this strange place. Kire and Kaos were probably still back in the White Forest, not even realizing that she wasn't with them anymore.

"Don't worry, Rose," Kire's voice suddenly said, even though it sounded strange. Like an echo. "We didn't leave you."

Charlie turned all around herself, trying to figure out where his voice had come from. Where Kire was hiding.

"Yeah," Kaos joined in. His voice sounded the same. As if it was echoing all around her. "We're right here."

She jumped in fright at a rustling bush and let out a little squeal.

You're supposed to be braver than this, Rose.

The bush continued rustling, and she continued stepping backward in terror. The branches parted, and out stepped Kire and Kaos. They looked like themselves, but only... something was off.

They were smiling at her. Wickedly. Their eyes were green and glowing. Almost as if their eyes were night lights. It was the only bright thing she could see inside this dark world around her. They were slowly creeping toward her with sinister expressions.

"What are you guys doing?" she asked.

"Don't be scared," Kire said. But the voice he used made Charlie feel like she should, in fact, feel *very* scared.

"S-stay away from me!" she cried.

"What's the matter, Rose?" Kaos asked, not listening to her request. He got closer and closer to her. Rose continued backing up until her ankle caught on something, and she fell backward onto her butt, right in the mud. She scrambled back to get away from them, but they still kept approaching.

"This isn't funny," she told them.

"Of course it isn't," Kire told her. "There's *nothing* funny about us trying to kill you."

"What—what are you talking about?" she asked, her teeth chattering. They couldn't mean it. They weren't possibly wanting to kill her. She didn't understand how this was happening. Who had somehow transported her into this other world?

Frightened and afraid for her life, Charlie clutched the Pendantix. Then she got back to her feet and focused on the vines around the two boys. She concentrated hard, and suddenly, they started moving and wrapping themselves around Kire and Kaos. The two angrily fought against the vines, but Charlie refused to let them go. And even though Kire was trying to bite and cut himself out of his, every time he made any dents in the vine, Charlie made the plant grow back twice as strong.

It was Kaos who kept advancing toward Charlie despite the vines holding him back.

"Kaos, stop!" she cried.

This couldn't be real. It had to be another dream. She had to have fallen asleep while looking at the Dwarf Lake Iris somehow.

But Kaos kept trying. He was much stronger than he looked, so the vines had a harder time holding him back than they did Kire.

So then, Charlie did the only thing she could think of to stop Kaos from attacking her. She made one of the vines wrap itself around Kaos' throat. It held on tight, choking him so hard that it was lifting him off the ground.

"What are you doing?" Kire asked. But when Charlie looked in his direction, it didn't sound like his voice had come from the Kire who was in front of her, trapped in the vines.

"Charlie! Stop!" he cried out.

Charlie turned around, and suddenly, she was back in the White Forest. Kire was in front of her, looking terrified as he ripped the vines free from around his body. He continued staring at Charlie. She didn't understand why he seemed so afraid of her. Just moments ago, he had been trying to kill her.

"Charlie, make it stop!" he shouted again.

Make what stop?

She heard the noise of someone struggling behind her. She spun around and saw Kaos. Just like she had been doing in her dream, she was choking Kaos with the vines of the trees above them. He was lifted off the ground, his face turning purple.

Panicking, she quickly made the vines release Kaos, and he dropped to the floor on his hands and knees.

He coughed and sputtered and inhaled oxygen into his lungs, glowering at Charlie as he did so.

"I don't know what just happened!" she cried. "I thought we couldn't use our powers on each other like that!" She was breathing heavily. "Where were we just now? I think... I think Rezin did something to us!"

"To *us*?" Kire asked, looking angered. "Kaos and I came back here to try and find you once we realized you weren't with us anymore. When we found you, you seemed to be in some weird sort of trance, and then out of nowhere, you were attacking us with vines!"

"You were trying to kill me!" she argued.

"Are you out of your mind?" Kaos asked. His voice was raspy as he rolled over to sit on his butt, still trying to collect himself. "Why would we want to kill you? We need all five of the Quintets in order to complete our duties, Rose."

"That's it," Kire snapped. "We're not coming back and doing this again unless we have all five Quintets together. We need to be able to look out for each other."

"I..." Charlie trailed off, not knowing what else to say about it. Apparently, all of it had been fake. A trick Rezin had played on her. He had tried to turn Kaos and Kire against her. And in turn, Charlie retaliated and attacked her own teammates.

"I—I'm getting out of here!" she blurted out, turning on her heel and running down the trail. She wanted to get out of the White Forest as quickly as humanly possible.

20

Charlie was slightly embarrassed to meet with Kire the next day to go to the library together. They agreed to meet at a park inside her neighborhood because she didn't want Kire coming directly over to her house where her sister and her parents would ask him a million questions about who he was and what he was doing with Charlie. Nor did she have any interest in going to Kire's house and talking to his parents. Heck, she hardly even wanted to talk to Kire at all. Especially now.

She reached the park first and sat on a bench, twiddling her thumbs while she waited for Kire to show. It was another cold day, but the sun was at least peeked out through the clouds this time. No snow or sleet was coming down on her. The grass around her was dead and dry, and there didn't appear to be a single kid out on the playground or anybody walking the path around the small pond. Charlie was alone until Kire arrived, his black backpack over both shoulders, his hands on the straps of them. He approached her and gave her a lopsided, close-lipped smile. "Hey, Rose. How are you doing this morning?"

Charlie got to her feet. "How is Kaos?" she asked, not bothering to answer his question. She had been too nervous to even try to text Kaos last night to reach out to him to see if he was feeling okay after she had nearly choked him to death with the vines. She felt terrible about what she had done to him. And looking down at Kire's wrists, which were visible underneath the sleeves of his navy blue hoodie, she could make out some scratches and red markings where the vines had gripped him, too.

"Kaos has perfectly healed already," Kire said. "I texted him before I went to bed last night to make sure. Our new healing abilities really are something else."

"Yeah. That's good to hear, though."

"So, do you want to talk about what happened last night?" he asked, running a hand through his hair. It gave Charlie the strange urge to run her own hand through his hair, but then she remembered how much she was supposed to be hating Kire right now.

"Not really," she said. "Clearly, Rezin was messing with me."

"He doesn't play like Heno and Jago did," Kire pointed out. "He plays these mind games. He's trying to mess with all of us mentally so that we fail physically."

"Apparently so."

"Well, at least it wasn't worse," he said, trying to be optimistic.

"I don't know why it seems like he's only messing with me," she said.

"What do you mean?"

"I've been having bad dreams because of him every night. I feel like he's making that cat follow us around. Or follow *me* around. It's like Rezin has me as his personal target, and I wish I knew why."

"You're not the only one having bad dreams," Kire informed her. "I have them, too."

She didn't know why, but for some reason, his words made Charlie feel a little bit better.

She cleared her throat. "Well, I feel sorry for you. Because they're terrible."

"What did he make you see yesterday?" Kire asked.

"I saw you guys," she admitted. "You and Kaos, in the White Forest. Only... it didn't look the way the White Forest normally does. Everything was black and this dark, hunter-green color. And your eyes were glowing. And... you both wanted to kill me."

"Uh, I *assure* you, that that's the *last* thing we want, Rose," he said. "So, if anything like that happens again, just try to remember that I said that. See if that can help you distinguish between what is real and what is fake."

Charlie nodded sheepishly and avoided his gaze. "Okay, then. Let's just get this over with."

They walked over to the bus stop together and stood underneath the awning. Thankfully, there were a couple of other people waiting for the bus as well, so Kire and Charlie couldn't make conversation about anything related to the Quintets and their gifts. And if it weren't for those things, they'd have nothing else to talk about—which is why they stayed silent.

As a bus pulled up, Charlie stood behind Kire to board it, but her eyes flew to his backpack when she noticed something peculiar. She could've sworn the thing just jiggled around as if a wild, loose animal was trying to make its way out of it.

She decided it must've been a trick of the light and continued following Kire onto the bus. They sat down next to each other in one of the rows of seats, and Kire put the backpack on his lap.

As the bus took off when everyone else was seated, it happened again. This time, Charlie was sure of it.

On Kire's lap, the backpack jiggled around almost violently.

Kire got a tight, firm grip on it.

"What's going on?" Charlie hissed quietly, not wanting anyone around her to see or hear them.

"It's—Halo—" he said as he struggled to keep the backpack still. "She won't stop moving around."

"Don't you think that's probably because she has something to tell you?" Charlie asked, arching an eyebrow.

"Probably, but this isn't really the place, is it?" Kire snapped back.

Charlie crossed her arms and sat back in the seat. The entire bus ride over to the stop where the Norduke Library was, just outside Montgomery, Charlie had the urge to snicker as people started giving Kire strange looks as he struggled against his moving backpack. No doubt they thought he was keeping an animal in there that he shouldn't be. They thought he was being an abusive pet owner, or that he was trying to smuggle an animal in somewhere he shouldn't. For some reason, it made Charlie feel slightly happier to know that Kire was being judged so hard by all of the adults around them.

When Charlie and Kire finally got off the bus, Halo was moving around so much that it was impossible to keep the backpack still. Every time Kire tried, his entire body wriggled with the backpack, and he looked in danger of falling to the ground as he wrestled with it.

Groaning, Charlie motioned for him to follow her. "Come on, let's just go in here." They went into an alleyway between two buildings in the cute downtown area they were in. Finally, Kire dropped the withering backpack down onto the ground and panted, out of breath.

"Good cardio workout?" Charlie joked.

Kire shot her a look, then he unzipped the backpack and took the book out. It burst open, and immediately began to write. Charlie tried to read what it was saying over Kire's shoulder, but Kire was apparently the only one that could understand anything it was saying. She watched his facial expressions as she waited for him to digest it all. He went from confused, to *more* confused, to anxious, to angry, to worried. Then he finally looked back up at Charlie.

"This isn't good," he told her.

"What is it?" she asked, her stomach dipping. Did Halo just tell him that Rezin was on his way to attack again? Was the same thing going to happen to Charlie as it had last night in the woods? She wasn't ready for it.

"It's the Albus Realm." Kire's head went back to the book as he kept reading.

"What about it?" Charlie asked, feeling impatient.

"Oh, man. It's in bad shape, Rose."

"What's going on, Kire?"

"It's... it's under attack. Yash sent all kinds of creatures to destroy all of the powerful ones in the Albus Realm."

"It's under attack? Like Albus mentioned when he said he needed to start preparing? Is Albus okay?"

"I don't know," Kire answered. "This is bad, Rose."

"Yeah," she agreed. "Really bad. Why are they attacking? I thought all Yash needed to do was just get to the portal in the Albus Realm so that he gets here to Earth."

"I guess he sent minions to destroy all of the Albuses and other magical beings. Apparently, he sent them all down so that everything gets destroyed so that there's nothing in Yash's way when he arrives in the magic realm."

Charlie swallowed, feeling terrible about this whole situation. They needed to find the portal to the magical realm, and they needed to find it fast. Albus' life depended on it. "It makes sense," she said bitterly. "He wants nothing in his way so that when he finally gets to the portal in the magical realm, there won't be anything trying to stop him."

"Exactly," Kire said. "Nothing to stop him at all."

21

"Ask Halo if she knows how much time we have," Charlie said quickly. She and Kire were still in the alleyway near the Norduke Library, the book pulled out to tell Kire about the horrible things happening in the Albus Realm.

Kire nodded his head. "Okay, I will." He dug around in his backpack to get a pen out, then he scribbled in the book. The waiting was torture. Charlie wished she could just read the words Halo was creating over Kire's shoulder as they appeared like he could.

"What's she saying?" Charlie asked, even though only a couple of seconds had passed by since Kire had written the question.

"She's saying that... *ugh*, of course. She's being vague again. She's saying that we don't have much time."

"Ask what that means!"

Not much time? Like I need to find the portal today? Tomorrow? When?

"Okay, okay!" Kire said, his voice getting shrill. But then

again, so was Charlie's—Kire's tone was probably just in a reaction to that.

Kire continued scribbling some more. Then he read Halo's reply.

"She said that we don't need to be too worried, but that we do need to speed it up a little."

"Can't she tell us anything more helpful?"

He wrote some more. Then he waited for her to answer.

"She doesn't know anything more," he told Charlie.

"I don't believe her," Charlie said.

"Well, I do," Kire argued. "I've already been talking to her about this a lot lately. I've gone over these questions with her. I'm going to ask her to give us more details about the attacks in the magical realm, at least."

"Fine. Yeah. Good idea," Charlie said, shaking her head enthusiastically. She wanted to know as much information as possible about what was happening in the magic realm.

Kire got back to scribbling. It took a while longer for him to be able to say Halo's reply this time because her response was a couple of paragraphs long.

"Okay, so to summarize, the creatures in the magical realm are different from how they were here on Earth. On Earth, Heno, Jago, Rezin—they showed up looking like alien figures, right?"

"Okay..."

"Well, apparently, in the magical realm, they show up as *mythical* creatures. As forms of werewolves and trolls and other beasts that they fear most. And there is talk that those beasts already *do* exist in that realm. But Yash's beasts are beasts like none other. They have magical powers. The ability to wipe everything out. So, what Halo is telling me is that Albus isn't trying to hide, and that the powerful ones—the Albuses—are trying to fight back because they don't all understand that these aren't the normal mythical creatures. They're from a different realm."

"That's horrible," Charlie replied. She tried to picture the mythical creatures.

"Yeah. There have been casualties already.

"Is Albus okay?"

Kire nodded. "He's okay—for now. But Halo said she can't give me a continuous read on him, either. That it drains too much of her energy."

"So, how are we supposed to know if he makes it alive or not? What if something happens to him, Kire? We need his help."

It was awful to think about. Sure, Charlie had only met Albus a handful of times, but she really liked the man. He didn't deserve to die. And if all of the other Albuses in the realm were like him, then they didn't deserve to die either. Yash had no rational reason for wanting to do this. For wanting to destroy Earth. Other than for the fact that he could. He was an evil, vile monster.

"Hang on," Kire said. He read something that Halo was writing out to him. "Halo says that she's done answering our questions for now. She needs some time to charge. Her last message is, 'Just hurry and find that portal. And find a way to close it. Multiple realms are counting on you five.'"

Then the book fell limp in Kire's hands. He closed it and shook his head. Charlie crossed her arms and leaned against the dirty brick wall in the alleyway. "That's it?" she whispered. "No more information?"

"At least not for now," Kire said. He put the book gingerly back in his bag and zipped it up. "I really hope Albus is okay."

"And that he *stays* okay," Charlie said.

"So, when we go to this library today. And if we find James Winterfell's journal, like your plant friend—"

"Ramoni," Charlie reminded him.

"Right. Ramoni. Like Ramoni said—if we don't find any hints as to where the portal is, then what do we do next?"

"Why are you asking me like I would have any idea, Kire? You're lucky I even came across this lead to go off. I'm apparently the only one who is trying with their gifts to get answers."

"Excuse me?"

"Beside you," Charlie said, adding an eye roll in.

"I know you're trying," he said. "And I'm grateful for it. The other ones, they just aren't taking it seriously enough. And Kaos... I don't know. I don't think he's getting the hang of his crown very well."

"Too bad," Charlie said, and bit snippily at that.

"Yeah, I know. Trace and I have been telling him that."

"Good."

Kire sighed. "I really hope we get some sort of information from this James guy, Rose. Otherwise, we have nothing else to go off. No other trails to follow. All we will be able to do is take that stupid colorful string into the White Forest and wander around hopelessly until we find something that might be the portal."

"And to make it *worse*," Charlie added, "we don't even know what the portal looks like."

"Exactly." Kire looked back at his backpack. "I just wish Halo could be a little bit more useful than she has been lately."

"Or that Albus could come back here and offer us his words of advice."

He chuckled softly. "Even if sometimes his words don't make a whole lot of sense."

"He is kind of kooky, isn't he?" Charlie asked, smiling a little too, despite the sad situation. Once she realized again how dire things were, she sighed. "When he told us he wasn't going to be able to be much help because he was going to be too busy preparing for this battle... I don't know. I guess I didn't realize the battle was going to be starting so soon. It makes me nervous about how much time we really do have."

"I know," Kire said, nodding and looking down at his dirty sneakers.

"We just... we'll find a way," Charlie decided, thinking one of them had to have some sort of optimism. "We have to."

"Yeah. Uh, I guess we should probably stop wasting time standing here in the alleyway discussing what we should or should not do. We need to get to the library and find that journal, don't we?"

"You know..." Charlie said, trailing off. She stepped away from the wall, seeing Kire in a sort of different light—like she used to see him back before he had hurt her. "You are really taking all of this stuff seriously, aren't you?" It seemed as if Kire was the only one besides her who did.

"Of course I do," he replied. "I don't want anything happening to Earth. And I don't want anything happening to the magical realm, either. So what that I've never been there? So what if I don't know anybody or anything about the other realm? Nobody deserves to die at the hands of Yash. For no reason at all."

Charlie said nothing and stood there staring at him instead. She just didn't understand it. Despite how poorly Kire has acted toward her lately, and despite the way he moved on from her and onto Angela in what seemed like the blink of an eye, he was still a really good human being. She couldn't deny it. So how could somebody as good and just and kind as Kire just drop Charlie like she was nothing? Like she didn't matter at all? Especially when right before he did so, it seemed as if he cared about her more than anyone else in the world?

It just didn't make any sense to her.

None whatsoever.

22

The exterior of the Norduke Library was much different from what Charlie had been expecting. For a place that held such an old journal, she expected something more old-fashioned. A stone exterior with stone steps, big marble columns, and a frieze on top. Instead, the Norduke Library had a more modern feel. It had floor-to-ceiling glass-paned windows and glass automatic doors. The sides of it were wrapped in a thick planked wooden paneling and cement, and there was a wide overhang with large metal lights built into the thin striped metal soffits underneath.

"Why doesn't Montgomery have nice places like this?" Kire asked Charlie as they made their way inside the library. For Saturday, it wasn't as busy as Charlie had been expecting it to be. She figured maybe other people had similar mindsets to Kaos'—they would rather be spending their Saturdays differently than inside some lame library. Why would anyone want to be reading books when they could be on their phones or tablets or computers or watching TV or playing video games in the comfort of their own homes?

They both went to a computer straight away to start looking

up where James Winterfell's journal could be. Then they scrambled around the sleek and clean rows and levels of stacks, trying to get their hands on it.

It was beginning to seem almost as if their efforts were hopeless, but then a book with a well-worn, peeling spine caught Charlie's eye.

She whacked Kire on his chest. Not even on purpose—she was just simply too excited about what she had just witnessed.

"Kire!" she cried, eliciting a "Shh!" from somebody a couple of rows of book aisles down. Charlie pointed to the book spine, ignoring them.

Kire's eyes widened. "I think that's it, Rose!" he whispered. Then he reached forward and pulled the book from the shelf. On the front of it, engraved in gold, were the words, "The private journal of James Winterfell. Do not open."

They wordlessly bounded over to a table and sat down. "What do we do now?" Kire asked. "Do we start reading it?"

"I guess so," Charlie said. "Start from the beginning."

He opened it up and blew some dust out of the pages. It seemed as if nobody had had any interest in opening up the journal in what felt like centuries.

"Why don't we take turns reading the entries," Kire suggested. "Like, I'll read one first, then while you're reading an entry, I'll jot down some notes from it and try to determine exactly what James Winterfell was talking about."

"Fine," Charlie agreed. "But I want to go first."

Before Kire could argue, she shot him a look and snatched the book closer to herself on the tabletop.

"What?" she asked him. "It was I who had this idea to find the book in the first place."

"Technically, it was Ramoni," Kire pointed out.

"Yeah, but Ramoni came from *my* gift. So still, technically, it's me."

He rolled his eyes but offered her a playful smile. She

started reading the first entry, which dated back hundreds of years ago. As she did so, she saw through her peripherals, Kire pulling his phone out of his backpack and composing a message to someone. It distracted her momentarily. "Are you letting the others know we found it?" she asked curiously.

"What?" he asked her, seeming to only half be paying attention. "Oh, yeah, yeah."

Feeling not quite sure she believed him, Charlie continued reading:

THIS IS MY RESPONSIBILITY. I was one of the chosen ones. One of the hand-selected. It's an immense honor. I should be grateful for the chance. But I feel an intense amount of pressure. An urge not to fail. But I'm worried I will. With a gift such as the sword and scabbard, I feel I am a stronger man. I feel everyone counts on me to be the strongest warrior. To lead the team to victory against these heinous, vile creatures: the earth walkers. The earth destroyers. That's why I feel I should keep this journal now. To document my progress. For if I fail, I know others will be called to complete the task. I just hope I get a handle on what gifts the great sword has brought me. And more importantly so, I hope that the Quintets are able to save all.

SHE SLID the book over to Kire. Then she wandered from the table to get some loose paper and pencils so that she could scribble down her notes. When she returned, she saw Kire doing the next reading. She *also* could see his phone face up on the table. When it lit up with a text, Kire spastically snatched it off the table and held it in his hand underneath, where Charlie could no longer see it.

That's suspicious.

Trying to ignore it, she made simple notes. The date the journal entry started. How James was the one given the sword and scabbard. She hadn't really learned anything useful to go off yet. She also noted that one, James had been hand-selected to do the task, whereas Charlie and the others just happened to stumble upon the gifts. And two, James was being very vague in his entry. He didn't name things specifically. He didn't say how he was chosen or for what. It gave Charlie the impression that James wanted to write in a sort of secretive code. That way, the journal could only be useful to those who got their hands on the Quintet gifts after he passed. It was as if he knew what his fate was going to be, and he wanted to help not raise any panic should the journal fall into the wrong hands after his defeat.

Kire finally looked up, and he finished reading. "Okay, your turn." He slid the book back over to Charlie.

"Did you find anything interesting?" she asked curiously. She didn't like this whole 'taking turns' thing. She wanted to read every single entry for herself.

"No. He was just writing about the sword and how he was trying to get the hang of his powers. Though I did write down some useful tips that Trace might find handy."

"Gotcha."

The day continued like that. Charlie and Kire kept exchanging entries and writing down what they thought might be useful. But they hadn't read any journal entries mentioning anything about a portal yet. And all the while, Kire's phone kept blowing up. Somebody was texting him repeatedly, and she knew it wasn't the group chat between him, Trace, Kaos, Amberly, and her because her phone would've been getting notifications, too. It made her worried about something—what if there was a different group chat? A group chat with just Trace, Kaos, Kire, and Amberly? What if they were purposely keeping Charlie out of the loop about something for some reason? For not being cool enough?

It wasn't for a few hours more when Charlie's started

getting *really* annoyed about Kire's repeated phone notifications and his constant texting.

"Gracious, Kire, isn't there a rule about not using your cell phone in the library?" she finally snapped, slapping her hand down on the table and eliciting yet another "Shh!" from people behind her.

"I'm only texting," he said to her. "My phone's on silent."

"No, it's vibrating all over the place."

"Whatever. Same thing. It's not like I'm making a phone call or letting it ring."

"Still, it's super distracting. Who keeps texting you?"

"My parents. Uh, no one."

She raised an eyebrow and squinted at him. "Well, which one is it then?" she asked. "Is it your parents, or is it no one?"

Just then, his phone screen lit up again. Charlie had had enough, so she leaned over him quickly to get a view of the name on the screen.

Angela.

"Oh," she said shortly, falling back in her seat. Of course it was Angela. Charlie didn't even feel surprised. The only thing that did surprise her was the fact that Kire was trying to hide it from her.

And just when I was starting to maybe like him as a friend again...

"It's... nothing," Kire said. "She just likes to text a lot."

"Yeah. She *is* your girlfriend. I think they like to do that kind of thing." Not that she would even know. She had never had a boyfriend before. She had never been somebody's girlfriend before. There had been a time when she thought maybe she was going to be Kire's girlfriend, but that already felt so long ago.

She continued reading. Entry after entry, they recalled detailed encounters of what James Winterfell went through to fight Heno and protect Earth. They read all about him getting used to his powers. Getting used to his group. Charlie did find it useful when she read that it appeared the Quintet's gifts all seemed to work well together when all five members were getting along. But as for a portal to the magical realm, there wasn't even mention of a magical realm at all.

"This is hopeless!" Kire eventually complained. "We're getting closer and closer to the end of the journal, Rose. What if we don't find anything?"

"Don't be so negative," Charlie tried, taking the journal from him. Instead of reading each and every word of each journal entry, she started scanning the next few pages, looking for keywords like *Magic*, *Realm*, and *Portal*. When she finally found an entry that looked promising, she tapped on the page so hard with her pointer finger that the tip of it turned white.

"There!" she cried out, completely forgetting she was even in a library at all.

Finally, Charlie and Kire were about to discover information about the portal, and hopefully, James Winterfell would lead them right to its location.

23

"Are you going to read this entry then, or am I?" Kire asked about the entry Charlie had finally discovered that mentioned stuff about a portal.

"It's *my* turn to read," she argued with him.

"But I don't want to wait for you to tell me what it says!" he complained.

"Funny! Then you'll know exactly how it feels when you're having your top-secret little conversations with Halo while the rest of us have to stand around and wait for you to translate it for us!"

Just then, a shadow loomed over them on the other side of the table. They lifted their heads slowly simultaneously and found themselves facing a tall, skinny man with a handlebar mustache and round spectacles. He was looking down at the two of them over the rim of the glasses, which were sitting down low on the bridge of his narrow, crooked nose. His nametag read *Peter Paulson, Librarian.*

Charlie gulped, not liking the look they were getting from him.

"If I hear one more person *kindly* asking you two to keep it down over here, I am afraid I am going to have to ask you both to leave," the librarian said in a nasal voice. He continued looking at them harshly, and it made Charlie get the idea that this man would have actually *loved* to kick them out of there. He looked like the type of guy who didn't have any idea why he held a job where he was forced to deal with the types of people he hated more than anything else in the world—kids.

"S-sorry," Charlie muttered in the faintest of whispers.

"Yeah. It won't happen again," Kire added in.

After one more long, sinister look, Peter Paulson finally pushed his glasses up the bridge of his nose, placed his scary, long, thin hands behind his back, and walked away from them.

"That was close," Charlie whispered.

"Imagine if we got kicked out before we had a chance to read the entry," Kire whispered back. James Winterfell's journal had been in a section of the library where the books weren't allowed to be checked out. They both shuddered together.

"Let's just read it together then, shall we?" Charlie suggested. Eagerly, but as quietly as possible, they pushed their chairs together so that they could both read James Winterfell's next journal entry at the same time:

I WAS TOLD something interesting today. By a wise one. One not from around here. Not one of the earth walkers. Someone entirely different. Someone with good character. Someone witty and charming and funny. What they told me was interesting. It was about their way of getting from their world to ours. The portal.

To defeat the evil ones, all portals need to be sealed off. Destroyed. They need to be nonexistent. We can't let anyone find their way here to Earth. Not even those funny little magical creatures like the man I met—if you could even call him that.

I was explaining to him how unfortunate I thought it was that the portal had to be destroyed. I thought it was a shame there was not a way to just block out the bad ones from getting through. And he informed me of just that. That maybe there was a way. A way to seal it off to those who don't mean well and those who do not want peace. He said that it is quite possible. But not completely possible. Now, what am I supposed to make of that?

That was nothing about this man, or whatever he was. The funny part of him. You see, he would not help me locate the spell. Or the ritual. Or whatever needs to be done to make it so that people like him can still access our earth and vice versa. So that we can just block out the dark ones. It wasn't a matter of him just simply not knowing, either. It was a matter of him just... not wanting to give me the information about it. It is sort of what makes it confusing about all of this. They are the magical ones. If they wanted to perform such a spell or ritual, why didn't they just do it? Why did it have to fall on us? Was that a part of this whole riddle about it? Did it have to be us for some specific reason? Or is he trying to prevent us from performing such a ritual because he does not want it that way? Because he wants the portals closed off forever to everyone. Maybe he does not want people in his world. Maybe he fears us coming over onto his side. Or maybe we are supposed to fear them coming over to ours. I cannot even imagine the amount of chaos it would cause. I suppose some secrets are better left hidden. Like the fact that another life form roams this earth. If I try to tell people about it, I would be considered crazy. Most would not even believe me. I would say in a room of about a hundred and fifty people, only three of them would take my word for it. But then the rest would have my head.

But no matter how helpful (or unhelpful) this curious man was. I guess I will just have to figure it out myself.

Kire and Charlie both looked at each other in astonishment after reading the entry.

"Well," Kire said.

"You got that right," Charlie whispered. She hadn't even

thought of that possibility—a way to just close off the portal to the bad people. To Yash and his minions. That way, Albuses could still come this way. They could travel freely back-and-forth between each realm. It was clear that the "mysterious man" James Winterfell had mentioned in the entry had been Albus.

"So... there could be a way so that Albus could still come to the earth realm? And we could potentially go to his?" Charlie asked Kire.

"I guess so."

"Unless Albus was just messing around with him."

"Maybe he mentions something more in a later entry," Kire said curiously. Both of them were silent for a long while as they considered it.

"Have you thought about what it would be like to go into the magical realm?" Charlie couldn't help but ask Kire as she daydreamed about it herself.

"All the time," Kire said. "I think it would be the coolest thing in the world. Especially because once we find the portal, we'll be the only ones in the world who even know about it. The only ones in the whole world who know it even exists at all."

"I just wonder why Albus wouldn't tell James how to do it," Charlie said with a sigh. "And why wouldn't Albus tell us that this was a possibility?"

"Maybe he feared it wouldn't work if we tried to do it that way," Kire suggested. "Maybe it's so desperate of a situation that he didn't want to take any chances and figured it was better off that the portal was destroyed."

"Do *you* think it's better off that way?" she asked.

"I don't know."

Charlie let out a slow breath and dropped her head on her hand. They had been here for hours, and she was thirsty, hungry, and sleepy.

"We should probably head back home soon, huh?" Kire asked.

"Yeah. Your parents are probably wondering where you are," Charlie replied.

"Like I care," he said. "Besides, aren't yours?"

"Wait," she interrupted, not wanting to answer his question. "Why don't you care that your parents probably want to know where you are?"

"I... I just hate it there," he explained. "You don't understand it, Rose. It's awful. And I tried explaining that to Amberly, but she just won't listen to me. Ever since I found out the truth about Dad, I'm noticing just how much of a horrible human being he is. I can hardly even take it. And I'm getting shorter and angrier and snappier with him, and he's getting angrier and angrier at me for my snappiness. Not to mention Mom... I've been telling her that she deserves better than him."

"Are you serious?" Charlie asked, surprised that Kire would insert himself into his parents' business like that. She couldn't imagine having a similar conversation with her mother. She couldn't imagine having a conversation of importance at *all* with her mother.

"Yeah," he said, looking at his feet. "I just don't understand it. Why would she even want to be with him? He's horrible to her. He's horrible to everyone around him. He's a miserable person. I'm so sick of putting up with his crap, Rose. I mean it."

"That sounds awful," she said, sympathizing.

"Yeah. It *is* awful."

Charlie could see how stressed-out Kire was about the whole situation. He was gripping the edge of the table so hard that his knuckles were white, and his jaw was clenched so tightly that she could hear him grinding his teeth.

"Kire, is everything okay?" she asked, feeling concerned for him. Then she hated that she felt concerned. But she just couldn't help it.

"Not really. I'm sure you want to get back home. But I'm not in any hurry to."

"Honestly, neither am I."

But it wasn't like Kire was paying much attention to her. "I swear, Rose. One of these days... I don't think my anger is going to be able to stay inside my head. I'm going to do something."

"What do you mean?" she asked.

"Like, once he makes me angry, I'm going to snap and really give him a piece of my mind. I mean it. And I don't even want to think about what's going to happen after I do that."

24

There were only two more journal entries in James Winterfell's journal after the one talking about the portal. And unfortunately, neither of those entries mentioned the portal again.

Charlie and Kire had come to a dead end.

"Great," Kire said as they walked out of the library together. "We're no closer to finding the portal than we were before we got here."

"But at least we learned *something*," Charlie said, trying to stay positive even though she didn't quite feel that way inside. It was truly disheartening that they didn't learn the location of the portal with all the effort they had put into going through that journal together. There were a million other ways Charlie would've rather spent her Saturday. And she was certain that Kire would've much rather been hanging out with his lovely cheerleader girlfriend, Angela.

"Yeah, something that we don't even know is true or not," he commented. "I'm not trying to be such a drag, but this really stinks."

"I know. But we tried. Maybe once Halo feels up to talking again, you can tell her what you learned and see if maybe she'll give you any information to go off based on that? Maybe once she finds out that we've at least been trying, she'll be able to give us more hints or something."

"Maybe."

Charlie dragged her feet as she walked home after separating from Kire when they got off the bus at the stop by the park. She would rather stand outside in the freezing cold and have to go in and spend time with her family. At least any day now, Lexi would finally be going back to college and getting out of Charlie's hair.

Thankfully, when she got home, Lexi, her mother, and her father were all cozied up on the large sofa in the living room, a box of pizza on the coffee table in front of them as they watched the movie Charlie had mentioned several times she had wanted to rent on the large flat-screen TV. They looked like a whole, complete family there like that on the couch. When Charlie walked into her home, she felt like a total outsider. Like she didn't belong there. Like she didn't belong with them.

I don't care.

She walked into the sunken living room and flipped the pizza box lid up to get herself a slice out.

Only, there was none left.

"Char, can you get out of the way?" Lexi asked over on her spot in the middle of Charlie's mother and father on the couch. "I think a good part is coming up!"

She couldn't believe her family hadn't saved her a slice.

"Go on, Rose," her father urged her. At least he was using her preferred name. "Sorry that there's no more left. We weren't sure what time you were going to be home. I think there is stuff to make a grilled cheese in the fridge."

Charlie's rumbling stomach was full of disappointment.

She was starving from not eating all day long. But she was too angry to make herself a grilled cheese. Instead, she marched right up to her room and went to bed.

25

Miraculously, Charlie was able to fall into a relatively easy, deep sleep. She had no dreams of Rezin or of world destruction or anything scary of the sort. However, she could not come up with an explanation as to why she awoke in the middle of the night. There was no sudden sound that made her bolt upright. It wasn't as if she had just woken herself from one of those terrifying dreams. And she certainly couldn't hear the noise of any of her family members' downstairs.

The first thing she did was pick up her phone from her nightstand and check the time. It was well past three in the morning. Groggy, she sat up in her bed and rubbed her tired eyes. Then she froze, still as a statue. In front of her window, with a bit of moonlight shining in and illuminating the silhouette of it, Charlie could make out the half black, half orange cat. Its tail swayed lazily back-and-forth as its green eyes stared at her, seemingly glowing in the dark.

I can't believe it, she thought. *It's back.*

This time, Charlie felt less afraid. Less stressed out about the chances of the cat being Rezin there to visit her. In fact, she found instead that she was more determined than ever to try to communicate with the cat—or to get some control over it so that she could get it to leave her alone, hopefully for good.

She rubbed her eyes once more so she could see more clearly, then she threw her legs over the edge of her bed and concentrated. The two made eye contact with each other, and for the faintest of moments, Charlie felt something. There was no way really to describe exactly what it was, but it was deep inside of her. A connection to the cat. Somehow, she just knew that's what it was. She couldn't help but smile to herself. Finally, she was getting somewhere. She was going to learn how to communicate or control this cat one way or another.

She continued trying her hardest to make the connection deeper and stronger within herself. But then, she and the cat lost eye contact. It turned away from Charlie and slid out the little sliver of a crack in the window, and disappeared out of sight, climbing down Ramoni, the leaves rustling as it went.

CHARLIE WAS STILL CONFUSED by the cat. All day long during school, she thought about it. About why it was continuously bugging her and not the others. About what it could possibly want. And above all, she couldn't stop thinking about her potential connection to it. How she was getting so, so close.

It was as if thinking about this cat all day long had somehow forced it to appear by the edge of the woods when school got out for the day. It was out there by the trees, and again, its green eyes were staring intently at Charlie, something she could tell even from far away. She couldn't believe the cat was back. That it was staring at her in that same way. She paused in her step, causing some of her classmates to stumble into her back behind her. They mumbled and grumbled at her to get out of the way, but Charlie didn't pay any mind to it. She wanted to feel that deep connection again. She wanted to finally be able to control the cat, or at least talk to it to see what it wanted. But as she stood so far, she couldn't concentrate as well as she could last night. And she was standing in the middle of a massive crowd leaving the school doors, too—it was quite a big distraction, and no doubt people would begin to wonder what she was staring at and why she was just frozen there in the middle of the walkway if she continued to do it for much longer.

So, she decided she had to get closer. She stepped off the school's paved streets and onto the grass, where she crossed by the soccer field and went over to approach the cat. Unlike most other cats, this one did not scurry away at her arrival. It merely sat there and challenged her to continue coming closer. She stared it down and finally stopped walking. Within seconds, she felt something deep in her gut. She couldn't even tell if it was the Pendantix working or if it was just her internal instinct. Or maybe her internal instinct had been changed because of the Pendantix. But all she knew was that the cat wanted her to follow it. She could just sense it.

Quickly, Charlie pulled out her phone and gave Kire a call.

"Rose?" he asked when he answered.

"Kire? Can you get the others and come meet me by the edge of the woods? You'll see me standing out here," she said to him.

"The woods? Right *now*?"

"It's an emergency. I'm not kidding. It's related to... you know what."

As much as Charlie didn't feel like talking to Kire, she knew she needed to assemble the team to follow the cat into the White Forest. If she went alone, she would likely run into trouble that she wouldn't be able to get out of. Besides, she still had a slight feeling about this cat. Like it could be Rezin.

"Okay, sure thing. I'll have them get there as soon as they can," Kire said.

"Great." Charlie did not offer a thank you or even say goodbye before she ended the call and put her phone back in her pocket, continuing to stare down the cat to make sure she didn't lose sight of it before the others arrived. When they did, they were full of questions.

"Why are we here?" Trace asked, sounding annoyed.

"What is that cat doing back?" Kaos added. "I'm starting to think you've landed yourself a new pet, Rose."

"Aren't you, like, terrified of animals, though?" Amberly asked, a hint of a sneer in her voice as she balanced in the grass uneasily in her four-inch heels. Why any girl would feel the need to walk around high school in high heels all day long was beyond Charlie.

"I've been communicating with the cat," Charlie told them all, feeling slightly like she was lying because she didn't know for sure if *communicating* with the right word. If she told them she just had a hunch, it was likely they wouldn't believe her and that they would leave.

"Okay?" Trace asked.

Giving him a glare, Charlie replied, "It wants us to follow it."

"Into the White Forest?" Amberly asked, looking unsure.

"I think so."

Charlie stared at the others as they all stared at the cat. Then, right in front of them all, the cat turned and began slowly stepping into the trees, moving to stare back at the five every so often as it went.

"What are you guys all doing just standing around?" Charlie snapped bitterly. "Let's go."

"I hope you all have your gifts on you," Kire said, following after Charlie as they began entering the White Forest.

As they walked, Charlie had to listen to Amberly and Trace arguing with each other about how Trace hadn't given Amberly a kiss goodbye in between classes at her locker when he stopped by to say hello earlier. It made Charlie roll her eyes profusely, but she was also glad that nobody was trying to talk to *her*. She just wanted to get this journey over with. She wanted to find out where it was the cat wanted to take them. And she was very on edge because if this cat *was* Rezin, it was possible that it was leading them straight into a death trap.

"Can you guys maybe just do that later?" Kaos finally snapped at the angry couple, sounding as if he had had it with having to listen to them argue. Kaos was around Trace and Amberly more than anyone, and for a brief second, Charlie almost pitied the fact that he had to deal with them so often. Pity that was gone once she remembered how horribly their little trio treated her.

"Yeah," Charlie agreed. "Maybe you guys can just not talk or something if you can't be pleasant."

"I don't have to talk," Trace snapped quickly. Then he swings his backpack around and pulls out his sword, which was hanging out at the zipper obnoxiously, making Charlie wonder how no one said anything to him about it all day long, and once it was in his hand, the whole thing burst into flames that didn't bother Trace as they trailed up his arm one bit.

As they got deeper into the forest, Trace focused on his sword. The trees above created a canopy, shutting out much of the cloudy sky above, and as the forestry grew denser, suddenly, Trace's sword seemed to be emitting brighter flames.

"Would you look at that?" Trace asked, sounding amused. "I didn't even really think about it, but this makes a pretty good torch if you have to go anywhere in the darkness. We don't even need flashlights. Just like the old times."

"*So* cool," Kaos said, but his voice was full of sarcasm.

"Don't be jealous, Kaos, that I know how to work my gift, and you can't figure out yours."

"I can, too, figure it out. It just doesn't do a whole lot," he snapped.

"Knock it off," Kire demanded.

"Why don't you mind your own business?" Amberly bit out of him venomously.

"Stop being so nasty to Kire," Charlie said to her.

"Stop defending Kire like you think he's eventually going to realize his mistake with Angela and fall for you instead," Amberly argued back. "It's honestly just pathetic, Rose."

Charlie crossed her arms and walked more quickly ahead of the group, closer toward the cat.

Why couldn't the Quintet group have been composed of me and any other four except them?

"What is that?" Kire asked suddenly, making Charlie's head snap up. Before, she had been so focused on just following the cat's trail she didn't even look at her surroundings. Hopefully, they would be able to figure out the way back out once they were done with all of this.

Up ahead of them, there was a giant opening. Charlie knew exactly where they were. They were at the caves. The very caves where they first discovered their gifts.

Charlie waited to see what the cat's moves were going to be next.

"It's not going in there, is it?" Trace asked.

"You're not being a baby, are you?" Amberly prodded behind him.

"I'm not afraid," he retorted. Then, sure enough, instead of turning left or right, the cat headed directly into the darkness of the caves, completely out of sight. They all stopped walking when they reached the front of the cave, Charlie feeling hesitant, probably just as the rest of them were feeling, too. Somewhere inside the darkness, the cat's meow echoed, making all of them twitch where they stood.

"I think..." Charlie trailed off, wishing it wasn't true. "I think it wants us to go into the cave."

"Great," Kire said, shaking his head as he stood next to Charlie. "Just great."

As much as Charlie did not want to be impressed by Kire as he led the way into the cave, proving to be the braver one out of the five of them, it was the main thought she had in her mind. Kire was smaller than Trace. Not as confident appearing as Kaos. And yet, he went straight into the cave without another word about it. As much as Charlie may not have been getting along with him right now, it was clear to her that he was the only other one out of the five of them that really wanted to do whatever it took to make sure they saved their planet and humanity.

Charlie, feeling empowered about how strong Kire seemed, followed in after him second. Then Kaos followed next. Charlie didn't look behind her, but she could hear Amberly complaining about not wanting to be last in case something behind them in the cave swallowed her up. So, she squealed and went in front of Trace instead.

"Wow, Kire," Kaos said. "If only Angela could see you now."

"Shut up," Kire said in response.

"What's going on with you guys lately, anyway?" Trace intervened.

"What do you mean?" Kire asked. Charlie wasn't quite certain, but there was something about Kire's voice that seemed off. It was almost as if he was uncomfortable talking about the subject. Maybe it was because Charlie was around? Or maybe it was something else.

"Are you guys still good?" Trace continued.

"Things are... fine."

"Sucks to be you, Rose," Amberly jeered.

"I don't care," Charlie tried.

"Yeah, right." Amberly's snicker was enough to make Charlie want to turn around and smack her silent.

"You know, you and Rose *did* seem pretty lovey-dovey and all of that, not that long ago," Kaos pointed out. "Man, this must be so awkward for you guys now."

"There's no awkwardness," Charlie said quickly. "There wasn't anything lovey-dovey between Kire and me."

"Um... are you forgetting that you two kissed?" Trace asked. The painful reminder stung Charlie, but she was determined not to show them that she was bothered.

"That was nothing," she answered.

"Nothing," Kire repeated, although he didn't sound as certain about it as Charlie had.

Trace was right about his sword being a great torch for them in the caverns. They could see the cat clearly, along with the cavern walls all around them. Charlie wasn't used to going in this direction. She didn't like to walk too deeply into the cave in fear of there being a cave-in or of her getting lost and not being able to find her way out. In fact, she was certain she had never been this far before. Ever.

"How much longer do you think?" Amberly asked. And just then, the cat turned around the corner.

"Hopefully not much further," Kire responded.

"I wasn't asking you," Amberly was quick to snap.

"Amberly, come on," Kaos complained. The gang rounded

the corner after the cat, and Charlie audibly gasped when she saw what they had been led to. They were inside a huge cavern. And before them was a massive pool of water. It was as if there was an entire lake built in here. She was amazed she had never seen it before. Nor had she ever even heard of it.

"What is this place?" Trace asked, looking around it all. Everyone else joined in. The pool of water almost appeared to be ice-blue in color. Shimmering rocks from the cavern's walls reflected down on the surface in the glow of Trace's flames. The whole scene was quite mesmerizing.

"Hey," Kire said suddenly, his voice loud and startling Rose a bit. "Where did the cat go?"

Charlie looked around herself. It was true; the cat had disappeared. Or it was hiding from them. Charlie couldn't see it anywhere. "I don't think it's with us anymore," she answered. Then scared, she swallowed, and the sound of it was very, very audible in the quiet cave.

"Well, this was dumb," Kaos finally stated to the group as they stood inside the massive cavern.

"Charlie, why did the cat lead us here? Can you talk with it and summon it to come back and explain itself?" Kire asked.

"All I know," Trace said, wielding his sword in front of him as if he was preparing to fight. "Is that I'm feeling that something bad is coming on."

"What do you mean?" Amberly asked, her eyes darting all around the cave.

"It led us here for a reason," Charlie tried, looking around the cavern for an explanation. "There *has* to be a reason."

"Yeah. The reason is that that cat is working for Rezin, and it just led us to our death," Kaos grumbled. Out of his backpack, he pulled out his crown and put it on. Following suit, Kire got out his book, and Amberly put on her gauntlet. Instinctively, Charlie grasped her Pendantix, feeling nervous. But what if the others were right? What if she had just led them all into a trap? What if, like so many others, this group of kids was going to fail to save the world too?

Suddenly, there was a great rumbling noise. It sounded far away in the cave, almost as if there were a few monster trucks driving around right outside the entrance. Amberly squealed. The sound was growing louder. Eventually, the floor beneath their feet started vibrating.

"That can't be good," Trace said. There was more fear in his eyes at knowing that whatever they were about to fight might not be anything Trace could use a sword for.

"I think this place is going to cave in!" Kire called out, his wide eyes huge with alert.

"No, no, no, no!" Charlie groaned. This couldn't be happening. She hadn't sensed that the cat was leading them to evil. As she followed the cat through the White Forest, she was getting some sort of sensation in her gut telling her that the cat meant *good*, not harm. The cat wasn't Rezin. If it had been, it would've done something to attack them much sooner than just now, wouldn't it have?

"Charlie, you've gotten us all doomed!" Amberly yelled out.

"Don't raise your voice," Kire said. "You're only going to make the cave-in happen quicker!"

The walls began rumbling around them. Charlie could feel the ground moving underneath her feet. Bits of rock and dust were falling from overhead, and instantly, Kire started to cough.

"Kire, do you think your shield will protect us all?" Charlie asked.

"Even if it does, what happens when I let the shield down?"

Fear rippled through Charlie. Kire was right. Halo's shield would stop all the rocks from tumbling and killing all of them, but as soon as he closed the book and the shield disappeared, all of those rocks would continue to fall and crush them to death.

"Too bad the rocks don't have minds," Kaos said. "Minds that I could convince not to do this!"

Amberly raised her gauntlet-clad hand. "I can try to move

some of the rocks out of the way! But I don't know how much good it is going to do if there's a million of them!"

Charlie chewed on the inside of her cheek and looked around the cavern frantically. The rumbling was growing louder and louder. It was nearly deafening to the point where she could no longer hear the others. She couldn't believe this was happening. She couldn't believe how stupid she had been. She couldn't believe she had caused this. The Quintets already didn't like her enough as it was. If they got out of this alive, how were they ever going to get past this grave mistake of hers? How miserable were they going to make her life from now on?

There was only one way, as far as Charlie could think, to ensure that they didn't become furious with her.

Charlie had to save them all.

28

Charlie Rose knew that the Quintets, the Unlikely Defenders of Earth, were practically seconds away from all being defeated. She had to do something to stop it. She had to save all of her peers from a horrible fate. Without them, there was a chance that the rest of humanity would cease to exist as well. A chance that Yash would come down and wreak his havoc. Burn everything to a crisp, just like Charlie saw in her nightmares. She might have not been very close with her family—she might have even had an extreme dislike for them, even—but she didn't want them to die. She didn't want *anyone* to die. Not on her watch. Not when she was capable of doing something to stop it.

"What are we going to do?!" Kire shouted, sounding more and more afraid with each breath.

"There's nowhere to run or hide!" Kaos added.

"We're done for," Amberly screeched.

No, Charlie thought. *We can't be done for. This can't be the end.*

Again, she continued looking around the rumbling and falling apart cave. At last, she spotted something. With the glow of Trace's sword's torch, Charlie spotted a bit of green. A weed growing through a crack in the rocks underneath her feet. It was the tiniest weed. Barely even sprouted. But it was the only plant around here, and as far as Charlie could tell, there weren't any animals to use for her manipulation. This was her only shot.

Charlie steeled herself and stared down at the plant. One hand gripped the Pendantix while the other was balled into a tight fist. She concentrated hard, and then suddenly, the weed in the ground was growing. Larger and larger, sprouting more and more. The stem then morphed into a tree trunk. One that grew far and wide. Roots rippled out under their feet, causing Trace to trip over one of them and stumble back on his butt. Kire nearly fell as well, but he dodged the root just in time. As the cavern continued to feel like it was caving in, the tree continued to grow. It shot upward, and Charlie was well aware of how this was the most massive thing she had manipulated so far. A single weed into a full-blown tree. Its branches continued spreading out of the top of it when the trunk stopped growing. Charlie could hear the ceiling of the cavern crackling above them. It was going to burst into a bunch of rubble any second. But she persisted with the tree. So many branches flew out of it. Thick ones and skinny ones, weaving in throughout each other. It looked almost as if it was creating a web-like pattern—a web-like pattern out of tree bark. The leaves on the tree were massive and acted like cloth patches over the webbing, covering every bit of the cavern's ceiling above them. Just when it seemed like, after one great big crackling noise, the ceiling was going to come tumbling down on them, only a few bits and pieces rained down as the tree stopped growing.

At last, Charlie relaxed, ignoring the blood dripping from her nose. Above her was the most magnificent thing she had ever created. The tree had made its own ceiling, keeping the rocks safely trapped above it, and its branches stretched all the way through the cavern, undoubtedly making it so that they had a clear enough path to get themselves out of here.

Charlie fell to the ground on her butt, amazed at herself. She couldn't believe she had done it. She had saved them all from dying.

Kire immediately raced to Charlie's side, as did the other members of the Quintet group quickly after.

"I'm fine," Charlie promised them.

"But your nose!" Kire complained.

"I promise, I'm fine," she urged anyway—and she felt it. Sure, her nose was bleeding, whatever that meant. But she felt strong. She felt sure of herself. The victory was instilling confidence in her that she didn't know she had.

"Well," Trace said, looking up at the massive tree Charlie had created. "This is probably the most incredible thing I've ever seen."

"Who knew your powers could do such crazy things?" Kaos added.

"It... whatever," Amberly said. It was the closest she would probably ever get to complementing Charlie. But Charlie would accept it. She even offered the weakest of smiles as Kire helped her back to her feet.

"You saved us, Rose," Kaos said, slapping Charlie on the back.

"You're amazing," Kire added in.

"It *was* pretty sick," Trace agreed. "Even though you're the one who led us in here in the first place."

29

While it had been nice getting the praise from her team after she saved everyone yesterday from a horrible death via tumbling sharp rocks, Charlie was still angry and upset at herself for putting Kire, Trace, Kaos, and Amberly in danger in the first place. She had been so stupid. But she was also glad she hadn't gone into the caverns alone. Without the desperate need to save the others, she probably would have never been able to produce such magic with the Pendantix. She probably would have died all alone, and without her, there was no Quintet group. They all needed to stick together, whether Charlie liked it or not.

At school, it was another rainy, dreary, cold day. Second period went by in a blur. Fourth period with Kaos felt strange to Charlie. The entire block period, Kaos acted as if Charlie was invisible. It was as if he, Trace, Amberly, and Kire had reconvened earlier this morning without Charlie about the incident that went down last night. Maybe Charlie was just feeling paranoid, but it felt as if maybe they had all talked about how it wasn't cool what Charlie had done to them, and saving their lives wasn't enough to make them not mad at her for leading them into that cavern in the first place. It *was* true, after all; Charlie had just made them all follow the cat on a *hunch*. She hadn't actually been able to communicate with it. Sure, she felt something deep in her gut telling her that they had to follow it, but what if her mind had just been playing tricks on her? What if the cat *was* Rezin, and it was making her think all the wrong things?

She was a nervous mess by the time it came to Economics, the last block class of the day. She sat at her desk and kept her head down, fiddling with the white daisy charm bracelet she was wearing on her wrist. It complemented the Pendantix well, along with the rest of her floral-themed outfit.

Kaos, Kire, and Trace entered the classroom altogether as if they had just been having a blast outside in the hallway, all of them with smiles on their faces. Charlie avoided their gaze, too worried she would catch the hatred for her in their eyes if she looked up.

Thankfully, the bell rang quickly, and Ms. Wright got straight into teaching her lesson for the day.

"Today, we're learning about trade agreements, class. Exciting, exciting stuff," Ms. Wright said. Yet, the class collectively groaned together. Nothing Charlie had learned in Economics had been exciting to her so far. It all felt like information she definitely needed to learn, but that it was all information she didn't need to know right *now*—especially if she wasn't going to pick any careers that had anything massively important to do with the economy.

"Can somebody tell me what they know about trade?" Ms. Wright asked.

Instantly, Kire and Kaos both raised their hands.

"Yes, Kire?" Ms. Wright asked, favoring him. It was something Charlie had noticed having this class with them—Ms. Wright very much seemed to prefer quiet, intelligent Kire over dark, ominous, bullying Kaos.

"It's basically a bunch of attempts from different nations to have some sort of exclusive advantage in the game that is trading goods and services by creating barriers. But there is the struggle to quite understand why creating these barriers creates resistance that in the economic logic, restricting trade prevents there being more wealth created."

Charlie was clueless about anything Kire had just spit out. Every day, she was amazed at how smart he was. But with him being smart, she also admired how he wasn't too braggy about it. He was a humble, intelligent man and didn't shove his knowledge into other people's faces like some others did. Kaos liked to do that.

"Well, barriers are a good start," Ms. Wright said, nodding her head approvingly to Kire. Charlie side-eyed Kaos and saw that he was rolling his eyes. "Restricting trade reduces the growth of wealth." Ms. Wright started a PowerPoint on the board. Bored of the lecture already, Charlie got out a notebook and pretended as if she was taking notes, like the rest of the class, but instead, she was drawing doodles inside the margins of her notepad. Flowers and plants—always flowers and plants.

Before she knew it, some time had passed, and they were deep into the lesson when Ms. Wright called on Charlie to answer a question.

"I know it was a couple of slides ago, but just as a test for your knowledge, Miss Charlie Rose, what is a quota?"

Shoot. She hadn't been paying attention.

"Isn't its purpose to protect the domestic product from competition by ensuring that foreign products are higher priced?"

The class chuckled. Immediately, Charlie knew she had gotten the answer wrong.

"You were *kind of* paying attention, but not quite. Stop drawing in your notebook, will you?"

Charlie gasped. "How did you—?"

"I have eyes in the back of my head, Miss Rose. You're thinking of a *tariff*. We just learned about that. A quota is the limitation of the quantity of products that may be important. Stay alert, because I might call on you again."

The class laughed at Charlie some more. She felt humiliated. Kaos and Kire were so smart and above her. Even Trace was laughing, even though Charlie was quite certain that Trace wouldn't have been able to answer the question if he had been called on, either. It felt even more true now—like the rest of the Quintets were still plotting against her. Even more so since she almost killed them all. She had a feeling she wasn't being paranoid, either.

CHARLIE COULDN'T WAIT to get home. Not to hang out in the living room and have to deal with Lexi or her parents when they got home from work, but to just go up to her room and talk to Ramoni—to get some stuff off her chest and hopefully have him make her feel better.

But instead, she got home to see that her parents were already there. It was so unlike them that Charlie froze as soon as she entered the house, eyeing the way her parents were setting up decorations and giggling with each other while Lexi flitted about the house in a happy manner, wearing a cute pink, flowing dress with a white collar.

"What's going on?" Charlie asked uneasily.

"They're throwing me a going away party," Lexi informed her, smiling happily. "Remember?"

"Nobody told me," Charlie answered. She hadn't been aware of the going away party at all. But the fact that her parents were home from work early and that they were setting this all up, instantly angered Charlie. Not even on her *birthday* had they come home early. They hadn't even gotten her a gift or birthday cake. And definitely no decorations. They had simply handed her a $50 bill and told her to go to the mall and buy herself something nice. That was it. Their *happy birthdays* had been in rushed tones as they scrambled about the kitchen early in the morning to get their coffee and breakfast before they dashed out the door to head to work. And here they were, throwing her older sister a party just because she was headed back from her break from college. She hadn't done anything exciting. It wasn't as if any birthdays of hers had come up. And yet, Lexi always received all the attention.

"Lance is going to come, too!" Lexi said, coming right up to Charlie and playfully toying with her hair, but Charlie quickly swatted her out of the way. "I'm so excited for you to finally get to meet him!"

"I am... I'm busy. Too busy for some stupid family party," Charlie said.

Lexi put a hand to her heart, looking deeply hurt. Of course, surely it was all an act that she was putting on a front of their parents.

"Charlie, you're not busy. Don't say things to upset your sister," her mom said.

"I'm not!" Charlie snapped. "I really do have a lot of things to do today. Homework. Projects. Sorry, but if somebody would've told me about this party earlier, I could've rearranged my schedule."

"So, what?" Lexi asked. "You're just going to stay upstairs locked in your room while we have the party? Are you going to say goodbye to me when I leave?"

"Does it really matter much to you?" Charlie asked. "Because the last time I checked, no one in this entire house gave a single crap about me. In fact, now that I think about it, I'm one-hundred-percent positive that you all still don't. It's always you, Lexi. Isn't it, Mom and Dad? Who cares about awkward, weird, quiet Charlie? You have the perfect daughter. I was just an accidental extra that you guys didn't know what to do with. You already used all of your parental energy to create the perfect daughter in Lexi. I'm just your pathetic leftover child. Don't even deny it."

"Now, Charlie, you listen to me right now," her father started. His finger was pointed at her as he angrily moved in her direction. His face was red and twisted up into a scowl. But Charlie didn't want to listen. She was the leftover child. She didn't want to talk to anyone in her family ever again.

"Just stay away from me!" she shouted. "All of you!"

Before her father could get any closer, and before Charlie could really get a good look at the stunned expressions on her mother's and sister's faces, she turned right back around and raced back out the front door.

Charlie didn't know whether it was her anger coursing through her veins or the fact that she had been practicing for a few days now on it, but as she stormed through her neighborhood and the half orange and half black cat reappeared in front of her yet again, Rose stood in front of it and stared it down, her chest heaving with her anger at her family. And suddenly, she understood the cat.

"There you are," the cat said in a low female voice.

"Excuse me?" Charlie snapped, her brows furrowing. She couldn't believe this was happening. Her mind was still half on the interaction she had just had with her family. She was still fuming over it. She didn't want to talk to the stupid cat who had almost caused her and the other Quintets to die.

"Oh, finally," the cat said, "we can converse."

"Who are you?" Charlie demanded, stepping toward the cat. It didn't move away. It just sat in front of her on the sidewalk. Charlie was still in the middle of the residential neighborhood, and the sun hadn't set yet. She shivered and realized that if anyone peeked out their windows, they would see her conversing with the cat. Yet, right now, she was so intrigued and desperate for answers that she didn't care if anyone thought she was crazy. Her family already did, so she might as well add in the rest of the neighborhood.

"I am Cordelia," the cat said. "My family has lived in the White Forest for generations. I know much about you and the other Quintets. About all of the ones before your group, as well."

"And you're on Yash's side or something, then? You know who *that* is, right?"

"Of course, I know who it is, but no, I'm not on Yash's side. Why would you even ask me that?"

"Are you kidding?" Charlie barked. "Do you not remember what you did yesterday? Did you not see what happened inside those caverns? You got us all trapped. You're so lucky that I was able to figure out my magic in time to stop us from dying!"

"It wasn't my intention at all to lead you into a trap. I'm offended that you would even think that. I was merely trying to help you, Charlie."

"If you've been stalking me like I know you have, then he would know by now that I like to be called Rose."

"Yes, that's right. My apologies," the cat said. "But I promise you, Rose, I did not intend to lead you into a trap. I did not want you to be attacked by Yash."

"Then why did you bring us into the cave?" Charlie didn't believe the cat one bit. She didn't trust it. Not yet.

"I wasn't trying to lead you to the cave specifically. I was trying to lead you to the body of water."

"The water?" Charlie asked. Then she clamped her jaw shut, deep in thought. *The water...*

"That's all I wanted. I know that you have been searching for answers. The water will help you find it."

Charlie wasn't sure if she should trust what Cordelia the cat was telling her now. Not after what happened to her yesterday.

But hey.

What did she have to lose anymore?

31

Cordelia the cat had been trying to lead Charlie, *not* to the cavern for an attack from Yash's minion, Rezin, but to lead Charlie to the water. Because apparently, the water held answers to some of the many questions Charlie and the rest of the Quintets had when it came to saving the planet.

Charlie felt particularly down on her luck, especially today. It felt like Kire, Kaos, Trace, and Amberly didn't like her and that they were angry with her for nearly getting them killed. She also felt like her family didn't feel any need to give her the time of day. She was just an extra in her own home. And at her own school. A complete and total outsider that nobody wanted anything to do with. And yet, somehow, it was up to her—even if just partially—to save the world.

Charlie decided to thank Cordelia for her help, and then she told the cat there would surely be plenty of scraps in the trash by the side of her house from the party that she would not be in attendance of at her house that evening. Happily, Cordelia jumped over the fence into Charlie's backyard, and Charlie went on her way. She decided to head to the White

Forest all by herself. She had managed to grow that magnificent tree inside the cavern that was keeping all the rocks from caving in. She had managed to figure out how to talk to Cordelia. Clearly, her powers were getting stronger, so she should be able to handle getting her answers in the body of water without the others. She felt confident and strong in her abilities. She had always been alone and could continue to be alone just fine. Charlie always valued her independence and her ability to find solutions to problems without needing anyone's help.

She had been to the cave so many times to do the bioluminescence project that she had been working on—even though it had been put on pause for a while now due to the whole 'universe about to crumble' situation—that she could get there with her eyes closed. When she arrived in the gaping mouth, she was glad to see that the cabin hadn't gotten any worse and that all of her tree branches and leaves from her creation were still holding it all together.

Using the flashlight app on her phone, she entered the cave and began the long descent, trying to remember precisely which directions it was Cordelia had taken that led them specifically to that body of water in that massive cavern. It was much creepier being in here alone. The deeper Charlie walked, the more she felt another presence. It was as if Rezin was near. As if he knew exactly what she was up to and that she didn't have the others' help. She felt that maybe she was more vulnerable here. More easily susceptible to being controlled by the mind games Rezin liked to use. But yet, she continued on. She was determined to find answers in that water. Then she would bring the results back to the rest of the gang, and they would all be impressed with her. Maybe it would even make them less mad at her for the situation she put them in yesterday. Besides, it was good that she was doing this alone and that she didn't risk putting them in harm's way yet again.

Every now and then, as she walked, a bit of rubble crumbled from the walls or the ceiling, and each time it was like a jolt of electricity and adrenaline ran through Charlie as she jumped slightly while walking. But of *course*, there would be crumbling noises inside the cavern. She was certain the tree could only hold up so much weight and for only so long.

She hadn't paid much attention when following Cordelia, so after a while of continuous walking, Charlie was beginning to feel as if maybe she had taken the wrong turn. But thankfully, eventually, she came around a bend and realized that everything still looked familiar. One more turn, and she would be in the cavern.

Sure enough, she took that turn and found that she was right where she needed to be. The water's reflectivity was a little bit different from the light from her cell phone compared to the lights of Trace's sword's torch yesterday. Still, she could see the large body of water clearly and its ice-blue murkiness. Some pebbles dropped from the ceiling every now and then, escaping through the canopy of leaves, vines, and branches that her tree had created. It felt ominous and a little bit scary because Charlie wasn't sure how much time she had before the tree gave out and the cave did indeed fall down on her.

I mustn't think about that now, though, Charlie thought to herself. *I have a job to do.*

Grasping her Pendantix, she looked up at the ceiling of leaves and branches. Using her powers, she managed to summon a vine down to her. She tied it around her waist and then kicked off her shoes. She wondered if maybe she should feel the water before she jumped right into the pool of it, but she was worried she would psych herself out if she did so, so she figured it was best that she just dove right in.

Taking a couple of deep breaths to prepare herself, she wobbled on her feet at the edge of the body of water, then finally, she took the plunge. From the surface, next to the body of water, Charlie's phone still had the flashlight shining up toward the ceiling. So, where she was now, she could still see light. But there was nothing around her. She had to go deeper.

She continued onward. But the deeper she went, the darker it got. She did not have any sort of underwater flashlight to help her see better. What exactly was it she was supposed to find out here?

She tried to feel along with her hands as she swam, but they grabbed nothing. She felt nothing. She was surrounded by complete and total pitch-black darkness.

Slowly beginning to run out of breath and quickly realizing this wasn't the best way to go about this since she could not see under here, she felt around for her vine so that she could manipulate it to pull her back out. But when she put her hand around her waist, she felt nothing. Just the T-shirt that was clinging to her body and simultaneously drifting off her in the weightless gravity of being underwater. The vine wasn't there.

Feeling more frantic, she felt around with her hands and feet, violently jerking herself and trying to grasp anything around her. The vine must have come untied and fallen off her as she was swimming. Now she couldn't see even her hand in front of her face, and she had no idea which direction was even up. She was going to drown like this. There was nothing she could do about it. No way she could get herself out of this. The vine had been the only thing she had been relying on to get her out of the water when she was so far in. And now that was gone.

She kept swimming in multiple directions, still grasping out. But her lungs were about to give out. She couldn't take much more of this. Still, she tried and tried and tried.

Eventually, Charlie's time ran out, and the blackness finally enveloped her.

32

When Charlie Rose came to again, she had it in her head immediately that she had awoken in heaven. That she had died down in that water and that she no longer existed. But something was confusing her about it. Why was she coughing and sputtering? Why was it so dark around her, and why were there so many eyes peering at her as she laid on a cold hard ground, her entire body feeling soaked? Was this what it was like to get to heaven? Was this what everybody had to go through when they first died?

Charlie continued coughing and sputtering. Somebody slowly helped her sit up, and she found that she was looking into the eyes of none other than Trace Henderson.

Wait a second.

As Charlie became more aware of her surroundings, she realized that she was not dead. That she was still in the cavern. That somehow, the Quintets had found her here and pulled her out of the water. Trace had saved her life.

Next to her, Trace was just as soaked as she was. Charlie looked around at the rest of the people in the cave, seeing that Kire, Kaos, and Amberly were all still dry to the bone. She was amazed that it had been Trace who saved her. And she could easily admit to herself that when she had felt hands on her back and somebody by her side, her mind had instantly hoped that it was Kire. She wished that it would have been Kire who saved her. Not Trace.

"Thank God you're all right," Trace said, slapping her on the back a little bit to get the rest of the water out of her lungs. It wasn't very helpful, but Charlie supposed she appreciated the gesture, nonetheless.

"Wh-what are you guys doing here?" she asked, still astonished that they were all standing before her. How had they known she was here? Had they been following her? Had somebody told them?

"It was Halo, actually," Kire answered for the group. He was holding the book in both of his hands, his face ashen in the glow of not only Charlie's cell phone, but Trace's sword that he was holding in his other hand. Charlie looked at it, shocked.

"You won't even believe this, Rose, but the sword's flames even work underwater! It's incredible!" He sounded excited. Both about having just saved Charlie and the fact that his sword kept revealing more and more special abilities it could do.

"What did Halo say? How did she know?" Charlie asked, deciding to ignore the cool fact about Trace's sword. There were more important things to discuss at the moment.

"Well, I was just at home, and suddenly Halo was going crazy. I opened her up, and she gave me a vision. She saw that you were in trouble. So I told the others, and we all came as quickly as we could. What the heck were you thinking, Rose?"

"I..." Charlie trailed off. She didn't even know what to say. She was a little bit touched that they would even want to come to save her in the first place. She had been certain they all hated her.

"I mean, are you honestly out of your mind?" Kire continued. He looked very upset by the whole situation. More upset than any of the others seemed. "As soon as I got here, I saw your phone on the ground, and I knew you were underwater. We pulled out the vine and saw that you weren't attached to it, and I instantly tried to jump in, but everybody stopped me."

"Yeah, Kire almost lost it wanting to get to you so badly," Kaos agreed. "But we all established that Trace is the more athletic one in the group. That if anyone were able to save you, it would be him."

"I could've done it just fine!" Kire complained. He had gone from being ashen and pale-faced in fear of Charlie being dead to angry about the fact that he hadn't been the one to dive into the water to save Charlie. She didn't know how she felt about it. All she could do was sit there on the ground, still in disbelief that she was even alive at all.

"Well, it doesn't matter now," Amberly said. "All that matters is that my boyfriend jumped in and saved your little ex-fling, or whatever, and now she's alive, and Trace is the hero."

"Yeah, he always has to be the freaking hero!" Kire cried out.

"Kire, dude, what's your problem?" Trace asked, sliding away from Charlie and getting to his feet. "You should be glad that I saved her. Are you not?" He started approaching Kire with an angry look on his face.

"Just stay away from me!" Kire shouted at him.

"Dude, chill out!" Trace continued.

"Don't tell me to chill out!"

"Guys, can you just stop?" Charlie tried, but her voice was too weak to really make an impact.

And then, right before Charlie's eyes, Kire was giving Trace a shove.

"You know what, I'm getting really sick of the way you've been treating everybody in this group!" Trace snapped, quickly going to shove Kire back. Because of his brute strength, Kire went flying, tripping over a rock and landing on his butt. He quickly got back up, and then, all of a sudden, both of their fists were flying.

Charlie scrambled to get to her feet, too. She would've never in a million years thought almost dying would've caused two boys to fight about her.

What on earth was happening?

33

As Trace and Kire continued to throw punches at each other, Charlie quickly grew enraged and irritated about the whole situation. Before she knew it, she was throwing herself in the middle of them, and they both had to stop fighting or else they would accidentally hurt her.

"Can't you just knock it off?" she demanded loudly. "I don't get why you're so upset anyway, Kire!"

Out of breath, Kire shot her a glare. "What are you talking about?"

Charlie didn't want to get in a fight with Kire about this. She didn't want him to know how affected she was by how he had ditched her for Angela. But suddenly, it was as if it was consuming her. She didn't know what was bringing it on. But she couldn't stop herself from letting it out. "I'm not yours to save!"

"Well, you're not Trace's to save, either!"

"You got that right!" Amberly interjected.

"Shut up!" Kire and Charlie both said to her at the same time. Then Charlie turned back to Kire. "I don't know why you were so freaked out about me almost dying anyway. I figured that's what you would've wanted! Save you the headache!"

"How could you even say that to me, Rose?"

"Are you kidding? Kire, I thought you and I had something! *Everyone* thought we did! And then, out of nowhere, you just completely ghosted me to go for Angela instead! I just don't get it!"

"Rose, you don't understand—"

Charlie held up her hand. "I don't even want to hear it. I'm sick of your excuses. You made your choice."

"Okay, maybe we shouldn't do this here," Kaos said, finally speaking up after a long while of silence and doing nothing but observing the chaos.

"Kaos," Kire said bitterly, "I thought you out of everyone would have my back."

"Why would he have your back over mine?" Trace asked. "I'm the one who saved Rose. *And* he's my best friend."

"Yeah, about that, actually," Amberly suddenly piped up to Trace. "You did seem *really* interested in being her savior. And what's with the whole 'Thank God you're alive' comment?" she demanded, both of her hands on her hips. "This isn't the first time that you've seemed to be clinging on to Ms. Freaky Plant Girl over there."

"Are you kidding me?" Trace asked, sounding as if he was in utter disbelief about the whole thing. "You can't seriously tell me you're being jealous of Rose right now."

"As if!" she snapped, avoiding Charlie's eye contact. "I could never be jealous of her. It's just disgusting that you're acting so interested."

"The only thing I'm interested in is trying to keep this group together!" he shouted. "You are the one who only started dating me in the first place so that you could manipulate me into hating Kire!"

Amberly gasped. "How could you say that? You know that's not true!" But for some reason, Charlie could see it in Amberly's blue eyes. It was true. Maybe she didn't feel that way now, but Charlie had no doubt in her mind that Amberly only started dating Trace because she knew he would be the perfect bully for Kire, whom she hated.

"Really?" Trace asked, picking his sword up off the floor and letting the flames emit around it again. "So, are you telling me you *don't* hate Kire or something?"

"Of course, I hate him!" she continued. "That's not why I dated you! How could I *not* hate him? He won't even tell his dad that he knows I exist!"

"Amberly, there's a reason for that!" Kire bellowed. "For the last time!"

"You guys!" Kaos shouted over everyone who had started bickering and yelling at each other at the same time. "Enough of this! It's getting ridiculous! We're supposed to be a team, for God's sake!"

The yelling and bickering quieted died down as Kaos continued on.

"Seriously, Rose, what on earth were you thinking? You would've died if we hadn't found you. If Halo hadn't warned Kire. We thought you were dead! It took us forever for the CPR to work! How stupid could you be?"

"Don't call her that!" Kire snapped.

"Don't defend me!" Charlie yelled at Kire. She knew she had made another dumb mistake.

"You would've ruined everything if you died, do you understand that?" Kaos asked. "Everything. If something happens to one of us, then the whole world crumbles. I'm not kidding."

"I didn't think it mattered if I died!" Charlie felt hurt as she said it. "I still don't think it matters! The only reason you're upset about it is that it would ruin your plans of saving the universe! It's not even about me as a person. I could be anyone, and you would be just as upset over their death because it would be a member of your perfect group missing."

"Rose, you just don't get it!" Kaos argued. "You act like this victim all the time. You're abandoned by everyone at school. You're abandoned by your own family. I know what it's like to feel abandoned by your own family! I know what it's like to have to do everything yourself! That's why I put in the effort to make friends at school. Because they're my real family! You never even put in any of that same effort. It's like you prefer to be on your own. You prefer people to feel sorry for you! It doesn't have to be that way! You don't have to be alone everywhere you go. We're a group. We're supposed to be a team. You need to realize that you're not alone and that you don't have to do things yourself. The sooner you figure that out, the more powerful we will be as a team!"

Charlie opened and closed her mouth a few times, trying to find the right words to say. She had never heard such a profound speech come out of Kaos' mouth. Everything he had said was true. Everything made total sense. And he had basically just admitted to her that she could be a part of their group in and out of school if she tried.

"Dang," Trace muttered under his breath, clearly saying what everybody else was thinking. Kaos sighed loudly and fiddled with the crown on his head, straightening it out.

"All the fighting that we're doing. All of this back-and-forth bickering and not getting along is not making us a strong team. Do you guys understand we have to stop doing this? We're not going to get anywhere if this is how we act every time we're around each other."

"He's right," Kire said. Together, everyone else nodded their heads. Then they all stood around in the creaking, pebble-dropping cavern, calming their breaths and trying to forget about the pain everyone had been causing each other. The Quintets needed to start acting more like a team. Charlie had a feeling there was a lot that depended on it.

34

As the Unlikely Defenders lingered in the cavern after having just got in their massive fight, a piece of the rubble fell through a space in the tree Charlie had made, which was holding up everything from crumbling down on them, and it narrowly missed Kaos' head. He jumped, startled by the loud noise as he looked down and saw what had almost hit him.

"I think it's time we just get out of here," Kire pointed out. The rest of the group mumbled their agreements, then the gang started walking together.

"So, Rose," Kaos started, leading right behind Trace, who was lighting up the way for everybody. "Do you want to tell us what you were doing in that body of water in the first place?"

"I-I ran into that cat again," Charlie confessed, deciding she might as well not keep any secrets from them. They *did* need to work as a team, after all. "And it turns out, her name is Cordelia, and I can speak with her."

"You learned how to do it?" Kire asked, looking at her and smiling, impressed.

Charlie rolled her eyes. "It's whatever." She was happy that she had figured it out, but she wasn't going to let Kire make her feel proud of herself. "Anyway. The cat wasn't trying to lead us into a trap. It's okay if you guys don't believe me, but I'm being honest. The cat told me it was leading me to the body of water because some of the answers to the questions we've been looking for are hidden in there."

"So then, did you find anything when you were down there?" Amberly asked.

"I didn't. It was too dark for me to see anything. I had used the vine to tie it to my waist so that I could pull myself back up if I got too far in, but by the time I realized the vine was gone, I was already too deep into the water. It was just a... freak accident."

"You're not going to try that again, right?" Kire asked.

"No, *Dad*," Charlie replied, trying to sound as sarcastic as possible.

"So, do you really think there's something down there then?" Trace asked. "Like a clue that will lead us to the portal? Or the portal *itself*?"

"What if that cat just sabotaged you again?" Kire asked. "What if it led you to the water knowing you would go alone, and then it's the one that ripped your vine away from you?"

"I know that could be true," Charlie said. But she didn't have a better way to explain herself. "I just have this feeling that the cat wasn't lying to me, though. She seemed like she genuinely wanted to help."

"Seems suspicious to me," Trace said. "You should be careful, Rose. You never know who you can trust."

"But you can trust *Trace*," Amberly interjected. "Because *he* seems to care a great deal about you." Charlie could clearly tell that there was bitterness and resentment in her voice. Amberly could say she wasn't jealous of Charlie all she wanted, but Charlie couldn't help but get the feeling that she indeed was.

"So, listen," Kire began. "I haven't had much time to talk to you guys with school and everything going on, but we should probably talk about what happened when Charlie and I went to the library."

"Anything helpful?" Kaos asked immediately.

"Uh... sort of..." Kire trailed off, afraid to give them the bad news that they weren't any closer to finding the portal because of James Winterfell's journal. Right now, that cat was their only lead.

"We learned that there might be a way to seal off the portal to those who don't mean well and don't want peace. So theoretically, we can seal off the portal to all the bad guys but keep it open for the good ones," Charlie answered.

"But that's not what Albus wanted," Kaos said. "He wants us to destroy the thing completely."

"But we haven't even found the portal yet, for one," Kire said. "And two, we don't even know *how* to destroy it once we do find it. At least we know that there is a way to do what James Winterfell's journal suggested if we can find out how to make that happen."

"It just seems to me like we're getting more and more things added onto our never-ending to-do list," Amberly said.

"It might sound never-ending, but we do have to start checking through it quickly," Charlie told them. "Just like how Yash sent minions to Earth to wreak havoc on us, he also sent more minions into Albus' realm to wreak havoc on them. Only worse. There's *more* of them, and they're doing total destruction. Yash wants there to be absolutely nobody in his way when he gets to Albus' realm and makes his way to the portal."

"You mean to say that this is *already* happening?" Kaos asked, stopping in his steps and causing everyone behind him to stop as well. Trace didn't notice right away and kept walking forward, and when he glanced around his shoulder, he rolled his eyes and re-joined the group quickly.

"It is," Charlie said uneasily.

"How much time then do we have exactly?" Kaos asked incredulously.

"We don't know," Kire answered, making Charlie glad because she didn't want to be the one to say it. "But we don't have much of it."

35

The rest of the gang had arrived in Kaos' car, and Kaos offered them a ride home, including Charlie. Charlie climbed in the backseat, followed in on either side by Trace and Kire. Amberly got in the front seat with Kaos, the driver.

"I think as long as we are all continuing to practice with our gifts when we can and trying to see if there's any use for them, that'll help us figure out how to get to whatever it is we need to find in that body of water in the cavern, we should be able to figure this out. I'm fairly confident." Charlie was amazed at how self-assured Kaos sounded. How sure of himself he seemed even though he was the one out of the group who could figure out his gift the least.

"So, you think we should go *back* to that cavern again?" Amberly asked, raising a perfectly arched eyebrow at him, looking as if she thought the idea was completely ridiculous.

Kaos shifted in his seat. "Well, Rose believes the cat was just trying to help. And if Rose believes it, then I'm going to trust her. We have to trust each other."

"I don't think we *have* to," Amberly disagreed.

"It's preferred," Kaos snapped.

"Babe, come on," Trace said, rubbing Amberly's shoulders from behind her. "You don't have to be so mean to people all the time. Rose is harmless. What has she ever done to you? Just give it a rest and try out this whole 'trusting team bonding thing,' will you?"

Amberly spun around in her seat, shrugging off Trace's shoulder massage as she did so and glaring at him wildly. "How could you say that to me?" she demanded. "How can you be on their side and not mine? You're supposed to be my boyfriend, Trace! You're supposed to agree with everything I want to do, or everything I say, or everything I think!" She seemed ready to smack him.

"I'm just saying, Amberly, calm down. We're a team, are we not? The Quintets? I'm not saying you have to *like* her; you can just try getting along with her."

"Why do you care in the slightest what I do with her? Since when do *you* like her? You've been, like, all over her lately! Everyone's seen it!"

If Charlie had been drinking a soda, it would surely have flown right out of her nose at the statement. "Absolutely not!" she yelled out. "Nobody thinks that! You're being crazy!"

"Stay out of it!" Amberly snapped. Then she turned around in her front seat, crossed her arms, and stared out the window.

Trace rolled his eyes, then he turned and faced out the window, too. Feeling awkward, Kaos turned up the volume on the radio.

"Rose," Kire said in a soft voice next to Charlie. She turned to look at him, not even knowing what was about to come out of his mouth next. "Look, I really do just want to apologize to you for everything."

"There's nothing to apologize for." She turned to face the front again.

"I'm serious, Rose. Please just hear me out?"

"Why should I bother? You didn't even give me an explanation in the first place."

They rolled up to a stop sign, and then suddenly, Kire and Charlie's conversation was interrupted by Amberly harshly unbuttoning her seatbelt and unlocking the car door. "I've had enough of this."

Before anyone could stop her, she opened the door and climbed out.

"Amberly!" Trace yelled through the cracked-open window. "Where are you going?!"

Charlie wasn't the biggest fan of Amberly, but she did have the right idea. Anything was better than being forced to be stuck in this car listening to Kire come up with some pathetic excuse about how he used to like her, but then Angela came along, and he decided she was the better choice. So, before she could think it more thoroughly through, she unbuckled her own seatbelt, climbed over Trace, and jumped out the side door, running after Amberly.

"Rose, wait!" Kire shouted, but Charlie did not turn around.

She did not want to hear it.

36

Amberly turned out to not be happy about Charlie following her out of the car.

"What are you doing?" she asked in a voice full of sass as Charlie caught up to her.

"I didn't wanna be in the car, either. Besides, if I've learned anything, it's not good to be alone out here like this. Not when Rezin could be anywhere at any time."

She crossed her arms and continued walking at a fast pace. It honestly impressed Charlie because Amberly was still in her heels, and Charlie was struggling to keep up even in her basic tennis shoes.

"I don't need you to protect me. Why don't you go be with your bodyguard, Trace?"

"I don't know where this whole thing came about with Trace, Amberly, but I promise you he doesn't like me."

She scoffed loudly and didn't say anything back.

"I'm serious," Charlie continued to try.

"Yeah. Why would he, anyway?" she snapped. "You're not even that pretty. You have horrible style. You're weird and shy and obsessed with plants. You're afraid of little, tiny animals. I really don't even see what there is to like."

Quickly, Charlie was full of regret about her decision to leave the car. She didn't have to stand for this. But also, her house was past Amberly's, so she didn't really have a choice but to walk Amberly all the way the rest of the journey back to her house so that she could continue on her way to hers after.

"I don't get why you're such a brat to me," Charlie muttered. "Trace is right. I didn't even do anything to you. Simply my existence seems to make you angry."

"You wouldn't understand."

"Try me."

"Absolutely not. I'm not confiding in you about anything. Ever. "

"Fine." Charlie found that she was crossing her arms too as they walked. She couldn't wait for Amberly to leave her and go inside her house.

When they arrived at it, Charlie had to admit it wasn't exactly what she expected. For someone as glamorous as Amberly, she assumed it would be a cute white house with a picket fence and an immaculate lawn with one of those tire swings tied to the tree out front. But instead, it was a small bungalow with a very poorly tended front lawn. All of the blinds in the windows were closed, and there was a huge oil stain on the driveway.

"*This* is where you live?" Charlie asked. She didn't mean for the question to come out mean; she was just surprised.

"Leave me alone." Amberly whipped her hair so quickly that it hit Charlie in the face before she could dodge it in time. Then the queen bee stormed up the flight of wooden stairs leading up to her front porch.

Rolling her eyes, Charlie continued on with her walk. Only a couple more blocks to go until she was home. And thank goodness she was alone again. Rezin wouldn't really try to attack her right here out in the open like this, would he?

Charlie continued to walk, caution filling her because she didn't want to have another incident where the Quintets had to save her yet again. She kept her eyes peeled for any signs of strange activity, which was new to her because usually, she kept her eyes glued to the floor under her feet as she walked.

She stopped mid-step when she heard an earsplitting scream emitting from inside Amberly's house.

37

There Charlie was, worried that Rezin might attack her out here out in the open. She hadn't even considered the fact that Rezin might have been inside Amberly's house, patiently awaiting her return so that he could attack her there instead.

Instantly, adrenaline pumped through Charlie's veins for the second time that day. She turned sharply on her heel and darted across two of Amberly's neighbors' front yards and into Amberly's. She had no idea what she was going to do when she got into the house and saw Amberly's condition and what was happening, but she knew she couldn't just stay out of the house and do nothing.

The front door was closed, but she burst her way through it, happy to find it unlocked. The foyer was dimly lit, and Charlie couldn't see a whole lot, but she raced forward, terrified of what she was going to find, for Amberly had stopped making any sort of noise at all. When she turned the corner and entered the living room, she had, just for a split moment, envisioned Amberly dead. However, there *was* somebody on the floor; it just wasn't Amberly. It was an older woman, unconscious, with

Amberly knelt down beside her, tears streaming down her cheeks, ruining her mascara.

"What happened?" Charlie asked, her voice high in pitch.

"I don't know!" Amberly whined loudly. "I just came in, and I... I found her like this! She won't wake up, Charlie! Why won't she wake up?"

Thinking quickly and realizing she didn't need any of her powers to do this next part, she pulled out her cell phone and dialed 911. "I'm going to get her help, okay?" she said to Amberly as she waited to speak with the 911 operator.

On the floor, Amberly continued to cry. "Mom," she said, shaking her mother. "Mom, you have to wake up!"

Charlie had never seen this side of Amberly before. She was quite certain that nobody in the entire world had ever seen the side of Amberly. Despite Charlie's feelings for Amberly most of the time, this sight was still one of the most heart-breaking things she had ever beheld.

38

When the ambulance arrived, they loaded Amberly's mom, Elizabeth McHenry, into the back of it. Amberly, still a mess, with a blanket from one of the paramedics draped over her, clambered into the back of the ambulance to be with her mother. Charlie didn't quite know what she should do. What she *did* know was that she didn't like the thought of Amberly being all alone in the hospital, waiting to find out the news of if her mom was going to be okay or not. So, she decided quickly that she would run home, grab her bicycle, and then take it over to the hospital.

It didn't take her long to get there, but when she parked her bike on the rack and went inside, she instantly found Amberly in the waiting area, her knees tucked up under her chin as she sat in a chair alone. She still hadn't even bothered to wipe the mascara from under her face from all the crying she had done since finding her mom.

Charlie made her way over to her and took a seat beside her.

"How are you holding up?" she asked in a soft, timid voice. The last thing she wanted was for Amberly to snap at her.

"I haven't heard anything yet," she explained to Charlie. "But the waiting is torture." She sniffed and hiccupped, and Charlie almost wanted to rub her back for comfort but decided she better not. She was probably already pushing her limit with Amberly right now by being here at the hospital with her and seeing her in her current state.

"I'm sure she'll be okay," Charlie tried, wanting to think of positive things to say to her.

"You don't know that," she said.

It was true. Charlie did not know it. But someone had to stay positive in the situation, didn't they?

"Well, whatever happens, I'm here for you."

They were silent for a long while. Then the doctor came out and wanted to speak with Amberly.

"You don't have to stay here and wait with me," Amberly said.

"I know I don't," Charlie replied. "But I want to."

Amberly stood, wiped a tear from her cheek, got mascara on her finger, and then went and talked to the doctor. Whatever conversation they were having, it looked serious. When Amberly came back, her spirits didn't look to be much higher.

"It's still too early to tell exactly what's going on," Amberly informed Charlie. "I don't even know why I'm telling you any of this."

"It's okay. You don't have to tell me anything. I'm just here for support."

"Thanks."

Charlie was shocked. *A thank you? From Amberly McHenry?*

"Yeah... don't mention it." She was certain that Amberly wouldn't.

"So, did you tell the others then?"

"Tell them what?"

"Did you tell them that I'm here? That you found me all freaking out in my house and that my mom is sick?"

"No, I didn't tell anyone." Charlie cocked her head and stared at Amberly. "Does Trace not even know?"

"It's... complicated."

"Do you want to talk about it?"

Amberly went back to tucking her knees under her chin again. She stared straight ahead, staring blankly. "Absolutely not."

"Okay, then. We can just sit here in total silence. Whatever you want, Amberly. I'm here for you."

They were silent, for only for a brief moment. Then, Amberly spoke again. "You have to promise me that you won't tell the others about this. Okay?"

"Are you sure?" Charlie asked. "I'm sure they would be a really good support system for you—"

"Promise me, Rose."

Charlie swallowed her next words and nodded her head. "Okay. I promise."

They were silent a little while longer. Then Charlie couldn't help herself.

"Why don't you want them to know?"

"Because. I don't want them thinking differently of me. Everyone sees me as this girl who has her whole life together. Who is perfect, and who has perfect things happening to her nonstop. If people saw that my life was like *this*, that I'm constantly dealing with my sick mother, and that I don't have a father who loves me, people would... pity me. I don't ever want to be pitied. I want to be liked. Feared even. I want people to look up to me. I want people to want to *be* me. And nobody wants to be somebody who hardly has any family to care for her."

"Wow." Charlie breathed. She would've never guessed that Amberly was going through anything like this. Of course, she already knew about the father incident. But she figured Amberly's mother was healthy and loving and enough of a parent to where Amberly never felt like she was missing out on having a father. "Thank you for sharing all of that with me."

"Yeah, and if you tell anyone, I promise you, I *will* beat you up."

Charlie snickered. "I won't tell a soul."

Charlie wasn't used to seeing this new vulnerable side of Amberly. But suddenly, Charlie felt as if she understood her a little bit better. As if she knew sort of where she came from and why she did the things she did. It was as if Charlie was seeing her in a whole new light. And in that new light, Charlie found a new appreciation for one of the Quintets.

39

While things at home still weren't all that great—Charlie's parents and her sister had given her the silent treatment last night, and then Lexi left for college this morning without even so much as a goodbye—Charlie felt like things were headed in the right direction in her life. She was getting the hang of her magical powers. She had her good plant friend, Ramoni, to give her words of encouragement and help her through the tough questions she had about herself and her life. And she vividly remembered, as she walked to school in the cold drizzle the next morning, Kaos telling her in the cavern that she could fit in with the others and be part of the group if she just put in the effort. Maybe that was what she was supposed to do. Put in the effort and try to be the rest of the Quintets' friends. She would even try to dress a little less weird for them so that they wouldn't mind being seen with her as much. She wouldn't dress herself up like her sister by any means—today, she had on a pleated white skirt and a floral top that she could picture Amberly wearing. She wore normal white sneakers and black tights with a black leather jacket she found in the back of her closet that she got at a vintage clothing store a while back. She felt normal in this outfit. Especially with her hair just brushed out and straight, nothing fancy done with it. But of course, she would always have the Pendantix around her neck.

When Charlie entered through the doors into the school before the bell for first period rang, she was greeted by that rush of warm air, which sent goosebumps down her spine from how freezing she had been walking out in the drizzle with no umbrella. She shook some of the wetness out of her hair and then headed toward her locker, deciding that if she saw any of the other Quintets as she passed, she would wave at them. Charlie could be different. Charlie could try. Kaos was right. She didn't have to always be alone.

When she turned the corner heading to her locker, she slowed her pace when she noticed one of the cheerleaders sniffling. It was none other than Angela, digging through her locker with puffy eyes and tear-stained cheeks.

Angela... *crying*?

Charlie couldn't believe her eyes. Why would she be so sad? What had happened to her to cause the crying? Had she been kicked off the cheer squad? Berated by Amberly, who was surely in an extra sour mood coming back to school today after everything she had to deal with at the hospital with her mother the day before?

Charlie was pretty used to minding her own business. She didn't care about anything going on with anyone in the school, usually. She wasn't interested in any drama or gossip, and she didn't partake in spreading lies or rumors about people. But when it came to Angela, she was curious. Immensely curious.

It's what led her to reach out to one of her classmates, Lily Peterson, during Physics class with Mr. Loch, to ask her if she knew anything about it. Lily was on the cheer team, but she wasn't anywhere near as popular as Angela or Amberly. She was only on the squad because she was really good at doing flips. Otherwise, she was sweet and well-liked and not a bully like the other cheerleaders. Charlie thought that was why she didn't fit in with them as easily.

"Hey, Lily," Charlie started as they were supposed to be working on a worksheet about how electromagnetic waves transfer energy by radiation.

"What's up?" Lily asked, seeming clueless about what to do with the worksheet. It was exactly how Charlie felt about it, too.

"I was just wondering if you knew why Angela Meyers was crying this morning by her locker."

"Why do you care?" Lily asked, seeming genuinely confused about Charlie wanting to know. Most likely, it was because Charlie so often kept to herself about those sorts of matters.

But Charlie had to know.

"Just curious."

Lily stared at her for a second with her boring brown eyes squinted, then finally she sighed before giving her answer.

"Well, if you must know, and don't go repeating it anyone either—"

"I won't."

Lily nodded. "Good. Unfortunately, this morning, Kire Hunter sort of... broke up with her. Dumped her. Right in front of the other cheerleaders, too. It was pretty sad."

"I'm sorry, I don't know if I heard you correctly," Charlie said, her heart picking up speed. "What happened?"

Lily gave her a weird look. "I *said*, Kire dumped Angela."

40

During her lunch period the next day, Charlie made her way to the cafeteria, not sure what to expect of the day. Her plan was to march up to where Kire and the others were sitting and ask if she could join them. It made her feel a little bit better because it wasn't as if she had to worry about Angela being at the table, throwing herself at Kire. Was that what Kire was trying to tell her in the car yesterday? If so, why? Why break up with Angela now? Did it have anything to do with Charlie, or was Kire simply just tired of being with her?

Try not to think about it. You're not supposed to care about Kire.

She nodded to herself and continued to walk into the cafeteria. She put her hand on the door handle but then was suddenly pulled out of the way by her other hand. She whirled around and saw Trace and Kire standing there, Kaos jogging behind them to catch up. Amberly suddenly came out the other cafeteria door with her arms crossed, avoiding everybody's eye contact and looking pouty.

"What's going on?" Charlie asked, wondering why they suddenly had an impromptu Quintet meeting in the middle of the busy hallway.

"A couple of developments have happened this morning," Kire said, dragging everyone away from the middle of the busy crowd off to the side where they could talk more privately.

"What kind of developments?" Charlie asked.

"Well, Trace has this theory, anyway," Kire started.

"Yeah," Trace nodded. "I totally think the new soccer coach is Rezin in disguise. That he's here at the school to keep an eye on us."

"I mean, it *would* make total sense," Kaos agreed. "He hates everyone and everything. He doesn't seem like he wants to be a coach. He hardly even seems like he knows what he's doing, and he relies on the captain of the soccer team to lead everyone else during practices and stuff."

"So, you think Rezin has been here on the campus this whole time?" Charlie asked, amazed and a little afraid.

"Well, if Heno could do it with Andrew..." Kire trailed off, looking down at his feet. Andrew's untimely death was still a sore subject.

"Okay, so what do we do with that information?" Charlie asked. "You don't think he would attack during school with everyone watching, do you? "

"We don't," Kaos said. "Which is why we think this is the perfect opportunity to ditch and go back to the cave."

"Excuse me?"

"If Rezin is supposed to be the soccer coach, he also has gym classes to teach, so he can't just leave campus to follow us into the woods," Trace said. "It was Kaos who came up with the brilliant idea for what we should do when we get to the cave. It involves our gifts and getting to whatever it was that cat wanted us to maybe find down there."

"I..." Charlie felt uncertain about it. She didn't want to have a repeat of the incident that happened yesterday.

"And that's not all," Kire said, looking a little energetic. He was bouncing on the balls of his feet as he spoke. Charlie realized it was the first time she had faced him since she had learned of him breaking up with Angela. Instantly, her stomach filled with butterflies. She hated it and wished they would go away.

"Okay, what?" she asked.

"Halo finally gave me a little bit more information last night! She told me—because I was so stressed about finding the portal and then finding out what ritual to do to close the portal and destroy it—that all we needed to do was just get to the portal first. And then she said that we might be surprised to learn that everything else will fall into place after that. That discovering it is the most important key to it all."

"That's great, then!" Charlie agreed, nodding enthusiastically. "Whatever is in that water is either a clue that will lead us to the portal or..."

Kire smiled at her. "...Or it's going to lead us to the portal itself."

DEEP IN THE CAVERN, the Unlikely Defenders turned the corner and came across the massive ice-blue lake. The whole walk over there, the boys had been joking around and talking excitedly, seemingly happy that they were getting somewhere with this journey of theirs. Next to them, Amberly stayed deadly quiet, her arms crossed. Charlie wondered if she had ever uncrossed them from yesterday. Charlie, of course, knew why Amberly was being this way. Her mom was sick, and she was worried about her. And she was probably also nervous that Charlie was going to say something to the rest of the room and let it slip that some stuff had gone down yesterday at her house. But Charlie wouldn't do that, no matter how much she disliked Amberly. If Amberly wanted to keep it a secret, then Charlie could do that for her.

Trace turned to Amberly. "Okay, do you know what to do?"

Amberly took the gauntlet out of her backpack and put it on her hand. It climbed its way up her arm and latched on delicately. It seemed as if the gauntlet was made just for her.

Then she nodded, her jaw tense. "I'm ready."

Kire took Charlie's hand and pulled her gently away from the edge of the lake. "It's probably best if you stand back for a little bit."

Lit up by Trace's sword of fire, Amberly was the only one who stepped closer to the water's edge. Then, pointing her whole fist at the body of water, she concentrated so hard that her hair started flailing behind her, an invisible wind picked up by her powers. Then right before Charlie's very eyes, the water started moving. It took Charlie a second to realize it, but the water was parting right down the middle and rising into the air, creating a sort of pathway leading deep underneath.

"This is amazing!" Kire shouted.

"I can't believe it worked!" Kaos yelled in agreement.

Charlie was too stunned to speak. And Trace was too focused on lighting the way for Amberly.

"Okay, Amberly, do you think you can hold it?" Kaos asked. Amberly gave a stern head nod. "Great, then I think it's time we walk down there."

Scared, Charlie stood close to Kaos and Kire as they began following behind Trace into the narrow pathway between the two massive walls of water that Amberly was holding up. At the end of the group, Amberly walked backward behind them all, keeping her focus on the walls of water so that she wouldn't accidentally let them drop. She looked strong, powerful, and fearless. She didn't look even in the slightest as if her powers were going to falter. She seemed a lot more secure in her ability with her gauntlet. More than Charlie was with her ability in her Pendantix, anyway. She wondered where that inner confidence came from.

It took them only a few minutes of walking through the narrow pathway, being careful not to slip on the slick surface of the muddy ground underneath their feet, then they came across two stone pillars.

Charlie was in amazement at what she was seeing.

"You guys think this is it?" Kire asked. "Is this the portal?"

"It doesn't look very exciting," Trace said.

"It looks like it's been untouched for centuries," Kaos agreed.

"What do we do now?!" Amberly called over her shoulder. "I'm hanging in there for now, but I can't do this all day."

"Right," Kire said. He dropped his backpack on the stone ground that the potential portal pillars were attached to, unzipped his backpack, and pulled out Halo. The book seemed to flip open on its own, and it emitted a small white glow from it. Charlie didn't even bother to read over his shoulder at what Halo was telling Kire because it was in a language only Kire seemed able to understand.

"Halo brought me right to this incantation," Kire said, sounding hesitant. "I mean, of course, I trust her, but I'm just not entirely sure what it's going to do when I say it."

"What do you mean?" Charlie asked.

"Like, if I destroy this portal right now, then we can never go into the other realm. We can never help Albus. It might destroy us, too, in the process. There's just no way to know for sure."

"I guess it's just a chance we have to take. We're not going to have many more opportunities to do this," Kaos said. "The tree that Charlie created isn't going to keep this cave from toppling on us forever."

Kire sighed and straightened up. "You guys are right. Are you ready for this?"

"Ready," Kaos and Trace said at the same time. Charlie admired how brave they were. The *ready* she emitted was much squeakier and quieter, and Amberly simply nodded her head as if she wasn't even fully paying attention because she was too busy focusing on keeping the water from staying away from them.

"*Zaest salleac impsis atenilum.*"

Suddenly, whether Amberly wanted it to or not, a stream of water was flying out from both sides of the walls she had created. They flew right in between the two pillars of the structure before them and filled it, creating a swirling water archway. It glowed a brilliant blue, so bright that Charlie closed her eyes for a moment, trying to adjust to it.

"We did it!" Trace cheered.

"Did we, though?" Kire asked. "I think all I did is merely activate it."

"Ask Halo what to do now!" Kaos demanded. "Hurry."

Kire quickly got out a pen and started writing. "She says... it's only open from our side. It has to be activated from both sides before the ritual to destroy it can work."

"You mean to say... we have to go over there?" Charlie asked.

"Hold on, she's still writing," Kire said, squinting to focus on it. "She says we're still doing okay on time and that she's proud of us for finding it. Yash hasn't reached Albus' realm yet. What we have to do is activate the other side and then find a way to make sure it stays closed for good."

"But how is the magical realm doing against Yash's minion's attacks?" Charlie asked. It felt selfish to just close the portal to protect their world from ending when another realm's world was potentially ending right before their eyes.

"I'll ask." Kire scribbled some more. When he replied, his voice cracked. "It's not good. Their minions are destroying everything."

"So we have a side quest!" Trace said, wielding his sword. "I'm more than fine with doing a side quest. I'm ready to fight."

"You *want* to help them?" Kire asked, astonished.

"Yeah?" Trace said. "Don't you?"

"You guys, come on!" Amberly complained.

"I..." Kire looked at Charlie. "Yeah, I do."

"I do, too," Charlie said.

"I'm down for it," Kaos agreed.

"Okay then. We're going through this portal. We're going to defeat some more of Yash's minions and help save the magical realm. And since we're good on time, we will close up the portal at the end of all of this. That's the plan?" Kire asked. Everyone nodded their heads yes. Kire closed the book and put it back in his backpack. Then he threw his backpack over his shoulder and stepped in front of the portal of swirling bright blue water. "Then it settled. It's time for us to go save Albus."

41

"Wait," Amberly called, her concentration wavering from holding up the water around them. "We're actually going to go across to the other side? Right now? Don't we need to... I don't know, tell our parents? Leave a note or something in case we're gone for a while?" It was like entering the portal was the very last thing she wanted to do.

Charlie hadn't even considered what Amberly was saying before she agreed to cross over into a different What if they got stuck over on the other side? What if something happened to them while they were trying to defeat more of Yash's minions? What if time in other realms worked like it did in space, and one hour on the other side was equivalent to five years on Earth? Their parents wouldn't know anything about it. Nobody at the school would know where they disappeared to. How would they ever be found? Would they just be deemed *missing* for the rest of their lives, their parents never able to finally be at peace with what their fate might've been?

Why do I even care? she wondered to herself as she thought about it. *My parents don't even like me. They'd probably be better off with me gone.*

She looked around at the others, thinking about how their parents would feel about them missing. She knew that Kire and his father weren't getting along. But what about the others? And didn't they care at all what they were risking by going in through that archway? There was no telling what would happen once they did. If one thing was for sure, Charlie was certain that the boys in this group were some of the bravest she had ever met.

Charlie looked back at Amberly. What about Amberly's mother, who needed her now more than ever? And Amberly was just supposed to agree to leave her behind in order to do whatever it took to close off the portal forever? Charlie could understand Amberly's sudden hesitation to go forward with it.

"There's no time for us to do any of that," Kire explained to Amberly.

This did not satisfy her. "What do you mean? Why not? I thought Halo said we were doing good on time," she argued.

"She did say that. And we are doing good on time. For *now*," Kire looked about ready to march up to Amberly, grab her by the wrist, and drag her through the archway with him. He looked like a fed-up older brother—even though technically Amberly was older than him. "But who knows when that will change?"

"What do you mean by change?" she asked. "Did Halo say there was a chance of the future changing or something?" Her focus on holding back the water slipped a little, and the walls of water started closing in on them.

"Amberly!" Charlie yelled, snapping her back into focus. She readjusted her position, and the walls of water moved back to their original position.

"I—it's complicated to explain," Kire answered. "And there's no time for me to do that right now, okay?"

"I don't like this," she said.

"Amberly," Trace said, taking a step forward. "You don't have to come with us."

She glared at him, ready to say something snotty back, but he held up his hand to allow himself the chance to continue.

"But I know that if the five of us stick together, we will have more of a chance of being successful at this—whatever it is we have to deal with when we get to the Albus Realm. We want you with us."

Still, Amberly looked unsure as she struggled to hold the water up. "But what... what if we don't come back?"

"I promise," Trace assured her, looking at her determinedly and adoringly. "If you come with us, I won't let anything happen to you."

"He's right, Amber," Kaos added in. "We'll look out for each other. The whole way through. Whatever waits for us on the other side, we have each other's backs. We will make it back through and back to our parents in no time. Heck, I bet no one will even really notice we've been missing."

"But what if we don't make it back?" Amberly asked again, looking wildly around at everyone. She seemed almost as if holding up the water was beginning to cause her pain. Charlie had never seen Amberly act so unsure of something before. It was as if she learned something new about her every day. It turned out that Princess Amberly didn't always know what was best, after all.

"I think it's better to live a life full of 'oh wells' instead of 'what ifs,'" Charlie decided to toss in. Everyone looked at her with their eyebrows raised for a moment. Charlie shrugged. She had heard that saying somewhere, but right now, the source wasn't coming to mind.

However, it seemed as if Amberly was changing her mind. And Charlie liked to think, as weird as the others thought she was for saying it, that her little saying was what made Amberly change her mind.

"Whatever," she finally said. "Let's just go then. I can't hold up this water all day, either. So hurry up before we all drown."

"Thanks, Amberly," Kire said.

"So not doing it for you," Amberly grunted with her struggle to hold the water back.

Kire ignored her. "So, we're all in agreement?" he asked, looking around at everyone in turn. When his eyes met Charlie's, Charlie felt goosebumps move down her spine. She hated that he had that effect on her. She wished she could just see Kire as she saw any other acquaintance of hers in the hallway. It didn't matter when he looked at her. Her body needed to stop reacting as if it did.

"Yes," Kaos answered first.

Trace nodded his head fiercely, a fire in his eyes—and not because of the flames on his sword.

"I'm in," Charlie said. She was surprised at how small and quiet her voice sounded when she spoke. But she tried to chalk it up to the water walls making enough noise to overpower her voice. It definitely wasn't because she was so uneasy and terrified.

"Great," Kire concluded. Then he began barking out quick instructions, taking charge with how he thought they should best go about this. "You guys go in first," he said to Charlie, Trace, and Kaos. "Then I'll go. Then Amberly, walk backward as you're holding the water back. You'll be the last one to go through right before you stop holding it up, got it?"

Amberly nodded her head sternly. But she made a constipated face like listening to Kire's orders was the last thing on Earth she wanted to do.

Good thing she wouldn't be on Earth much longer.

Kire turned to Trace. "You're the fighter. You go across first so that you can attack anything that might be waiting on the other side."

"Wh-what's going to be waiting on the other side?" Trace asked. He sounded slightly squeaky. But then he rolled his shoulders back and cleared his throat. "Not that I'm worried about it, though."

Kire gave him a suspecting look before answering. "I don't know," he said. "We have no idea what to expect from this Albus Realm. All we know are the few things Albus told us."

Trace nodded. When he spoke again, he sounded surer of himself this time. "You got it, boss."

"I'm not the boss," Kire said at the same time that Kaos muttered, "He's not the boss." Then the two smartest boys at St. Bernard High exchanged looks.

Charlie had to refrain from rolling her eyes. Instead, she beamed around at everybody, feeling warmth and appreciation for them. "We totally have this, you guys," she told them. "I know we can do it."

"Me, too," Kire said. The others nodded in agreement.

Then Charlie felt the strangest sensation on her chest. It was where the Pendantix was touching it. It was humming. And giving off a warming sensation. It almost tingled. It made her gasp as she reached her hand out to hold the Pendantix. Then as she did so, her hand warmed instantly, and it, too, felt the humming and the tingling sensation. It quickly swarmed through her entire body. When she looked around at the others, she noticed them staring at their gifts as well.

"Do... you guys feel that?" Kaos asked as he held his crown closer to his skull on top of his head. Charlie figured it wasn't often that his gift made him feel any certain sort of way—it hardly did anything at all.

"What's happening?" Amberly asked, staring at her arm, which was engulfed by her gorgeous gauntlet. "My whole arm feels weird!"

Kire held his book in his hands. "I feel something weird in my palms!" he called.

"Whatever is happening," Trace called as he stood in front of the arch with his sword. "It's definitely a new thing!"

Charlie couldn't describe the situation. She had no idea why it was happening. Her only guess was that it was a group effort. The fact that they had all agreed about something.

Maybe their working as a team was causing their gifts to react in a specific way. That had to be it. Because in the first time since they received these gifts, they were finally in agreement about what they wanted to do.

They wanted to go to the other side of that archway.

42

Charlie was in a state of disbelief. They were really doing it. One by one, the Unlikely Defenders began stepping through the swirling water-filled portal before them. Trace went first, his sword drawn. Everyone watched him disappear before their very eyes with no idea what to expect. With no idea what he was dealing with once he was on the other side. Charlie didn't know if he was okay. Or if he even went to the right realm. Or if she was ever going to see him again. Right now, nothing was certain.

After Trace, it was Kaos' turn. He stood before the archway, his eyebrows furrowed, making him look mean. "Albus Realm, I hope you're ready for me," he said. Then he turned around and gave everybody a steely head nod before, at a bit of a run, he became the second person to disappear through the watery blue arch.

Kire looked at Charlie. "Rose, you're up," he told her.

Am I really going to do this?

She carefully stepped in front of the arch next. Her entire body was trembling with her nerves. What would it feel like?

Would it hurt? Was there danger immediately on the other side? What was going to happen to her?

"I-I'm scared," she admitted.

"You're always scared!" Amberly whined. "But right now, we *really* don't have time for that!"

"Just ignore her," Kire said, speaking reassuringly to Charlie. "You can do it."

Charlie nodded, then she turned away from him to face the floating water. She could do this. She had to do this.

"Hurry *up!*" Amberly shouted. "I'm losing strength! If you don't go through that dang portal right now, me, you, and Kire are going to die, and Trace and Kaos are going to be stuck in the Albus Realm with Yash and all of his minions for good!"

Amberly's loud voice gave Charlie the little jolt she needed. Charlie forced herself to finally push through it. She stepped into the vertiginous blue oblivion, holding her breath without even realizing it. Inside the arch, she didn't feel wetness at all like she suspected she would. Instead, she felt a feeling far different from what she had anticipated. It was a slightly dizzying sensation, and for a moment, it seemed as if all gravity had disappeared, and Charlie was just floating through a cobalt blue nothingness. Then before she could even begin to wonder if there even was any gravity in the Albus Realm—who knew what that place would be like, after all— suddenly her feet were on the ground again, and when her eyes regained their focus and she inhaled a deep breath of air. Before her was the greatest, most curious expanse of land she had ever seen in her entire life.

Charlie Rose had officially entered a different realm.

And to think she used to not even believe other realms existed at all.

Trace and Kaos were busy staring around at the place and hadn't even seemed to notice that she had arrived. Charlie did the same thing, not paying attention to anyone coming in through the portal behind her.

This place was magnificent. Magical, yet dark. She could see so much from where she stood. It was as if this world worked on an incline, and the portal was stuck somewhere firmly at the bottom of it, in the middle of an empty field. She could see rolling hills. Rocky cliffs. Bodies of water. Thick patches of woods.

But among it all, she could see something else, too. Something that made her stomach clench and her heart ache.

Destruction.

Smoke. Flames. Everything around them was coated in a thick mask of smog from fire, some of which were still going and some that had been recently extinguished. Of course, Charlie had no idea what to expect the Albus Realm to look like, but she was pretty sure it wasn't supposed to look like this. Without the fire and the smoke, she figured this would be the most beautiful place she had ever been.

Charlie looked up because she wanted to know if the sky was blue like it was back on Earth. However, she couldn't even see the sky above her because of the smoke. She coughed a little as she tried to breathe in it. It wasn't easy to do.

This saddened her. Chills erupted down her arms and made the hairs on the back of her neck stand up. It was as if she could sense that it was bad here. Really bad.

"Where are we?" Kire asked suddenly from behind Charlie. She whirled around, for some reason relieved to find that he had made it through the portal. He looked just as awestruck as everyone else had, but when he saw that Charlie was looking at him, he suddenly appeared to only have eyes for her.

Then before anyone could answer him, Amberly flew in backward through the portal, slamming into Kire's back and nearly knocking him over. When she turned around to face everybody, the front of her was completely soaked.

"I *so* did not sign up for this," she said miserably as she shook some of it out and wiped the mascara from under her eyes. Trace was quick to go to her side to comfort her and wipe some remaining water droplets off her arms.

"Did everything go okay?" he asked her. Before she could even answer, he put an arm around her and looked off in the distance. "Babe. Do you *see* this place? Isn't it amazing?"

Amazing is an understatement.

"It's... something," Amberly said, shivering. "Cold."

"Your clothes will dry," Trace told her, sounding comforting. But all his words did was cause Amberly to shoot him a dirty look and step away from him. Charlie wasn't sure what exactly she expected Trace to be able to do for her. It was as if she was upset that Trace didn't keep an extra outfit on him at all times for Amberly to change into. She thought Amberly held expectations of people that were far too high for anyone to be able to reach.

"Aw, come back," Trace whined, going after his girlfriend.

"I think we're in a cornstalk field," Kaos suddenly pointed out. Charlie looked closer around her at the high stems surrounding them. She could see husks of corn, but they weren't yellow like she was used to seeing on Earth. These ones were all different kinds of colors. Ruby reds. Violets. Indigos. Some were multicolored, as well. They were the most unique things Charlie thought she had ever seen, and she had only *just* entered this new Albus Realm. She wondered what else was out there, waiting for her to find it. How else did this realm differ from Earth? Charlie knew that the wonders of being in a new realm weren't what she should be focusing on right now, however, and she forced her thoughts back to the task they were really here to tackle.

"And look—you guys see over there in the distance?" Kaos asked. Everyone followed his finger to where it was pointing. "I think there's a castle up on that mountain."

It was hard to make it out through the smog, but Charlie could see what Kaos was talking about. There was a tall, charcoal-colored mountain, and it looked like a magnificent—though slightly ominous—castle was carved right into the side of it, made out of the same material as the rocks that made up the mountain. The whole thing was a massive mound of black surrounded by endless green.

"I see it," Kire and Charlie said at the same time.

"Same. What about it?" Trace asked, looking around himself wildly as if he was expecting something to pop out of the corn at them at any moment to attack. Charlie was glad he was on edge—they needed somebody like that. Someone ready to fight and protect them at all times. She was also glad that responsibility hadn't fallen on her.

"I think we should make our way there," Kaos answered. "We need to try to find Albus—*our* Albus. He might be there. Or we might find someone there that knows where he is."

"I agree. I think we should go in that direction. And I'd like to find a ritual or spell that will keep the portal open to everyone except people like Yash and Rezin," Kire added in. "Like we read about in James Winterfell's journal."

Charlie was surprised to hear him say this. "I don't know if that was part of the plan," she said uneasily. It already seemed impossible enough to try and figure out how to save this realm and close the portal off so that Yash could never get to Earth. Now he wanted to add this task in?

"But if we can do that instead of closing off the portal for good, it's worth a shot," Kire replied. "I think the portal between here and Earth should remain usable. I'm sure others want it that way, too."

"You know what?" Trace said, looking eager. "I'm game."

"Same. I want to be able to come back here," Kaos said. "This place is seriously sick."

"Just add it to the never-ending list of things we have to do," Amberly said as she sighed.

"Hang on," Kire said out of nowhere, making the others look at him. In his hands, Halo was twitching. He set the book on the damp ground, and it flew open. Halo started writing something, which Kire squatted down to read. "Finally, some good news," he said.

"And what might that be?" Amberly asked. She was still shivering from being soaked by the lake in the cave back on Earth.

"She was telling me that there's one thing we don't have to worry about while being in the Albus Realm. Rezin can't follow us here."

"Are you sure?" Charlie asked. It sounded too good to be true.

"How does Halo know that?" Kaos added, skeptical.

"According to Halo, Rezin has been forbidden to ever leave Earth. He's to stay there to fight all of those who take on the Quintet gifts."

"That really doesn't make me feel that much better," Amberly complained. "I'm drenched, in another realm, with no idea when we're going to be able to head back into *our* realm, with a bunch of other minions of Yash's ready to try and destroy us unless we can destroy them first. Sure, we don't have to worry about Rezin, but we have about a million others just like him to worry about instead."

Charlie swallowed. Fear was trembling through her body, but she didn't want the others to see it. "Who knows," she said, wanting to be optimistic. "Maybe it will be different here. Maybe the aliens will be easier to defeat. Maybe they won't be like Jago, Heno, or Rezin."

Instead of supporting her in her answer, Trace and Amberly snickered sarcastically.

"Yeah, right," Trace said to her. "But it's whatever. I'm ready for it." He waved his sword around, slashing it through the air to show off his fighting moves.

"That's one thing we all need to be," Kire said as he stared at everyone. "We all need to be ready. We have no idea what's coming, but I get the feeling we're going to need all of us to be as capable with our gifts as possible if we have any chance of defeating these things."

Charlie was terrified. But Charlie was also ready.

43

Charlie had no idea how to gauge how long the journey to the mountain where the castle was would take them. From her eyes, it appeared as if it was days and days away from them. Would that mean days and days of fighting off aliens and trying to stay alive? The thought of it made her shudder. She didn't even know if she had the capabilities to make it through one day of fighting, let alone multiple. Was she strong enough? She knew she had her Pendantix to help her, but still, Charlie felt unsure.

Could she really do this?

The five teenagers walked through the cornstalks, all of them on the lookout for any rustling or noises that could be aliens preparing to attack them. But it had been dead quiet around them so far. Who knew how far away these aliens were? Who knew how long they had until they found themselves under attack? Charlie didn't have the slightest clue how long it would be until they had their first run-in with one. She wondered what they would be like. How they would compare to Jago, Heno, and Rezin. Would they be physical fighters, or would they be more like Rezin, who preferred to play mind games?

"I really think we're in the middle of nowhere," Kaos said after a while of all of them being silent. "That's probably why the portal is where it is. Nobody comes out here."

"Nobody except farmers," Charlie guessed. There was vegetation out here, after all. Did this realm even have farmers? Or did they call them something different, maybe?

It was so quiet around them that it made Charlie uncomfortable. And as they trekked along, there was nothing but the high cornstalks around them for miles. Every so often, they went taller than Charlie's head. Than *everyone's* heads. When that happened, there was no way for them to see in front of them except for the first couple of feet. But it did help that there was no wind, so if any of the cornstalks around them started swaying, they would know there was potential danger coming.

"Well, I guess while we don't seem to be in any immediate danger, we should all probably be figuring out how our gifts can help us in the wilderness. Not just in the fighting aspect of it all," Kire said.

"What do you mean?" Amberly asked. Her voice sounded wary like she had an idea of what Kire was going to tell her next but didn't want to hear it.

"It's going to be a multiple-day trek to get to that castle," Kire admitted.

"We're going to be in here for *multiple* days?" Amberly asked.

"Is that not okay? Do you have something else you need to do instead?" Kire asked back, sounding annoyed. Charlie wished she could tell him to cut it out. He had no idea what her mother was going through. In fact, she couldn't even believe that Amberly was here away from her mom doing this with them in the first place. But Charlie had to keep quiet about it. Amberly didn't want anybody to know what had happened to her mother. What had *been* happening with her mother—Amberly didn't like to seem weak.

"The whole city is going to be looking for us. Our parents are going to be worried sick," Amberly protested.

"I think there are more important things than people being worried about us." Kaos took his crown off and stared at it as he walked. "We're kind of doing something a little more important than being good kids getting home by curfew and doing all of our homework."

"Just a little bit," Kire joked.

"Isn't there like, a faster way for us to get to this castle?" Amberly's voice had become whiny. Charlie almost wanted to cover her ears.

"What, like a magic carpet?" Kire asked. At that, Trace laughed.

"This isn't funny, Trace!" Amberly snapped.

"We need to lay low," Kaos said. When he turned his head to the side while they walked, Charlie could see that he was smirking. "We can't be tracking people down and asking them for a ride. We have no idea what the aliens here will look like. Who they might disguise themselves as."

"Yeah," Kire agreed. "And even if they're not Yash's minions, there still could be other dangerous people in this world."

"People who don't like finding foreign strangers from another realm on their land," Kaos finished.

"This sucks," Amberly muttered, crossing her arms. "And I'm still not dry yet."

"It will be okay, babe," Trace said. "We'll get to the castle, we'll find the spell to close off the portal to the bad guys, we'll find a couple of aliens along the way, and then we'll be back home. Easy peasy."

Amberly laughed incredulously. Charlie was with her, though—nothing about any of this seemed easy.

"This is crazy," she mumbled.

They continued walking, but Amberly fell to the back of the group. Noticing it, Charlie fell back, too.

"Hey, are you okay?" she whispered to her. "If you need to go back, I'm sure the others would understand the reason why."

"Can you shut up?" Amberly snapped at her loudly. "I'm fine. I don't need to go back. I'm not a scaredy-cat whiny baby like you."

"Um, right now, you're the only one who is whining about anything."

She shot Charlie a dirty look. "Didn't you hear me? I said shut up!"

"What's with the hostility?" Trace called. "Amber, we're supposed to *like* Rose now."

"We don't have to like her," Amberly clarified. "We just have to accept her as our teammate. And she's annoying me."

"You could at least try," Kire reminded her. "Liking each other probably helps our chances of being stronger as a team."

Amberly narrowed her eyes at Kire. "That sucks because there's a fat chance of me never liking *you*, either." Then she crossed her arms and continued glowering at him as he looked over his shoulder at her. All Kire did in response was simply shake his head and turn back around. "Yeah, that's what I thought."

"You know what?" Charlie asked as she clutched her Pendantix, feeling her irritation toward Amberly grow. But she didn't want to snap at her. The girl was going through some rough times. It was probably why she was being even more undesirable to be around than usual. "Let's all do what Kire said. Why don't we walk in silence for a bit as we try to think of ways our gifts will help us survive a couple of nights out here in the middle of nowhere."

"Look at you, Rose," Trace said, turning briefly to shoot her a smile. "Taking charge!"

"And what makes you think anyone should listen to you?"

Amberly asked. It was as if Trace being nice to Charlie was only making her angrier.

Keep your cool, Rose. Just let it slide. She probably doesn't mean it.

Right?

"You don't have to," Charlie said to Amberly through her teeth. "It was merely a suggestion."

"I like the idea," Kaos said, earning a growl from Amberly behind him.

But then everyone fell silent, and Charlie hoped it was because they were all thinking about how to use their gifts like they were supposed to be doing. Charlie could do things with plants. She could make them grow and move. And she could sometimes speak to animals and manipulate them into doing things, too. Only, that part of her powers was a little bit more difficult to get the hang of. At least she had an endless amount of plant supply out here to manipulate, and she couldn't see any animals anywhere in sight.

Kire had Halo. Maybe Halo could give Kire advice on how to come up with meal ideas from the limited food items that were around them in this strange wilderness, or on how to start a fire to keep them warm. Already the air outside was starting to get chillier. And it would only get colder the higher up they got. And if Charlie was dry and beginning to feel cold, and Amberly was still damp, she could imagine how the princess was holding up.

Kaos had his crown. If Charlie was being honest with herself, she couldn't even really figure out what it was that Kaos could do with his powers. Read people's minds—and only sometimes? Even if he got control of his powers and could use them during their journey to the castle, how would that help them in the wilderness when there was nothing around them? She wasn't sure. But he made a decent leader, and he was incredibly smart and cunning, so maybe that would at least help them out.

Trace had his flaming sword. If anything, if they couldn't figure out how to start a fire of their own, maybe they could all crowd around his weapon for warmth. And maybe if they needed to kill some of Yash's minions—or wild creatures trying to eat them for dinner—then he had his sword to do that.

And Amberly had her gauntlet. Her kinetic powers. But what would they need her to move in order to help them through the night? Maybe if boulders, smaller rocks, or fallen structures were in their way as they made the hike to the castle, she would be able to clear pathways for them.

And hopefully, as the group walked along, they were thinking up some more creative ideas in their heads as well.

Charlie took a break from thinking about it and found herself looking at Amberly again. Sure, the girl still wasn't being nice to Charlie despite what she knew about her now and despite the fact that Charlie was holding in a secret of hers from the rest of the group and could let it out any time she wanted. But still, Charlie felt bad for her. And she didn't want to tell the others about Amberly's secret. She could tell them when and if she ever became ready.

Charlie wasn't the biggest fan of her own parents, but if one of them was in the hospital because of a sickness, Charlie was pretty certain she would feel a little distracted and irritable being so far away from them, not knowing if things with her sick parents were getting any better or worse. If one thing was clear about Amberly McHenry, it was that she was one strong chick.

44

So, the Quintets continued to walk through the beautiful, smoky nothingness. Eventually, the cornstalks turned into a thick, dense, dark-looking patch of woods.

"Do we really want to go through here?" Charlie asked, feeling hesitant.

Nothing good happened in the woods.

She was used to the White Forest back home, but it was because she had spent her entire life adventuring through it. She didn't know anything about these woods. Especially since they were woods of a different realm. A dangerous, magical one.

"Maybe there's another way around?" Trace asked, looking to his left and right to see.

"Any detours are only going to make it take longer for us to get to that castle," Kaos said matter-of-factly. "And we don't want that, right?"

Charlie swallowed.

"We'll be fine," Trace said. He held his weapon in the air. "I've got my sword."

"You act like you're the only one who has a powerful magical gift," Kaos said.

"I know you guys have gifts, too," he claimed. "Mine is just the best out of all five of them. That's all."

Kaos scoffed, then turned his attention back to the forest. "How bad could it be?" he asked, more to himself than to the other teens. "If Yash's minions could attack out in the open or when we were in the cornstalks and they didn't, then my guess is they're not going to attack us in here either."

"Or they are waiting in the woods because it's a better place to hide until we get into their path," Charlie pointed out.

Then Kire joined in. "Not that I disagree with you at all, Rose, but maybe there won't be any of the aliens in here because they know we'd be most on guard in the woods, expecting them to be here. Does that make sense?"

Charlie shrugged. "Do Yash's minions even know we've entered the Albus Realm?"

Kire smiled. "Touché."

"Okay," Trace said, sounding annoyed. "Enough of the back-and-forth. I'd like to get to that castle as soon as possible, so let's get a move on." He took the first step into the dark trees. Amberly followed snootily, her nose in the air.

"Wait up," Kaos called, racing to be back at the front of the group.

Then behind them all, Charlie and Kire followed in together.

But still, as they began the next phase of their travels, it seemed as if they were entirely alone—a thought that equally relieved and terrified Charlie. What if the reason they were so alone was that Yash's minions had already destroyed everything in the Albus Realm? What if they had already killed every living creature?

Come on, Rose. Don't think like that.

In front of Charlie, standing behind Trace and Kaos—who

were leading the group—Kire opened Halo and began reading something. From what Charlie could see, it seemed as if Halo was writing him something.

"What's happening?" she asked curiously.

"Halo's predicting the future. She said that a short while from now, we're going to come across a moon oxbeast."

Charlie stopped walking. The others did, too.

"A what?" Amberly asked, sounding tense.

"I don't know. That's what she said. A moon oxbeast."

Trace spun about himself in a slow circle, almost as if he was ready for it to pop out right then and there.

"Don't worry, I can defeat it," he told the others.

"What do we do?" Charlie asked.

"Nothing we can do but keep going forward."

"Can't Halo tell us how to defeat it?"

Kire wrote something. They all waited.

"She doesn't know."

"Bull—!" Trace snapped.

Amberly interrupted him by swatting him on the shoulder.

"Trace!" she warned.

They all continued walking, slower this time. Then they heard a rustling noise over to the right. Again, they all froze, bumping into each other as they turned to face what was surely the moon oxbeast coming toward them.

Charlie was terrified. Were they all going to count on her to get into its head and make it leave them alone?

"Everyone be ready," Kaos said.

"I know I am," Trace said, his eyes narrowing as he stared at the rustling bushes that were moving closer toward them.

Then the critter came into view.

And that's all it was. A critter.

The moon oxbeast was about the size of a mouse. But it had four back legs and curved upward, revealing that it also had two short arms. Its tail was merely a nub on its behind, and its soft-looking skin was covered in thick fluffy fur in the shade of dark, rusty orange. It had a narrow nose and short pointy ears. In comparison to its little body, its head was massive, but in a general sense, it was still very small.

When it saw them before it, it gave a strange high-pitched snarl and stretched itself a little bit taller. But it didn't try to attack them. It just stared them down.

"That... *that's* the moon beast?" Trace asked, lowering his sword.

Kire chuckled nervously. "I think so."

Even though it was nothing like Charlie had ever seen before, she found it to be quite cute. Normally, she was terrified of animals, but since she had been beginning to learn how to talk with them, she was curious. So, she took a step forward and focused with her Pendantix to try to communicate with it.

However, at the sudden movement Charlie made, the not-so-terrifying moon oxbeast made the high-pitched snarl again and then dove to its left, trying to get away from the teenagers. But in doing so, it ran straight headfirst into a tree trunk. So hard that it flew onto its back and wiggled there for a moment before it got up, shook its head out, and then dove back into the bushes.

"That's what Halo wanted to warn you about?" Amberly asked. Then she snorted with laughter. Charlie and the others couldn't help it as they joined in on the laughter too.

They kept walking, feeling a little bit more at ease now. Maybe all of the creatures Halo was going to warn Kire about would be like that. Harmless. Friendly. Small.

As they walked, Charlie suddenly found herself next to Kire. She had been so entranced, looking at all of the plant life around her—bushes and trees and flowerbeds that she had never seen before or found in any textbook—that she hadn't noticed him walking in step with her.

"Hey," he said in a quiet voice.

"Hey," Charlie replied in an equally quiet way. As they walked, she did not look at him.

"I, uh—are we still not speaking?" he asked.

"We're speaking right now," Charlie replied, raising an eyebrow.

"That's not what I mean."

"I know."

They were silent for a bit. Then Charlie decided to continue the conversation.

"You broke up with Angela." It wasn't a question. It was simply a statement.

"Yeah," Kire said with a shrug. "I don't know. I don't even know what I was ever doing with her. We didn't even have anything in common."

"It's hard to resist a cheerleader."

"It's not really... that."

"Then what is it?" Charlie looked ahead of her and saw that she and Kire were the furthest back from the group. It didn't seem as if any of the others up ahead could hear any part of their conversation. Charlie was grateful for the bit of privacy.

"Look," Kire told her. "I suppose I just want to come clean to you about it."

Charlie tensed. Was this really happening? Was Kire finally going to tell her the reason that he randomly ditched her for Angela in the first place? She waited patiently for Kire to seem to find the words.

"I just thought... that night, after we defeated Heno—or Andrew—you and Trace... I know it sounds crazy, but you two were all over each other. He wouldn't stop complimenting you, and you kept blushing and smiling at him. Then you sat next to him in the car on the way home. It seemed like... I don't know. Like you were far more interested in him than you ever were in me. And I don't know. I was stupid, and I got jealous. I figured that you didn't actually even like me in the first place. I felt stupid for kissing you. Like you didn't even want it to happen because you had your sights set on Trace from the get-go. I think I just overthought things too much."

"You too?" she asked.

"What do you mean?"

"Amberly was getting jealous of Trace and me, too. Remember in the cave?" She let out a small laugh. An incredulous one. "It is crazy to me because there wasn't, and never will be, anything between Trace and me."

Kire sighed. "I'm a complete idiot. And I totally understand if you hate me."

Charlie didn't want to hate Kire.

Before she could say anything to him, in between the gang ahead of them and Kire and Charlie, who hung back, something flew down from the tall trees above and fluttered between the separated groups, a scowl on their face as they stared at Kire and Charlie directly.

"Uh, guys?" Kire called. The others in front of them stopped and turned around. Amberly cried out in fear. The thing in front of them seemed to echo. It was fluttering in the air still, with great big wings that looked to be made of crystals. Their dark eyes were hidden behind long orange and black striped hair. Still, they were staring at Charlie and Kire intensely. It made Charlie feel unsettled. Strangely warm. Around them, the forest brightened with the creature's glow. Their elongated body hovered with solemn energy and was clad in a hanging, white cloth. They carried a lantern that shined a golden light, and Charlie couldn't stop staring at it.

"What do you want?" the thing asked. It looked angry to see them there. But something about it didn't seem... dangerous.

However, Charlie was just going off a hunch.

"We're here to save you," Trace called from behind it. The creature, which seemed like a fairy if Charlie had ever seen one, turned to him.

"Save us?" she asked skeptically. "We can't be saved. We're all doomed. Where do you come from?"

"We came from another realm," Kire said. "But we have the tools to help. And Albus—one of the Albuses—has been in contact with us. You can trust us."

"What... are you?" Trace asked the thing curiously, scanning the creature up and down.

The fairy squinted at him for a long while before answering. "I am a tiger fairy. You don't have any of me where you are come from?"

"Definitely not," Kaos said. "There's nothing magical at all in our realm except for the gifts we were given."

"I see. I hope what you say about these gifts is true. Because we need all the help we can get. I did come down here to slaughter you all to save my kind and others in our world, but... I'm going to go ahead and trust that what you say is true. You may carry on."

Charlie and Kire exchanged looks.

Slaughter?

While the fairy did look intimidating, it was still somewhat small and didn't look capable of slaughtering five teenagers who held magical gifts. But what did Charlie know?

Wait," Kaos said as the fairy started fluttering back upward. "Are these woods dangerous? Should we be on guard? We know that Yash sent his minions down to destroy your world. Are any of those vile things near here that you know of?"

"You are safe... for now. They tend to be more where civilians are. But you should still always have your guard up. Anyway. I trust that you want to help. But I don't trust you fully enough to answer a bunch of questions. Best of luck." Then the fairy drifted upward and out of sight.

The group continued walking, Charlie wanting to stick closer to the rest of them this time in case they were separated by somebody—or something—again. But that meant that their conversation was a little less private now.

"Um," Charlie started. "You should know, Kire. I don't hate you. Or at least, as of right now, I've chosen not to."

When Kire turned and gave Charlie a huge grin, she was powerless against the butterflies that started swarming around in her stomach. It felt as if those crystallized wings on that tiger fairy were flopping around inside of her, no matter how much she didn't want to feel that way about Kire. The feeling was so strong that it almost made her stop walking.

"Are you okay?" he asked.

The others, having heard Kire, turned and looked over their shoulders at Charlie.

She shook it off.

"Fine," she said to Kire as she eyed the others. "Just fine."

45

The tiger fairy had been right about them not coming across any of Yash's minions while they were in the woods. At least, it had been true so far. But since their encounter a while ago with the first fairy Charlie had ever seen, it had turned to nightfall, and everyone was exhausted—especially Amberly, who hadn't stopped complaining about it for the past hour. She kept saying stuff like, "How much longer are we going to go today?" and, "My feet hurt. These shoes weren't made for walking," and, "What is the percentage of humidity in this place? My clothes are *still* wet!"

Charlie had been trying her hardest to keep her cool with Amberly, but the longer they walked and the more tired and hungry Charlie got, she was finding it increasingly difficult to do.

"I guess we can stay here for the night?" Kire asked everyone as they came upon a clearing in the middle of the woods. "Does this look fine?"

Charlie thought it looked more than fine. The bed of mysterious wildflowers looked like a very comfortable mattress to her aching body. And the clearing was beautiful. Not only because of all the flowers, but because of the way the tall trees had all somehow grown in a way that created almost a perfect circle of wide-open ground. And in the distance, she could hear the sound of running water. A creek.

"You want to stop here? Just out like this... in the open?" Amberly asked. "Where is our protection? Our shelters? A fire?"

Charlie snorted.

"Did you just think we were going to magically come across an unslept-in little cabin in the woods or something?" Kire asked, the annoyance showing in his voice. "One with a fire already somehow magically going in the fireplace?"

"Don't start with me, Kire. I didn't ask you," she said.

"Why do you think Kire suggested we think of ways to use our gifts to help us survive in the wilderness?" Kaos asked.

Charlie held up her hands. "You guys, stop," she demanded. She was sick of hearing them bicker with each other. In fact, she was sick of hearing any of them talk at all. All Charlie wanted was food, water, and sleep. "We can make this work. It's like you said, Kire. We can use our gifts to create a perfect camping spot."

"Go on then," Kaos said, nodding his head at Charlie. "Let's see what you can do now."

Charlie, more than willing to accept the challenge, spun about the space, her index finger to her lips as she thought. Then she clutched her Pendantix and concentrated. With the leaves from the trees and bushes around them, along with long sticks and branches, she conjured up five individual tents formed in a perfect circle around the opening for them all to sleep in. Then she had Amberly move some fallen logs around in another half circle in the middle of the clearing. In front of those would be where they would make a fire pit.

When Trace caught on, he was easily able to make the fire by gathering tinder, twigs, and logs with Amberly and using his fiery sword to spread the flames onto them in a little pit Kire dug.

"I think Halo might be able to help us, too," Kire said, rubbing the dirt off his hands. Then he scribbled something into Halo with his pen. He laid the book open on one of the logs, and Charlie felt a whooshing sensation go through her body. Looking around at the others, it was clear that they felt it, too.

"What was that?" Trace asked.

"He had Halo put up a shield," Charlie deduced.

"She's right," Kire said. "It's around the entire campsite. Just in case anything tries to attack us while we get some sleep."

"You mean no one will be able to see us?" Amberly asked eagerly.

Kire gave her a strange look. "Uh, no... it doesn't work like that. Attackers will still be able to see us. The shield doesn't come with an invisibility charm. It will just make the attackers unable to hurt us."

"Whatever. I don't know how I'm supposed to get any sleep lying on the ground like this," she spat out, peeking inside of her incredibly cool tent that Charlie didn't think she was appreciating nearly as much as she should be.

"Fine," Kire hissed at her. "Don't sleep then. That's your choice."

Amberly rolled her eyes and crossed her arms while Charlie and the others tried not to laugh at Kire's comment.

CHARLIE HAD BEEN RIGHT. With Halo's help, the gang was able to collect some non-poisonous berries in the woods for them to snack on. They didn't look like any berries Charlie had ever seen, however. Some of them were square-shaped. And some were more trapezoid shaped. But they were all full of delectable tasting nectars that Charlie could hardly get enough of.

The five of them sat around the fire, ate their food, sipped water from the creek nearby, and fell into an easy silence. When Charlie looked at Kaos from across the flames, she felt sad. Kaos wasn't looking at anybody. He was sitting on a log with his elbows on his knees, holding the crown in his hands and staring at it intently. He had been trying all night to wear the crown and figure out if he could sense any minions nearby so that he could read into their minds. He even tried to sense other Albuses, or any civilians, too. But he wasn't getting anything. And it was infuriating to him. As far as Charlie could tell, Kaos thought his powers were pointless. And it seemed like some others in the group thought so as well.

Eventually, Kire decided he wanted to make small talk with everyone. But what he decided to say was somewhat out of the blue. "Halo's predictions aren't totally reliable," he quipped out of nowhere, interrupting their long-lasting silence.

Trace snapped his head up and looked at Kire. His arms were around Amberly, rubbing her shoulders to warm her up. Amberly put her head on Trace's shoulder. "What?" he asked, looking slightly alarmed by Kire's random news.

"I don't know. She has predictions. Like you've heard. And they've all been right for the most part, but they seem to change a lot, and I'm not really sure why."

Charlie could gauge the look on Kire's face. He seemed worried about it. And if Kire was worried about it, then Charlie was, too. But no one needed to know that she was. She could be different from what Amberly was always calling her. She wasn't a scaredy-cat. Besides, would a scaredy-cat have gone into the cave in the White Forest to try and find the portal all by herself? Sure, it had been stupid. But Charlie thought it had been pretty brave as well.

"I'm sure it's fine, Kire," Charlie tried. For some reason, she felt a need to reassure him. She didn't like one of the leaders of the group being worried. It would make everybody else worry, too.

"Great," Amberly said, lifting her head from Trace's shoulder. "So, your book is unreliable? How is that useful to us? How are we supposed to trust anything it says?"

"I was just letting you guys know," Kire said, not even bothering to look at Amberly.

"Well, now I am more terrified than I was when I first agreed to come here," Amberly continued.

"Babe," Trace tried. "I'm sure it's not a big deal. Things change all the time. And if Halo's predictions do change, she'll let us know. Then we will regroup, change the plan, and carry on. No biggie."

"I don't even know why I came." Amberly got to her feet, ignoring her boyfriend.

"I wasn't looking to start another fight with you, Amberly." Kire glared at her from over on his spot on the logs next to Charlie. Charlie had sat there first; it was Kire who had decided to sit next to her. Something that she made a mental note of as soon as it happened.

"We have no idea what we're doing," Amberly said. Charlie was not ready for her to have another one of the whiny rants. It was too late in the night to hear one of those. Why couldn't they all just sit there in peace? "We have no idea how to defeat these things once we come across them. We have no idea where to even find a spell to close off the portal to *just* the bad guys. I know you want to save Albus, Kire, but I'm having second thoughts. I feel like maybe there's a reason we should've just listened to Halo and activated closing off the portal from the other side and let that be that."

"How can you say that?" Kire asked, getting defensive. "Albus has done so much for us. Why don't you care about somebody besides yourself for a change?"

She stepped closer to him, her eyes on fire. "Excuse me?"

"Guys, knock it off," Kaos snapped. Apparently, he was sick of them bickering, too.

Amberly tossed her blonde hair behind her shoulder. "Whatevs. This is stupid. I'm going to bed." She shot everybody one last glare, her eyes lingering on Trace as if she was hoping for him to tell her not to go, and when he didn't, she got even angrier-looking and dashed into one of the tents.

"About dang time," Kaos said quietly. Charlie and Kire snickered in agreement. Trace, on the other hand, shook his head and poked the fire with a long stick.

46

———————

I t was awkwardly silent for a moment after Amberly retreated into her tent. But then, on the log next to them, Trace dropped the long stick he was holding and let out a frustrated sigh.

"What?" Kire snapped a little bit louder than he needed to. It was as if he could tell the sigh had been directed at him, and he was ready to get on the defensive.

"Why do you always have to get into it with her, man?" Trace asked Kire. He looked tired, like he didn't want to be having this conversation but needed to have this conversation — for his girlfriend's sake.

"Are you kidding me?" Kire snapped at him. "Do you not hear yourself? Do you not see the way she talks to me for no reason at all? I'm trying to help you guys. I want to save Albus just like you guys do. *She's* the one that's not with us. Ever. She always has some argument to make about every little thing. And she complains nonstop. I don't even know how you can stand being her boyfriend. I would hurl myself off a cliff."

"Are you kidding me?" Trace asked. He looked less tired now and angrier. Macho. Like the man in charge of St. Bernard

High. "I know we're on the same team now and all, but did you forget who you're talking to you, Kire Hunter? I can end you in a second. So you watch your mouth. Especially when it comes to Amberly."

Charlie looked over at Kaos to see if he was going to interrupt them at all to get their bickering to stop. He sat there silently, still not looking at anybody. Apparently, Kaos was in a mood of his own.

Charlie decided she didn't want to get into the middle of it, either. She didn't want to give anybody a reason to think that she or Trace had feelings for each other. It was already embarrassing enough that both Kire and Amberly had gotten jealous for no reason at all.

"Look, I'm sorry," Kire said a couple of breaths later, seeming as if he was cooling down. As if he suddenly remembered that Trace was stronger and scarier than him and that he needed to be more careful about how he acted around him.

"No," Trace spat. "I'm sick of it. Tell your dang father about Amberly."

"No," Kire said simply. Charlie internally cringed. This was only going to lead to more arguing—she could just feel it.

"Dude, if you don't do it soon, I will seriously ruin your day. Multiple of them, actually. I might feed you to one of Yash's minions myself. "

"You just don't freaking understand it!" Kire bellowed, getting to his feet. "If I do tell my dad, that will 'ruin' not only *my* day, but Amberly's day too! Everyone's day! So just back off about it, okay?!"

So much for Kire being careful about how he acted around Trace. As Charlie sat there on that log, she almost wanted to cover her eyes.

Trace got to his feet, too. It somewhat seemed as if the two of them were going to get into a more physical confrontation. It made Charlie grow tense. But instead of Kire taking a step toward Trace, who seemed like he was at the ready, Kire turned sharply on his heel, digging it into the dirt on the ground, and then he, too, stormed off into one of the tents.

"Man! I just don't get that kid," Trace seethed, sitting back down on the log next to Charlie's. No one said anything. They were silent for a few beats, then on the other side of Trace's log, Kaos suddenly flung his crown to the ground and stood up.

"Kaos, what's going on?" Trace asked. "What's up with you?"

"Yeah, you've been really quiet all night," Charlie added. She didn't necessarily care much for Kaos, but she found that she was slightly worried about him regardless.

"This thing," he said, motioning to his crown exasperatedly. He shook his head and balled his fists. "It's useless. Completely useless."

Then he, too, turned and entered a third tent.

It left just Trace and Charlie out on the logs in front of the slowly dying fire.

Charlie didn't know what to do or say. She felt awkward and shy, especially after hearing about Amberly being jealous of Trace's interactions with her, and Kire being jealous about the two of them as well. She wondered if Kire or Amberly were still awake in their tents, and if they knew it was just the two of them out here together like this. A log in the middle of the woods with a roaring fire and a small pile of leftover berries in front of them? It seemed a bit like the romantic sort of set-up when only two people were present.

"It's... kind of strange here, huh?" Trace asked randomly, probably in an effort to make small talk, which Charlie appreciated. She wasn't good with small talk. Heck, she was hardly good with any sort of talk. She only liked talking to plants. The thought of it made her miss Ramoni. It also made her wonder if he was worried about her.

"Yeah," Charlie replied in a soft voice. She didn't look at Trace. She didn't want to seem interested. The last thing she needed was for Trace to go to Amberly in the morning and say something like, "Rose wouldn't stop staring at me last night. I think she might be into me."

Amberly would for sure kill her if that happened.

Realizing that Charlie wasn't going to add any other words onto her *yeah*, Trace continued. "I mean... it's a lot like Earth with the green and the forests and fields and stuff, but there are so many little things about it that are different. Like the berries and the colorful corn and the random creatures we ran into."

Charlie felt differently, and she wasn't afraid to voice it. "In a way, it's kind of exactly like what I pictured," she told Kire, looking up at the sky. She still couldn't see it behind the layer of smoke that seemed as if it was never going to go away.

"I have no idea *what* I even pictured," Trace said. "Maybe something fantastical. Like floating islands surrounded by lava or something. I don't know. Who would have even thought other realms existed, ya know? It's crazy to think we might be the only humans on Earth that know they do."

Charlie chuckled. Then she realized just how *alone* she and Trace were. And how she had once, recently, witnessed Trace doing something that made her curious. Suspicious of him. She wanted to think that underneath all of the bullying and trying to stay on top of the school, Trace had some goodness in him. That he knew right from wrong.

Which is why she decided she wanted to confront him. Right here and right now.

"Hey, Trace?" she started, trying to sound casual yet brave.

He nodded his head at her as his response.

"So... the other day, when we all came to the soccer game after it ended, I saw you leave the crowd. And... on a whim, I decided to sort of... follow you."

"Uh, okay..."

Charlie sucked in a breath and continued. "I watched you dive under the bleachers, and when I spied on you there, I saw you meeting up with Billy Michaelson, that scumbag. And he was giving you money. And I guess I just wanted to make sure that it wasn't anything... sketchy."

Trace eyed her carefully before he spoke. "And what if it was?"

"What?"

"What if it was something sketchy?"

"I..." Charlie's heart sank. Of course, Trace Henderson would be up to no good. She should have known better than to think he was capable of being a decent human being.

Trace continued before she could say anything else. "Here's the thing, Charlie Rose. There's a lot you don't know about me still. But I have to do some things that I don't always like doing for my family. My mom, mainly."

It was news to Charlie. Trace had issues involving his mother like Amberly did? Charlie wondered if Amberly knew that. That if maybe the couple would just communicate with each other, they would find an incredible support system between themselves.

"So... what was the money for? What did you have to do to get it?" Charlie asked. "And why?"

"I don't usually talk about it."

"Okay..." Charlie trailed off. "But it would make me feel a lot better if you would just explain yourself so that I don't have all of these secret hidden judgments that I'm making about you in my head. These... assumptions that you *are* the bad guy everyone makes you out to be."

Trace nodded his head slowly, taking in what Charlie had just told him. Then he cleared his throat. "My mom... she had an alcohol problem. For a really long time. And because of it, she ended up developing liver disease. And we don't have health insurance because her job doesn't offer it, and she says we don't make enough to afford it. So she needs medicine. And we don't have the money to buy it. So I do what I have to do to get it."

Charlie's heart ached for Trace. She had no idea about any of it. I made her wonder. What lengths would *she* go for *her* family? Sure, she didn't even like them, but they were her *family*. And aren't you supposed to do anything for your family?

"So, the game..."

"... was thrown on purpose. I lost on purpose." He hung his head. Charlie was so shocked she nearly gasped out loud. "I know, I know," Trace continued. "Like I said. I do some crappy things in order to get the money to help my mom. She is... she's all I have, you know?"

Charlie took a second before answering. "Well, that really does help me see you in a better light," she said. The two chuckled together.

"Well, good," he told her. "But hey, I don't want this to be a reoccurring conversation. I don't want you checking up on me and stuff. I don't need it. I told you why I do what I do, and that's enough, right?"

She put her hands up in the air in surrender. In a lot of ways, Trace and Amberly were so alike. "You won't hear me say anything about it again."

And just like that, Charlie was now seeing a third member of the Unlikely Defenders in a different light. One that made her appreciate Trace just a little bit more.

47

The next day, the Unlikely Defenders freshened up at the creek by their campsite, plucked more berries to eat for breakfast, and then decided to carry on with their journey toward the castle on the mountain. Charlie could tell that everyone felt uneasy about not only the fact that they were getting closer to civilization—or where civilization *should* be, anyway—but also because they had stayed somewhere overnight without notifying anybody back in their realm about the fact that they wouldn't be returning home last night. Their parents were probably worried sick by now. No doubt the police had been notified as well. Charlie wondered about her parents. She knew the others would be worried about their kids, but would hers really be? Or would they be relieved? Charlie had this sickening, bad feeling all these years that her parents secretly talked to each other in the confinement of their bedroom when they were alone about how they wished they never had Charlie and how she had been their greatest mistake. Would they even go to the police at all? Would they join the search parties? Would they cry to the media and make an announcement about how all that mattered was getting their precious baby home safely?

Charlie highly doubted it. And she tried to tell herself that it didn't matter. That she didn't care.

But it did matter.

And she did care.

Everyone seemed tired and groggy at first as they walked slouchily through the forest. Nobody was in the mood to talk to each other. Charlie figured they were all still grumpy from their conversations last night. Either that, or no one simply had anything to say.

Charlie, however? She felt good about the last conversation she had had last night. The one with Trace. And she was walking in a comfortable silence next to Kire, and it made her think about how he also felt good about the last conversation *they* had had. She hated him a lot less now. In fact, she sort of wished he would strike up a conversation with her again so that they could keep talking to each other. She just couldn't help herself. She liked talking with him. No matter how much of a smart-aleck he could be.

Finally, maybe after an hour of walking or so, the gang followed a dirt path that led them into their first village. The sights around Charlie had her mystified. It looked like something straight out of a medieval movie or TV show. Tudor-styled buildings lined dirt and cobblestone streets. There were wishing wells randomly scattered about every so often. Some structures were half in rubble, some just looked old, and some were in pristine condition, looking as if they had just been constructed yesterday. The ones that had been completely destroyed or half destroyed, however, gave insight as to the reason why there didn't seem to be any living beings around. This village had been attacked. And the attacker was more than likely one of Yash's minions, sent here to clear the path so that he didn't have anything in his way when he came to this realm, found the portal, and got to Earth.

"This is so... horrible," Charlie muttered as they slowly and cautiously walked through the main road of the village. There was destruction everywhere. In fact, some small fires still lingered. The attack here must have been recent.

"It really is," Kire agreed. Charlie watched him swallow and look away from what looked to be a destroyed family home. There was a stroller on its side in front of it.

"Where do you think everybody went?" Trace asked, his hand on the handle of his sword that was currently in its scabbard.

"If there's even anybody left alive," Kaos added morbidly.

"You think..." Amberly trailed off and stopped walking. Kaos turned her. Her next word, she squeaked out. "You think Yash's minions killed all of them?"

Kaos simply shrugged. As if it was what it was. "I highly doubt anyone who lived here saw the attack coming. If they hadn't had a warning like Albus had, anyway. I don't know what it is, but something about this village seems a little... lower class. Like peasants lived here. Like nobody with magic abilities lived here like the Albuses have. Maybe they didn't have the luxury of being warned about an oncoming attack."

"That's all just hearsay, though," Charlie felt the need to reassure. "We don't know anything for certain."

Kaos saw the look on Amberly's face and nodded. "Right. That's all it was. A simple guess. What do I know? It's not like I've ever been here before or like I know anything about this place."

Charlie had to admit—she was surprised to see that Amberly seemed bothered by what Kaos was saying. Scared, even. Could it be possible that her high school queen bee had a heart after all?

"Let's try not to think too much about it," Kire said as he stood next to Charlie, then forced them to continue walking. "We can't change the past. Our gifts haven't given us that ability. We just need to keep going and find Albus."

The group nodded in agreement and continued on their way. Charlie couldn't get out of this abandoned, ruined village fast enough. She probably would have loved it if it hadn't been attacked. Everything about it now just gave her the heebie-jeebies.

Eventually, they left the village and were in the wilderness again, but it wasn't long before they entered another very similar town with a very similar, horrible situation. They urged each other to keep going, and they walked through village after village, finding them all deserted and a lot of them mostly destroyed. With each one they entered, Charlie's heart broke a little more. All of this chaos that Yash had caused... it was unimaginable. Unthinkable. Too horrifying for words, even.

How many had died so far? How many were dying right at that moment? How many more were going to die before the five of them were able to do something about it?

Eventually, Kaos, who was leading the group with the crown on his head, spoke. By this time, it was a bit into the afternoon, and the sun was beating down harshly on all of them. "We need to talk about strategizing," he announced.

"I agree," Kire said, seeming happy to have something to talk about that would distract him from all the horror around them.

"Of course, you agree," Kaos said. "Yash's minions could pop out at any point. And we need to be ready when they do."

"What are you suggesting then, leader?" Amberly asked. It seemed enough as if she meant the words, but there was also something about her tone that made her sound the slightest bit sarcastic.

"Whatever you want, I am your guy." Trace said happily. Now, his words were genuine. He was loyal to Kaos through and through.

Charlie snuck a peek at Kire. Even though Kaos led their high school with Trace, and even though he had a crown on his head and was walking ahead of the group, Charlie still had the feeling that Kire was more of a leader in this group than Kaos was. At least *he* had a gift that gave him actual powers. And Kire always seemed to have the best ideas, and he had the most knowledge, too.

Kaos brushed some stray dirt off his all-black ensemble. "Well... I am open to your suggestions," he said to everyone.

This is exactly what Charlie meant—Kaos didn't have a clue about how they should prepare for battle.

Kire snorted.

Charlie had a feeling that Kire knew exactly what they should do. Like a true leader would.

Amberly harshly turned to look over her shoulder at Kire. "Got something to say?" she asked.

"I just think it's funny that Kaos is our quote-unquote *leader*, and yet he has no idea how to 'lead' us."

"And you do?" she asked, challenging him with a sneer. Charlie didn't get how anyone who didn't have to be could stand being around Amberly. She was so mean and negative one-hundred percent of the day.

The gang was in the middle of nowhere again. There was nothing but rolling hills on either side of them as they walked along a dirt-paved path. One that appeared to be leading them the entire rest of the way to the castle.

"Of course I do," Kire snapped to Amberly. He puffed his chest out and held his head high.

"We all need to be getting along, remember?" Charlie asked, acting again as the mediator between the two of them.

She thought vaguely of the ominous warning Albus had given her when he last talked to all of them. The stuff he had said about the consequences of her not letting the others in.

"Sorry," Kire said quickly, nodding his head in agreement with Charlie. "Rose is right. Kaos, if you know what you're doing, then let's hear what it is you think we should do."

"Kaos is a better leader than you could ever dream of being," Amberly continued, clearly not done arguing with Kire. She never listened to anyone. It made Charlie roll her eyes. "I'm embarrassed for you that you think you could *ever* be in charge of us."

"Amberly, you really need to stop being so nasty to Kire," Charlie interjected. She was sick of her snapping at him. She couldn't take it anymore and had to say something. The way she treated Kire all day long just wasn't right.

"I'll do what I want," Amberly hissed venomously at Charlie. "He's my brother, after all."

"Can't you just drop it about that?" Kire asked her, groaning loudly and looking up at the still-smoky sky.

"Not until you tell *our* father the truth about me!"

"Ugh, you're relentless, do you know that?!" Kire asked in an exasperated tone. "How many times do I have to tell you?"

"Just give me one good reason why, Kire Hunter!" Suddenly, Amberly was acting a lot different. She was yelling differently than she normally did. She seemed truly... upset. Almost like she was on the verge of a mental breakdown. And Charlie could guess why. She was already worried about her mother. And probably worried about the fact that she was away from her right now dealing with this. And on top of it, she probably was thinking about how horrible it would be if something happened to her mother and she had no father to fall back on. If Amberly's mother died, she would truly be all alone in the world. How terrifying was that?

"Fine!" Kire suddenly bellowed. Apparently, he was sick of this, too. "All *our* father really is, is a sack of garbage! You just don't get it. The reason I haven't told him about you and the fact that I know is that I'm protecting you! You don't have any idea what he'll do or how he'll act when I tell him! But *I* do! I'm the one who's had to live with him my entire life. You should consider yourself lucky that you never had to! He's a horrible, horrible man, Amberly! He doesn't even love *me*. So he could never love you! And I just don't want him hurting anybody else, okay?"

The group was totally silent. Kire's words seemed to echo through the air, getting carried away in the wind. Charlie stared at Kire, astonished at his outburst and admission. When she glanced at the others, she saw that nobody else was making eye contact with him, including Amberly. Kire stood there, his fists clenched tight, and his jaw hardened. His chest was rising and falling rapidly with how angry he had become talking about his father.

Amberly fiddled with her fingers while she looked down at them. Charlie watched her swallow a few times, looking conflicted as if she was having some mental battle with herself inside her head. Then when she spoke again, her tone was a lot quieter. "Kire... I don't care how he reacts, okay?"

"Well, you should," Kire insisted. "You're only going to experience disappointment."

She nodded and cleared her throat. "I don't know if you know this or not, but I'm a lot stronger than I look. I assure you, I can handle it."

Kire didn't seem sure at all. But Charlie figured he was right. Kire was the only one who truly knew what his dad was like. He would know if it was best for his father to know that he knew about Amberly or not. "Amberly..." he trailed off.

Amberly stood a little taller. "No. I'm serious. I can. I still want him to know. Can't you please just do it? It's all I want. It's all it will take to get me to stop hating you. That's it. Just tell him."

Kire let out a long, slow breath. His shoulders appeared to be relaxing. He licked his lips before responding. "If that's really what you want, Amberly. But if I do... don't say I didn't warn you."

"I won't."

"Great!" Kaos interrupted. "Now that we've gotten that strangely resolved argument over with, can we resume our journey? We can't keep making stops all day. We'll never make it to the castle."

Charlie watched Kire and Amberly exchange stares for a while. Then Amberly nodded first, so Kire followed suit.

"Excellent," Kaos said, clapping his hands together. "Onward we go."

They only walked for about maybe fifteen more minutes when Kaos stopped walking so abruptly that the other four all bumped into the backs of each other. Kaos outstretched his hands to prevent anyone from going any further. It was strange because the next village wasn't for a while away, and they could see that nothing was around them, so Charlie had no idea what had Kaos suddenly so spooked.

"I... I don't believe it," Kaos muttered, staring at seemingly nothing.

"Kaos, dude, what's going on?" Trace asked, looking uneasy.

"I am... I'm hearing the inside of somebody's mind. I think it's... it's one of Yash's minions."

"No way!" Trace called happily, glad his buddy's powers were finally working for him.

"What is he saying?" Kire asked quickly.

"What does it mean if you can hear him?" Charlie added. "Does that mean that he's close?"

Kaos stayed silent for a moment. Charlie figured it was

because he was still listening to whatever the beast was thinking.

"He's with others. They're in a group."

"Great," Kire said bitterly.

Kaos continues. "And... they're in the next village."

48

As the five teenagers moved now, they moved with great caution. Charlie's hand refused to leave her Pendantix. Trace held his sword out high. Amberly was flexing her fingers inside of her gauntlet. Kire held Halo in his arms as he walked instead of keeping it in his backpack like he normally did.

All of them were deadly silent. Not only did they not want to be heard by any of Yash's minions, but they also wanted to be able to hear everything going on around them. They were approaching the next village, which also appeared as if it had mostly been destroyed. And as they walked on toward it, the sun above them was slowly beginning to lower in the sky.

Charlie could barely even so much as cough without the others turning to give her a dirty look. But it wasn't fair. It was still so smoky here in this world that it was impossible not to. Charlie wasn't the most in shape and didn't have the healthiest lungs. She wasn't a very active girl.

Finally, feeling terrified of what was possibly to come, the Quintets entered the village. So far, from where they walked, they couldn't hear anything. Anything except for the crumbling noises of buildings still slowly decomposing from fires and blasts. And the noises of strange birds cawing in the sky as they passed overhead. Charlie couldn't get a good look at them when they were so high up, but they were a majestic purple color, unlike any bird she had ever seen back on Earth.

If only I could stay here, lay down on the ground somewhere, and bird watch instead of fighting a bunch of terrifying creatures.

The group crept along. Any time they came across an intersection, Kaos stopped everyone, then he peeked around both corners to make sure the coast was clear before motioning to the group so that they could continue. And it was the same when they approached alleyways, too. At one in particular, he stopped everyone from moving, shushed them, and made them hide against the wall before the alley's entrance. Charlie could faintly make out a fire's glow reflecting on one of the walls in the alley as she waited for Kaos to give them their next move. But he seemed to be concentrating intently, both of his hands gripping his crown. Charlie figured he was listening in to what the beast was thinking now. It took him a few moments before he finally turned to the rest of them.

"They're down this alley," he said quietly to everyone. "It leads to some sort of square where they all seem to be hiding out together."

"What do we do?" Amberly asked. She looked scared. They all did. It was one thing fighting one of Yash's minions. But multiple of them at the same time?

"I say we go see what they look like. And how many of them there are," Kire said. "We need to know what we're up against."

It sounded terrifying, but Charlie knew Kire had the right idea. Kaos did, too. He nodded, and the five carefully turned around the corner and entered the alley. As they walked down it, they could hear voices growing louder. Some were snakelike. Some more baritone. And some were soft but menacing.

They all lined up against another wall and huddled over

each other so that they could peer around the corner at the same time to see what was in the town square. Against the wall they were leaned on, they were safe from view, tucked away in the shadows.

Charlie tried not to gasp out loud at what she saw around the corner. She had expected to see more alien-like creatures. Yes, they would have seemed out of place in this realm, but it was what made sense to Charlie. It was what she had seen with Jago, Heno, and Rezin. But these things—and there were five of them—they were different from aliens. *Vastly* different. Each one of them was different from the other, too. These beasts were not aliens at all, but instead more like... mythical creatures. They fit perfectly in a little fantasy medieval village such as the one they were currently in. It was as if they were made to be in this world.

But it didn't make them any less terrifying.

Charlie looked them over as they huddled together around a fire made of wood pulled from the destroyed houses around them. She wanted to try and figure out what each one of them was. Knowing this would better prepare her for when she was trying to figure out how to defeat them.

One of the creatures was a tall, one-eyed monster. If it was supposed to resemble a cyclops, it looked nothing like any cyclops Charlie had ever seen in any book, TV show, or website image. Usually, those cyclops, while they looked massive, they also tended to look a bit... stupid.

But not this one.

This one had gray skin. It also had rippling muscles. It stood at about seven feet tall at *least*. But the strange thing about it was that his one eye, right in the center of his face underneath his forehead, was practically minuscule and not like the huge bulging eye she would have expected. However, his eye was such a shocking shade of blue that it wasn't easy to miss, despite its small size. The thing that overtook the rest of its face was its mouth, with huge, sharp teeth that stuck out in every which direction no matter how he opened or closed it. He also had no nose, large pointy ears, and a shiny bald head. Charlie did *not* want to take him on.

The next creature was what looked like a bull. One that could stand on two feet. Charlie had learned about these things in school. A minotaur. It was crazy to her that while she had been learning about them, it never occurred to her that she'd ever see one in person—they were called *mythical* for a reason!

The minotaur had gray-brown fur coating its entire body, but Charlie could still tell that the thing was well endowed with its muscles. It had large pointy hooves for feet, and his massive hands were curled into fists with sharp fingernails. Its horns curved out of the top of its head and were wider in circumference compared to any other bull Charlie had seen back on Earth. And in certain spots on its chest, back, and arms, its hair was coarser, almost like hay protruding out of the otherwise soft-looking fur that coated the rest of him. He had green eyes with no pupils and wore a shield covering one of his forearms and a draped cloth on his waist to conceal himself. Looking at him made Charlie feel woozy and helpless. He looked much too strong for her to take on, too! How on Earth were they supposed to defeat these things and save this realm from Yash's arrival?

The next monster was the first female version of any of Yash's minions that Charlie had encountered. This woman was thickly built with massive curves and a huge chest. She wore a red and gold laced bustier that had gold chains dripping from it down her exposed belly. She had large gold cuffs with blue diamonds on each wrist. Her long black hair fell in curls around her shoulders, and she wore a crown on her head. She was quite beautiful. The frightening thing about her was that her torso turned into what appeared to be the bottom half of a snake. This creature was half-woman, half-serpent. Charlie had no idea what she was called. But she wondered if the fact that this creature was female made her any less strong than the other things around the fire. And maybe since she was half-animal, Charlie would be able to manipulate her? Would she be the one Charlie took on?

The fourth one was as close to an alien as any of them got. And it was female as well. Her skin was ghostly white. Her white, waist-length hair floated behind her even though there was no wind blowing. Her face was purely terrifying. The stuff of nightmares. Her mouth was a gaping hole, and her eyes were black with dark veins protruding from the sockets. She floated instead of stood, and her feet were not visible underneath her long Victorian-looking gown. She seemed otherwise human, except for the fact that her body was all skin and bones and her fingers were the length of rulers with sharp white nails at the ends of them. Based on the gaping mouth, Charlie had an idea of what it was.

A banshee. A shudder rippled through her as she forced herself to look away from it and on to the next... *thing*.

The last one, Charlie knew what it was straight away.

A werewolf.

And it looked like the ones she had seen in every horror movie. It was a massive beast, able to stand on its hind legs. It had a long, furry tail. Its ears were pointy. It had a terrifying bite. Its gaze was piercing. Long talon-like nails were at the ends of its feet and hands. It was the simplest creature there out of the other five, but the sight of it still sent a ripple of terror through Charlie's body. These creatures were terrifying. Each and every one of them.

This is what they were up against? Five huge, horrifying mythical creatures who looked like they could tear the Quintets from limb to limb in a single second?

Charlie wasn't so sure this was a good idea anymore. All she wanted to do was go back home, curl up under her comforters, and talk to Ramoni. Maybe even her parents.

Charlie suddenly felt a hand tugging at her shirt, and when she hid back around the corner, she saw that the others had started walking away. She had been the only one who had stayed, surveying the horror before her around the corner in the courtyard.

"Let's go," Kire whispered to her, having been the one who was tugging on her. His face was a ghostly pale color, almost as white as the banshee.

"W-what are those things?" Charlie whispered. "How are we supposed to go against them?" She felt hopeless as they made their way out of the alley and followed Kaos.

"Where are we going?" Charlie asked, even though it seemed as if nobody wanted to answer any of her questions. What had they been thinking, coming here and hunting those things down? It didn't matter that they had special gifts. They had to be out of their minds to be doing this. Legitimately insane.

They hurried down the street, then Kaos turned sharply, retreating into a two-story building that was mostly still standing. It was one of the only buildings they had seen in this village like it. And there didn't appear to be anybody inside of it.

"So those are what Yash's minions are like in this realm?" Trace asked the others as they watched to see what it was Kaos wanted them to do next.

Charlie wasn't having any of it. "But they didn't look—"

"Yeah, they didn't look anything like the ones back on Earth," Amberly finished for her.

"I think I might have a possible explanation for that," Kire said, talking a little bit louder now that they were far away from that square containing the beasts. Kaos motioned for all of them to go upstairs, and so they followed him upward. They came upon an empty loft that served as somebody's bedroom. Amberly and Charlie collapsed back into the bed, exhausted from their fright. Trace looked too antsy to move. Kaos sat on the ground, leaning up against a rotting wood wall.

"Go on then," Kaos said to Kire, wanting him to continue with his explanation. He looked deeply unsettled about what they had just seen, just like the rest of them looked. Charlie couldn't see anything else but those beasts whenever she closed her eyes, even to just blink.

Kire nodded. "If you think about it, back on Earth, I don't think people typically fear running into mythological creatures as much as they fear running into aliens. There's more of a following of humans thinking aliens exist over those things. So Yash has his minions take the forms of alien-like beasts there. But here, in this fantasy world where there's magic, the civilians probably fear *those* types of creatures the most. And it makes sense for them to exist here. It's like we walked onto the set of a movie."

"So then all of Yash's minions can shapeshift and be whatever they want to be at any given time?" Amberly asked as she bit down on a fingernail.

"It's just my theory," Kire replied.

Charlie glanced outside, to where she could see that the sun was setting further. It would be dark soon. She didn't want it to get dark. Just like bad things happened in the woods, bad things also happened in the nighttime.

"I say we rest up here for a bit," Kaos said. "Work out our strategies and figure out how we're gonna go about attacking them. Because we *have* to attack. We can't let them keep doing this."

"A-are we sure this is what we want to do?" Charlie squeaked.

"We have to," Kire said.

"I agree," Trace said.

"Yeah, whatever," Amberly said. Charlie was too scared to reply.

So Kaos continued with his idea. "Then, when it's fully dark out and we have a game plan, we're going to retreat into their courtyard and defeat them all."

Charlie and the others rested up, but to Charlie, her rest was barely a ten-minute nap. It was nearly impossible for her to sleep. Not when she had this impending battle coming up. When she would have to be using her powers to defeat not just one of Yash's minions, but *multiple* of them. Multiple terrifying-looking creatures. And sure, there were five of Yash's minions and five of them, which meant it was equal; each one of them could just take on one. But it didn't make it any less scary. When they fought the other minions, it seemed like all five members were needed just to defeat it. And now they were going to take on five at once?

When Charlie finally gave up on trying to get some rest and decided to get back to her feet inside the slightly deteriorating two-story building they were in, she looked outside and noticed that the sun was getting lower in the sky.

She figured it was best she got started with her training.

She was up longer than the others, getting a head start at using her Pendantix to play with some weeds growing through the cracks in the ground. She manipulated them with rather simple ease, making them turn into tough restraints and swinging vines and whip-like weapons that she could use on her attackers. But how could she take it further? Could she manipulate small weeds to grow into giant tree trunks that entrapped the bad guys in it, maybe?

Could she force large, great big trees to topple on top of them? Would there be any creatures around while they were fighting that she was going to be able to manipulate to join in the attack as well? She rather hoped so, because she knew her team needed all the help they could get.

The sun was starting to set by the time the rest of the Unlikely Defenders woke up from their rest. Charlie had taken a break from her training and had gathered some food from the village that she scrounged around for. She currently had a fire going in a little metal portable stove-looking thing she found downstairs, and she was cooking some strange-looking vegetable she had never seen before on top of it.

"That actually smells really good," Kaos said, rubbing his tired eyes and stepping toward the food.

"Thanks, Rose," Kire said as he plopped down in front of it.

Amberly didn't seem to care for the food. Instead, she walked over to the window. "How much time do you think we have? The sun is starting to set now."

"It's not going to take too long for us to brush up on our training." Trace joined her at the window and wrapped his arm around her in a comforting side-hug. But Amberly pulled away from him.

"I don't even know how you guys can think about food right now," she said with an eye roll as she retreated to the other side of the building and started using her gauntlet to move things around. Items as large as cots she could move with what seemed like ease. It made Charlie jealous. Whenever she manipulated things that were large, it took a toll on her. But maybe since they were all finally fighting as a team again, she wouldn't feel so weak.

Charlie and the others ate quickly while Amberly focused on her training instead of joining them. Then they all got up and started practicing on their ends as well. Kire was scribbling in Halo, probably getting as much information as he could on the beasts and the best way to go about defeating them. Kaos was focusing severely with the crown on his head, but what it was he was doing, Charlie wasn't quite sure. Trace found some coal to draw some outlines of figures on the rotting wooden walls, and then he drew targets on them and used those targets for practice with his sword.

Now that she wasn't worried about waking the others, Charlie made her vines bigger. They went from weeds to flowers to bushes to trees. Trees sprouted through the house and made everybody look at her with wary eyes, as if they were worried the tree roots growing through the ground were going to make the place collapse on them. But Charlie felt like she had a hold on what she was doing.

Their training went on for a while. Everyone seemed focused on their own powers until Amberly let out a ferocious growl, and suddenly, there was a large thud heard over on the other side of the building.

When Charlie looked up, she saw that Amberly had fallen to her knees, her blonde hair falling in front of her face, which was all red and splotchy.

"Amberly!" Trace cried out, quickly running over to her. Everybody else went over and joined.

"Are you okay?" Charlie asked, full of worry for her as Trace helped her get to her feet.

Amberly brushed herself off and shrugged out of Trace's grasp. "I'm not okay!" she suddenly shouted. "I'm miserable! You guys have *no* idea what I'm going through!"

"What do you mean?" Trace asked.

"Is this about our father?" Kire added.

"It's more than that!" she hissed, shooting Kire a look. "It's everything! My entire life is falling apart, and I'm not even on Earth to deal with it!"

"Babe, what's going on?" Trace asked, stepping toward her again. But she simply backed away from him again.

"You guys don't understand."

"Understand what?" Kaos asked. "You can talk to us, you know. We are a team."

Amberly sniffled. "I lost my job."

"Oh... I'm sorry, Amber," Trace said, looking like it wasn't that big of a deal and that there wasn't much reason to be upset about it.

Amberly rolled her eyes, which were still watery. "It's a *big* deal, actually," she said. "Because I helped pay for a lot of the bills around my house. My mom can't work. She's too sick to work. She's too sick to do *anything*, actually. Right now, she's in the hospital. And I'm not there with her. And I have no idea what her status is. If she's going to be okay or not. And on top of her being sick, she's going to discover that I'm *missing*. And she's going to have to add that to all of the stress she's dealing with, and what if it kills her?"

Charlie was surprised that Amberly was admitting it to everyone. Not just to Trace. But to the whole group. She had told Charlie not to tell anybody what she knew. And Charlie had kept her secret. And as surprised as she was, she was glad that Amberly was finally letting it out. Already, she could tell that it seemed like a weight had been lifted off Amberly's chest with having confided in them. She understood how that felt. It was not good to deal with things alone.

"I had no idea," Trace said. "Why didn't you ever tell me?"

"Because... it doesn't matter," Amberly decided. "It wasn't anyone's business but my own. But being here and trying to not get killed while defeating Yash's minions so that the earth doesn't get destroyed... I'm just worried it's more than I can handle. I'm worried that we're not going to be able to do this."

"You don't think we'll be able to do this?" Kaos asked. Then he motioned around at everybody. "Look around the room, Amberly. We're all here. We're all together. We all are in agreement about how we're going to go down there and defeat those guys. Since when have we ever been in total agreement about something? Since when have we ever acted like a *true* team? I think this gives us more of a benefit than ever."

She sniffs again and avoids everyone's eye contact. "I'm scared."

"Me too," Charlie said quickly. She wanted Amberly to know that she wasn't alone in her feelings. "This is a terrifying thing that we're doing. But what other choice do we have?"

"She's right," Kire said. "Who else is going to defend the world? Nobody even knows that it's on the brink of devastation. We're the only ones who do. We're the only ones that can do anything about it."

She nodded her head. "I get it. But it doesn't make it any less scary."

"I just wish you would've told me about all of this," Trace said, still stuck on the fact that Amberly had been hiding so much from him. "I would've been there for you, you know? I would've never judged you, Amber. I would've helped you get through it all. I could even help you take care of your mom. I could get a job and help you pay bills. I don't ever want you to have to stress out like this."

"I don't need anybody's help," she said stubbornly.

"I wish you wouldn't say that," Trace muttered. He no longer seemed interested in trying to give her a hug.

"Amberly," Kire said, stepping slightly toward her. "All we have to do is defeat these guys. Get to Albus. Do what we came here to do, then we will be back home. Your mom won't have reason to worry anymore. And as long as we all think positive, I'm sure your mom is going to be fine. We don't know anything for certain until we get back. So you have to keep that positive mindset. We'll be out of here before you know it. Let's just try and focus on one thing at a time, okay? Can you do that?"

Amberly took a long, deep breath, then she finally met Kire's gaze. Slowly, she nodded her head at him. "Yeah. I think I can do that."

"Great," Kire said, clapping his hands together. "Great, Amberly. We got this, you guys." Then he led them all in the topic of discussion about how they were going to go about their attack. About how they shouldn't try to go one-on-one with the beasts. How they should all work as a team to try and defeat them all at the same time. How they should use their powers to work together. Then the teens practiced a little more.

Eventually, everyone broke off into their separate groups again. Kire was working near Charlie in the corner of the crumbling building.

"I feel horrible for Amberly," Kire muttered to Charlie.

Charlie nodded her head. "It's pretty awful."

"I just... I had no idea. It's terrible, the life she got handed. I feel bad for her. It seems like she's all on her own, you know?"

"That's because she is," Charlie replied. "I found out about her mom being sick by accident. But she didn't want anybody to know. She prefers to deal with this kind of stuff alone. I think it's because she wants everyone to always think of her as powerful and on top of things. As somebody who never has any issues. As somebody who has the perfect life. Somebody to be jealous of. Finding out that she has to pay a bunch of bills and that her mom is sick and that her dad doesn't want her doesn't exactly make her enviable. Does it?"

"That's true," Kire agreed. "It's just crappy the way things turned out. I mean, I know my life isn't perfect. I know I have a horrible dad who is a drunk and treats my mom poorly. But at least I have my mom. At least I have somebody who has it together. Somebody who cares about me and who is actually a good person."

Must be nice, Charlie thought to herself. But she didn't want to say it out loud to Kire. She didn't want him to know that she couldn't relate. That both of her parents ignored her. That they favorited Lexi over her. It was embarrassing to talk about. And it made Charlie feel more relatable to Amberly—she also didn't want Kire's pity.

They continued working on their gifts together until after the sun went down. Amberly seemed much more put together by then. But as Charlie watched her as they gathered around together and had some last-minute discussions before they gathered up their gifts and prepared to head down to their battle, she couldn't help but still be slightly envious of Amberly. Sure, Amberly's mother was sick, and that was a terrible thing. But at least Amberly's mother still loved Amberly. At least she still wanted to do everything for her—she just simply... *couldn't.* Charlie, on the other hand, had two very capable parents who had all the love in the world to give, but they only wanted to give it to one daughter.

Oftentimes, Charlie felt like there was nobody in the world who could ever truly love her.

50

"So, gang," Kaos said, his hands on his hips with his fists balled as he stared around at the other four. "The time has finally come."

"I'm ready to fight," Trace said, his sword in his hand instead of in its scabbard. That was the thing about Trace. He was always ready to fight. In some cases, like now, that was a good thing. Other times... Charlie thought the opposite.

Kaos nodded. "Good. Because we have a big one ahead of us."

"Are you going to lead us into us in some sort of pre-battle speech?" Amberly asked in a mocking tone. "Some sort of pep rally talk? Get us all hyped up to defeat these monsters?"

"Hey, I don't think it's such a bad idea," Kire said, looking around at everybody with a shrug. "I think we could use some words of encouragement before we head down there."

"I was kidding," Amberly said. "We really have time for that?"

Kaos shrugged, too. "Maybe a pre-fight speech could help us in the long run," he agreed. Then he looked back to Kire. "Do you want to start us off?"

Kire cleared his throat. "Um... yeah, sure. I think... I think that we should focus on the reason why we're doing this. Not just because we are the saviors of Earth. But because we want to save the Albus Realm as well."

"Here, here," Trace said dramatically. Charlie stared at him, thinking he would fit in well in this kind of land.

Kire smiled slightly and continued. "And we're going to bring these guys down. And then, after that, we are going to go on a rescue mission to save Albus. Because I don't think he's dead out there, do any of you?"

Everybody shook their heads.

"I think he's still alive," Charlie decided to say. "I think we would just... somehow know if he had died. I don't know how else to describe it. But I think we would just know."

"I agree with you," Kaos said with a stern nod.

"Right," Kire said. "And without Albus, we wouldn't have known about any of this. We wouldn't have known that we even were supposed to do something with these gifts we were given in the cave."

"You know?" Trace piped up. "I know that the gifts were given to us at random. But I like to think that Albus wanted *us* to have them. That he knew we would make a good team. He could see us for all of our differences, but he knew we could put our differences aside and come together to create one unstoppable team of superheroes."

"We're hardly superheroes," Amberly complained.

"No, we kind of are," Kaos argued. "All we're missing is our outfits."

Trace chuckled. "I still think we should wear red."

This got a smirk out of even Charlie. Red wasn't really her color. She was more into green. Into earthy colors. But maybe she could make an exception for being part of the Unlikely Defenders. Maybe she needed something different.

Suddenly, even Amberly was laughing slightly. "Do you guys remember the first time we met Albus?" she asked.

"You mean that horrible noise he played?" Trace asked.

"And how he greeted us by calling us conquerors of planet Earth?" Kire added.

Amberly continued giggling. "And he thought the noise was *powerful.*"

"And he didn't even know what the word 'sonic' meant," Charlie said. Then they all laughed together.

"Also, what's up with that weird French wig he wore?" Trace asked.

"Do you think he's required to?" Kire wondered.

There was more laughter.

"But remember what he told us?" Kire went on. "About how the Albuses and humans used to live in harmony. And then the Albuses went through that wormhole and decided to keep an eye on Yash's ship, Chaos, so that every time Chaos tried to approach Earth, they could do something to stop it. The Albuses care about Earth. And they care about the people on it."

"That's very kind of them. They have their own little world here. They didn't have to keep worrying about ours. And yet... they did." Charlie could almost cry because of how thoughtful it was. "Does anybody else think it's strange how Albus seemed to know things about all of us?" she added.

"Things we didn't even know about ourselves," Amberly said.

"He gave us tips," Kaos said. It seemed as if he was just suddenly remembering it. "Tips on how we could conquer our gifts. Remember?"

"He told me that I would be able to control plants and animals. But he also said... that on days when darkness ruled my heart, my fellow humans could even crumble to my will. And he hoped that day never came. Which is good. Because I hope that day never comes, either. I don't want to control humans."

"And he said I have a journey of self-discovery ahead of me," Trace said. "That to control the fire of my Pentfire, I must learn to master the raging flame inside of myself. I'll never forget it. I was surprised he knew I had so much anger inside me. He took one look at me and knew everything."

"And me with Gomora," Amberly said, her voice soft. "He said that I have hate inside of me and that I shouldn't let Yash's men sniff it out. And in order to prevent that from happening, I need to remove it and be free of it."

Kaos slightly smiled. "He could tell that I always had a desire to be in charge. I don't know how he knew. But he said that the crown would let me do that. Would let me be in charge by getting into the minds of others. But he told me that wouldn't be as much fun as it sounded. And he's been right about that. I've had great difficulties trying to get the hang of this thing."

"There was something else he said," Kire added. "Don't you guys remember?"

Charlie thought hard. But it was Trace who spoke.

"*'As the founders of your world, you must seek unity like never before.'*"

"*'Only all of you, not one or four, can face what is to come,'*" Kaos finished.

So Kaos had had the right idea. They all needed to work together to be the best versions of themselves in order to properly face everything that was coming before them.

"It's a good thing we're finally taking Albus' words seriously," Kire said. Everyone nodded along in agreement.

"We might not have all gotten over our own personal issues, but we are united," Kaos said. "Albus would be proud of us for that."

"Yes, he would," Charlie agreed.

"The things he told us terrified me," Amberly admitted. "I know I didn't act like it. But it did. That's why I was so hesitant to join you guys whenever you wanted to have those little meetups. That's why I relied on having to go to work so much. But... I'm glad I'm here now. You guys are right. It's good that we're doing this together."

Kaos cleared his throat again. "As your leader, I want to be the one to tell you that we are going to win this battle tonight."

All the others nodded in agreement.

"We're going to go down there. We're going to rush that courtyard. And we're going to fight with everything we have. Got it? I mean it. *Everything* we have. Albus said himself that one of Yash's minions has the power to wipe out thousands. And there are *five* of them down there. It's going to take a lot of work. But we are powerful. We *have* powers. And we know how to use them. We might be young and stupid and foolish, but we are more capable than anyone else who has tried to be in our shoes thus far. So I think we're going to be victorious. Don't you?"

"Heck yeah, I do!" Trace said, pumping a fist in the air. Amberly looked like she was trying her hardest not to smile.

Kaos nodded enthusiastically. "Good. When we go down there and fight tonight, let's try to remember what it is we're fighting for."

"Easy. I'm fighting for Albus. And so that I can get back home and do what Amberly has asked me to. To tell my dad that I know about her."

"Thank you," Amberly said to him.

"*I'm* fighting for Albus. And because I don't want innocent people to die back on Earth," Charlie said.

"I'm fighting because I love fighting," Trace said. Then he chuckled. "And for Albus, of course."

"And I'm fighting because it's the right thing to do. For Albus." Kaos said.

Everyone looked at Amberly and waited for what her answer would be.

"I'm fighting for Albus, of course," she said with an eye roll. "But I'm also fighting so that I can get back home and take care of my mother. It's what's most important to me. More important than anything."

"There we have it," Kaos said. "We're fighting for our lives, for other people's lives, and for Albus."

They all took their gifts and held them in their hands at the same time. They clashed them together in the middle of the circle they had formed, and at the same time, all of them shouted two words.

"*For Albus!*"

Now it was time for the battle to finally begin.

51

The Unlikely Defenders left their building and crouched down the alleyway once more. They hid behind the wall, and all waited until Kaos gave them the signal. Charlie's heart was pounding fast. She couldn't believe she was about to do this. Already, she was looking all around herself for any sign of plant life that she could use to manipulate into weapons. Thankfully, there were vines and weeds and bushes in the courtyard that she was going to be able to use to her advantage.

"Are you guys ready for this?" Kaos whispered.

Everybody nodded their heads. But Charlie didn't know how ready she was. This was going to be a terrifying battle. They might all die. But she had to remain positive. They were strong enough to be able to defeat them. They may not have been chosen for a specific reason to be the saviors of the earth, but they knew what to do with their gifts, and they knew it well.

Suddenly, Kaos puffed up his chest. Then in a loud, booming voice, he yelled out, "CHARGE!"

The five of them sprinted into the courtyard. They approached all of the beasts that were standing around a fire.

The one-eyed freak. The serpent snake lady. The werewolf. The floating ghost banshee. The minotaur.

All of the creatures quickly stopped what they were doing and turned to look at the teenagers at the same time.

"This should be fun," the snake woman said.

"Didn't we get rid of you fools?" the minotaur asked.

"They are not from this world," the banshee replied. "They come as a favor to one of the Albuses."

"A favor?" the minotaur asked. "Do these little things think they can defeat us?"

"Oh, I *know* we can," Trace said, his sword out. Then he ran at them, full speed.

The battle had officially begun.

Charlie barely dodged in time as the one-eyed monster shot a laser beam out of his one eye. It was made of bright blue light, and it blasted a hole into the wall brick wall behind Charlie. But she was quick to her feet and made eye contact with a weed, sprouting it out of the ground.

A shadow flew over her head, briefly blocking the moonlight, and she saw the minotaur jumping at great heights, its great hooves looking like they were going to land on her. Again, she drove out of the way. She had a vine wrap itself around the animal's horn and threw it off to the side, but it barely had any effect on the minotaur.

"Kire, look out!" she shouted over in Kire's direction when she saw the half-snake woman coiling up and getting ready to attack him. Her mouth was wide-open, and it looked as if she wanted to eat Kire in one whole bite.

Luckily, having heard Charlie's warning, Kire quickly whipped open the book, and the shield popped out. The snake who flew at Kire bounced off the shield as if it was a bubble, and it caused the serpent lady to be blasted backward, where it nearly knocked Charlie over as she ducked out of the way yet again.

"I have to figure out what kills them!" Kire said inside of his shield, taking the pen out from behind his ear to write something to Halo.

"Hurry!" Kaos yelled. The werewolf was swiping at him with its great claws, but Kaos was able to dodge it easily, probably because he could read its mind with his crown in order to anticipate what moves the werewolf was going to make next. This seemed to be infuriating to the werewolf, who was growling hysterically.

Then suddenly, a screaming unlike anything Charlie had ever heard blasted through the air, making Charlie instinctively put her hands over her ears. The scream hurt. It made her feel like she couldn't do anything other than fall to her knees because of the sound of it. It made her feel like she was going crazy. It made her feel like she wanted to do anything to make the screaming stop. Tears trailed down her cheeks, and she cried out in pain. She could hear the cries of her friends' voices, too. It seemed everybody was powerless against it.

When the screaming stopped, Charlie suddenly felt herself again. That had been the banshee. But Charlie couldn't see where it went. It was probably floating up in the air somewhere above them. She didn't have time to focus on that now. She needed to kill something.

"The snake's coming for you next, Trace!" Kaos yelled after having hurled a rock at the werewolf, which made it cry out and back away from him.

And Kaos had been right. The serpent woman was slithering her way toward Trace, who had been busy fighting off the cyclops. He turned quickly and wielded his sword around, keeping the snake back. But with this, the cyclops was able to take his laser beam eye and shoot it in Trace's direction.

Trace looked as if the laser beam was going to get him right in the head until a great big rock started moving behind the cyclops, then it rose in the air and dropped on the monster's head. The laser stopped, and the cyclops wavered uneasily, dazed. Charlie realized Amberly had used her kinetic powers.

"Kire, what is Halo telling you?!" Kaos yelled as he scaled a collapsing staircase on the side of one of the buildings and got onto a platform a few stories high.

"She's telling me how to kill them according to old mythology!" Kire said.

"Well, what are those ways?" Amberly bellowed, picking up a wooden bench and holding it in front of her like a shield while the minotaur blasted its horn through it and nearly gouged her in the stomach.

"Amberly!" Trace cried, turning away from both the snake woman and the cyclops to rescue her.

"Okay, okay!" Kire cried out, safe in his shield. "Kill the cyclops by stabbing it through the eye!"

Charlie heard a loud breathing sound behind her. A panting noise. She slowly turned around in horror and saw that the werewolf had left Kaos alone for now and was right behind her. It looked like there was nothing human in it. It was just a beast with an animal-like instinct. An instinct to kill.

"Rose!" Kire yelled. Then as the werewolf raised its claw in the air and went to strike it across Charlie's face, its hand rebounded off some invisible force. Charlie screamed and fell to the ground, thinking she was done for. But when she felt no pain, she looked behind her and saw that Kire had tossed Halo in her direction, and the shield was now around her.

Charlie quickly brushed herself off, picked up Halo, and ran back over to Kire so that he could read the unfamiliar language that Halo was writing in. She stayed by Kire's side so that she was in the shield, too. But in the shield, she could still manipulate the plants around her.

"We have to work together!" she cried. "We're not being very strategical right now!"

"You're right," Kire said, still scanning through the book.

"To kill the serpent, we need to throw rosemary and salt on her and set her on fire!"

"Where the heck are we supposed to get rosemary and salt?" Amberly complained loudly, she and Trace fighting off the minotaur together. It had jumped in the air and landed on the wooden bench, and it burst into a bunch of splintering pieces. Amberly quickly picked a piece of wood up and used it as a sword, jabbing it in the minotaur's direction.

Then the cyclops came at Trace. He turned around at the last second and stabbed the thing straight in the stomach.

"Nice!" Kire and Charlie yelled at the same time, cheering him on. When Trace pulled the blade out of the beast, the sword was covered in purple goo. The cyclops staggered backward, but it still didn't seem like it was dying.

"The eye!" Kire shouted. "That's the only way!"

Trace made his sword burst into flames, and then he aimed his sword right at the cyclops' eye as its laser beam was shooting around everywhere. The thing with the cyclops seemed to be that its eye was so small he had a hard time focusing it on exactly the target he needed to.

"Trace!" Amberly yelled behind him, still trying to keep the minotaur away from her. "Hurry!"

The sword shook, and then suddenly, a ball of fire emitted from it. It blasted right into the cyclops' eye.

The beast let out of wailing noise and stepped backward before falling on its butt. There, it continued to writhe and shriek until it fell all the way on its back and stopped moving.

"We killed one!" Trace cried out triumphantly.

"Nice work!" Kaos yelled. "But we have to—"

The loud screaming erupted again. Everybody dropped to their knees. The sound was torture. Pure torture. Charlie felt almost like she wanted to die herself in order to just stop having to listen to the banshee's scream.

Then it stopped again, but the banshee was nowhere to be seen.

"Ask Halo about that next!" Charlie demanded. "We have to get rid of that thing! Fast!"

Kire nodded, and with his hand shaking, he wrote some more into Halo.

"Charlie, I need you and Amberly and Trace for this!" Kaos called from up on the balcony.

Charlie nodded, steeled herself, and left the shield. Immediately, the snake lunged for her, but she quickly had vines wrap themselves around the woman's throat, and it held her back long enough for Charlie to get over to Trace and Amberly.

"Charlie, make a catapult with whatever you can!" Kaos demanded. "Amberly, you help!"

Charlie looked at Amberly, who nodded, and then the two of them got to work. Charlie manipulated the plants around her, and Amberly used her kinetic powers to gather a bunch of rocks and to force bits of wood to fit together in just the right way to where they had what they needed to complete the mechanism.

"Trace, can you make firebombs?" Kaos yelled, ripping out a piece of rotting wood from the wall behind him and using it as a shield to protect himself from the werewolf, which was again making its way up the crumbling staircase toward him.

"Kaos, be careful!" Charlie cried, worried about him. He only had his crown. He didn't really have a good weapon other than that pathetic piece of wood.

Trace didn't even answer Kaos. He already understood the idea and thrust basketball-sized fireballs into the catapult holder from his sword. Quickly, Amberly launched the first one, and it flew toward the wolf. It hit him right on its back and made it whimper and scurry away back down the staircase in pain.

Charlie and Amberly high-fived.

But there was still that banshee that Charlie needed to get rid of. It rendered them unable to do anything whenever it screamed.

But in order to kill the banshee, they would need time to look up into the air without the snake lady lunging for them.

So suddenly, Charlie ran. She ran away from the courtyard.

"Rose!" Kire shouted out to her. But Charlie would be back.

She ran back to that nearly demolished market she had gone to earlier to get food for them that morning, and there she found it: rosemary. There was only a little bit of it left, but of course, Charlie manipulated it so that there was plenty. She quickly grabbed it and ran back to the circle of fighting down the alley. They had to get the serpent woman out of the way so that it would stop lunging at them while they looked around for where the banshee was hiding.

"Amberly, I need you to blast that rock apart. Blast it into a million pieces!" Charlie called to Amberly. "There's got to be salt inside of it. Rock salt!"

Amberly did as she was instructed and threw a boulder at a brick wall. She did it repeatedly until it crumbled. Then Charlie approached the snake.

"Rose, what are you doing?!" Kire called. But Charlie had to get close enough so that when she threw the rosemary, it stuck to her. The snake coiled up.

"Rose!" Kaos yelled, not liking her being close to it either.

Then just as it lunged at her again, Charlie threw a fist full of rosemary at it. It stuck to the snake and made a sizzling noise, and then Charlie rolled out of the way and missed being bitten by it. However, as she rolled, she moved out of the snake's path and right into the way of the werewolf's path, where it swiped at her, and this time it got her right across the arm. She screamed out in pain.

"Amberly!" Kaos yelled. "The salt!"

"Rose, are you okay?!" Amberly yelled.

"Don't worry about me!" Charlie called, having manipulated more vines to keep the werewolf's arms away from her.

Amberly did as she was told and dragged her pieces of rocks through the air and hurled them toward the snake. She tried to slither away, but Amberly ended up being successful, and the salted rocks stuck to her.

The serpent woman had the salt and the rosemary on her. The last thing they needed to defeat her was...

"Trace, another firebomb!" Kaos yelled.

Trace did as he was told. He threw the fireball into the catapult, and then Amberly launched it. It hit the snake square in the middle of where her stomach met her snake tail.

"No! You imbeciles!" she cried as the end of her tail started burning into ash. The smell of it was terrible. "How did you even come across the information on how to defeat me?!"

Before anyone could even answer her, the tail had burned up until her torso was on fire, and then it quickly engulfed her entire body until she was nothing but a pile of ashes on the ground.

"The banshee next!" Charlie yelled. "If she screams again—"

And just like that, the banshee did scream again. They all fell to their knees again. Kaos rolled off the platform he was on, and somehow, with Charlie not even thinking about it because she was in so much pain, she was able to manipulate vines to catch him before he hit the ground. The vines then lifted him back up onto the platform, where the werewolf, who didn't seem affected by the banshee's scream, was coming up the stairs toward him.

That werewolf is practically all animal, Charlie thought to herself after the banshee stopped screaming again. *Does that mean I can control it?*

"We have to rip out the banshee's vocal cords to kill it!" Kire yelled.

Trace nodded his head. "I got no problem with that. Amberly, I'm going to climb on top of that barrel. Then you lift me up!"

Amberly nodded, and the minotaur ran at her with its horns pointed toward her face, but she quickly used her powers to grab a different barrel to block herself. One of the minotaur's horns got stuck in it. The minotaur bucked and shook itself around, and when it finally pried itself free from the barrel, one of its horns had been ripped out of his head and was stuck in it.

"No!" the beast yelled when he realized it.

Trace jumped on the other barrel. Amberly quickly lifted it into the air with him on it. She was careful about it as Trace held on carefully, trying to not fall off. Higher and higher in the air it went, where the banshee was flying around above them.

"I don't think you want to test me," the banshee said to Trace.

Trace smiled wickedly. "But I do," he replied.

Then suddenly, so many things were happening at once. Trace was lunging off the barrel, fifty feet in the air, right at the banshee.

Amberly was plucking the minotaur's horn out of the barrel. Now she had a weapon.

The werewolf was still coming toward Kaos up the crumbling staircase, and then it finally stood on the balcony where Kaos was.

The minotaur was bleeding but still looked like it wanted to find a way to get that horn out of Amberly's hand.

Thinking quickly and concentrating hard, Charlie tried to control the werewolf.

When she opened her eyes, she saw that it was working. The werewolf was frozen. It couldn't move anywhere. Up above them, Trace and the banshee were wrestling with each other, Trace clinging onto the banshee for dear life.

"Stab the minotaur with its own horn!" Kire was yelling at

Amberly.

Charlie was surprised that she had such a good handle on the werewolf. She was actually controlling it.

Fall off the platform, she commanded mentally.

Then the incredible happened; the werewolf did just that. It hurled itself over the edge, squealing on its way down. When it hit the ground far, far below, it stopped moving.

"Whoa, Rose, did *you* do that?" Kaos asked, his chest heaving as he looked over the platform down at the dead beast below.

"It's no biggie!" Charlie called, even though she felt like it was a quite big deal indeed. She had controlled something that weighed more than double her!

Annoyingly, the banshee above them was suddenly screaming again. It was so painful this time that Charlie was nearly ready to throw herself headfirst into a wall. And just as she was standing up, getting ready to actually hurt herself because she just wanted the screaming to stop, the screaming was cut short. "Rose!" Trace was now screaming instead. Charlie looked up just in time to see that he was falling through the air with the banshee, who was no longer able to fly.

Charlie quickly manipulated a bunch of leaves to come together and create a canopy for him to land on. The banshee missed it and fell flat to the ground with a loud thud instead.

Slowly, Charlie lowered the canopy to the ground, and Trace was fine. In his hands, he held what looked like a grayish, dripping body part. Charlie figured it was the vocal cords of the banshee.

Amberly still had the horn in her hand. The minotaur was eyeing her carefully, knowing that Amberly now knew how to kill it. "I'd be careful if I were you, little girl," the minotaur said in its deep voice.

"I'm through with being careful," Amberly spat. Then she

let go of the horn. But instead of it dropping to the ground, it floated in mid-air. Amberly used her gauntlet to control it, then she pushed her open palm forward, and the horn flew dart-like through the air. The minotaur had no time to jump out of the way. The horn pierced him right in the chest.

With a single grunt, the minotaur collapsed, and finally, it, too, was dead.

The five teens stood around and stared at the defeated minions of Yash's.

Charlie couldn't believe it.

"We killed them all," Kaos breathed, coming down the steps from the balcony.

"You guys are incredible!" Kire yelled. He closed Halo and set the book on a barrel, and his shield disappeared. "I feel like I was no help!"

"Are you kidding?" Amberly called, dusting herself off. "We would have had no idea how to defeat those guys without you. "

"Yeah, it was good that you were in the force field," Trace agreed. "Every one of our powers had helped us in different ways. We were the *ultimate* team."

They all high-fived each other and congratulated each other on their victories. Around them, all of the creatures had now turned into goop—the clear sign that the teens had been successful in defeating them all.

"Kire," Charlie said, noticing something.

"What?" Kire asked. On top of one of the barrels behind him, Halo was shaking. Then she burst open, and Kire ran over to her.

"Crap," Kire said as he read whatever it was she had to tell him.

"What now?" Kaos asked.

"We have to get to the castle. One of those creatures somehow notified Yash that this was happening. He sent more down to attack."

52

"You mean..." Charlie trailed off, feeling weakened. "We have more fighting to do?"

"I'm afraid so," Kire said, closing Halo and putting her in his backpack. "But they're not here yet, so we have time. We have to make it as close to the castle as we can before they arrive."

Charlie was exhausted. She was worried, too. How much more fighting could she do? All of the manipulation she had done; controlling the werewolf, making it kill itself. She felt like it had been almost too much. She felt dizzy. Lightheaded. She felt like she needed some water and to sit down.

But apparently, there was no time for that.

"All right then," Kaos said, straightening his crown on his head. "Are we good to move on?"

Charlie looked down at the cut on her arm. It was bleeding pretty heavily. Maybe that contributed to the reason why she felt so weak.

She manipulated some leaves to wrap themselves tightly around the wound to seal it up.

"Ready," she said to Kaos.

The others were beaten and bruised, too, except for Kire. But they seemed to still be a lot more alert and energetic than Charlie did. She heavily envied them. Why did she have to feel this way right now? Sure, she hadn't gotten as much rest as the others had, but that couldn't be the reason why, right?

"Are you sure you're going to be okay?" Kire asked, looking at Charlie with concern.

Charlie started walking. "Let's just get to that castle."

"That's one brave chick," Trace said. Then Amberly shot him an annoyed look.

"Not as brave as you are, though, babe," he clarified.

Then together, the Quintets took off out of the courtyard. They left the strange goop of all of the defeated minions behind.

It was a straight path to the castle. They could still see it from where they were. They just needed to keep following the road. The long, winding, never-ending road.

The first beast arrived about ten minutes into the next part of the journey. But within this one beast, to Charlie, it looked like there were three of them. At first, she saw the great big lion that appeared to have dropped from the sky out of nowhere, and it was running toward them from a field in the distance. But then it looked as if a horned goat was *riding* the lion. It was a strange, obscene scene to Charlie, and all she could do was stop and stare at it in wonder. As it came closer, and she saw the thing's tail, she realized it wasn't a normal tail. For the tip of it ended in the head of a snake. And as a lion ran on, she realized that the goat was *part* of the lion.

"What on earth is that?" Trace asked, his mouth hanging open, his sword at the ready.

"I've heard of that," Kire said. "I read about it in a Greek mythology book."

"Well, you better hurry and get Halo out and have her tell us how to defeat that thing!" Kaos said quickly.

"It's a chimera," Kire said. Then he pulled Halo back out of his backpack and immediately pulled her open.

"Hurry!" Amberly yelled, looking afraid. The beast was gaining on them. She used her kinetic ability to start throwing any pebbles around at the beast that she could find. Trace started throwing his firebombs that were emitting from the tip of his sword, but the lion creature was doing a good job at prancing around them, and not a single thing hit it.

"He's going to come for you first, Amberly," Kaos said, reading the chimera's mind. "It says you are the weakest link."

That's weird, Charlie thought. For she felt weaker than anybody. She tried to manipulate the snake, goat, or lion part of the creature to get it to do something, but nothing was happening. She simply felt like she couldn't.

Just as Kaos had foreseen, the lion lunged at Amberly, who screamed loudly. But Kire quickly threw the book in her direction, and it landed at Amberly's ankle, and a shield shrouded her just in time. The lion rebounded and rolled off it, the snake hissing and trying to lunge out at Charlie as it passed.

Trace ran at it with his sword out while Kire went back to the book and started reading from it.

"I got it!" Kire yelled. "Trace, catch this!" He tossed a pencil from his backpack at Trace, who caught it with a funny look on his face.

"Get the pencil into the lion's mouth!" Kire instructed. "Then, with your sword, light the pencil on fire! The lead will turn into lava and melt down its esophagus and go straight to its center where it will kill it!"

Trace did exactly as he was told. Thankfully, the plan worked effortlessly. As the lead melted and slid down the lion's mouth, it roared. Then when the lead seemed to hit the center inside the chimera, all the animals shrieked and hissed and cried, and then the beast fell to the ground, dying nearly instantly.

It was the fastest the group had killed any of Yash's minions yet.

"We have to get to that castle!" Trace yelled as he put his sword away. "Let's go!"

They kept going toward the castle. The closer they got to it, the more beasts there suddenly were that came out of them. And the more fighting they all had to do to kill them.

One was a ghoul that they had to feed normal, human food in order to get it to die. Then there was an undead Viking-looking man. It needed to be beheaded. Next was a spider-like creature that needed to have a boulder dropped on its back to squash it. Then there was a three-headed dog that needed its heart ripped out.

One by one, the Unlikely Defenders continued to defeat these creatures as they made their way to the castle. And Trace was right. It really did seem as if they were unstoppable. No matter how exhausted Charlie was. No matter how much she had to let them take the lead because she felt that she just didn't have it in her to keep fighting, they still managed to always win.

Then, when it seemed like they were out of the greenery of the land they were in and were newly surrounded by nothing but lava rocks and smoke at the base of the mountain where the castle was, they came across one of the hardest to defeat creatures yet.

It was called a chupacabra, according to Kire. It was a gray creature that stood on its hind legs with spikes on its back.

It fed on blood.

It was wickedly fast, so no matter how many things Amberly tried to throw at it with her powers, and no matter how many firebombs Trace shot from his sword, and no matter what Kaos tried to predict with his crown, there just seemed to be no defeating it.

"It's just too dang fast!" Trace yelled. The chupacabra

leaped toward Kaos, and Kire quickly tossed his book to save him with his shield. But now that Kire didn't have a shield, the chupacabra flew through the air again, looking like it was going to land on Kire with his back first, its sharp spikes out.

Kire tried to drive out of the way in time, but some of the spikes on the thing's back locked into Kire's leg, and he screamed out in agony.

This seemed to be what gave Charlie a renewed source of power. She stared at the beast, thinking with all of her might that it was an animal. One she could control. She balled her fists and focused hard. So hard that her head felt slightly like it was going to explode. But thankfully, the beast got off Kire, ripping its spikes out of him as it moved away from everyone. She had a hold on it.

Kill yourself, she thought to the beast.

It looked like it was fighting against everything it could to keep itself from doing what Charlie demanded. But it couldn't stop its own clawed hand from reaching into its mouth and forcing its way down its throat. Then there was a horrible squelching noise, and the beast had plucked his own heart out right before falling to the ground, dead.

"Kire, are you okay?" Amberly called as Charlie fell to her knees. The gang ran over to Kire to help him with his bleeding leg. No one even appeared to have noticed Charlie, who wiped her nose and saw that both of her nostrils were bleeding. Then she felt wetness on her cheeks and wiped that, too. More blood was on her hand. Were her *eyes* bleeding?

"Oh my God!" Amberly looked in horror at Charlie, finally seeing the state she was in.

"Rose!" Trace yelled.

"Where's all that blood coming from?" Kaos asked, his eyes wide in alarm.

Charlie tried to stand herself up. She didn't understand what was happening. She was having trouble remembering what occurred even thirty seconds ago. Everything felt so hazy and blurry. Where was she? How did she get here? Why was everyone staring at her like that?

Then as Trace, Kaos, and Amberly started running over to Charlie's aid while Kire was still on the ground clutching his bleeding leg, Charlie collapsed and faded into darkness.

53

When Charlie woke up, she found it was to herself muttering Kire's name.

"Uh, no," Trace's voice said awkwardly. "You got me here, though."

Charlie tried to figure out what was going on in her surroundings. She couldn't tell where she was and how she got there. It seemed like she was slumped over something.

Quickly, she came to the right realization that she was slumped over Trace's back. He was giving her a piggyback ride, and they were making their way up the mountain toward the castle.

"What's going on?" she mumbled, concerned about how weak her voice sounded coming out of her. She looked over Trace's shoulder and saw that just up ahead of them, Amberly and Kaos both had their arms around Kire and were helping him walk, too, due to the injuries he got with the spikes from the chupacabra.

"You sort of... passed out," Trace pointed out. "You were bleeding from, like, every single hole in your face, dude."

"I... I was?" Charlie asked. Then, sure enough, when she

looked down on Trace's shoulder where her head was rested on, she saw that she had gotten it covered in blood. And when she tried to move the muscles in her face, they felt tight. Dried-up blood was all over her.

"Yeah, you look kind of terrifying," Trace said, chuckling lightly.

"You... you don't have to hold me," Charlie said, feeling awkward about it. "I can walk. I'm fine."

"Not a chance I'm letting you down, sister," he told her. "I'm just glad you're even awake. We were beginning to think you were dying."

Charlie sort of felt like she was. She hated this. Why did she feel so weak when everybody else seemed to be doing fine? Everyone except for Kire, who had sustained some injuries from the chupacabra. But that made sense. Sure, she had been scratched by the werewolf, but it didn't even hurt that bad. She had a feeling that her injury from the wolf beast had nothing to do with the reason why she felt so weak. Why she was bleeding so much?

"How much further?" she decided to ask instead of replying to him. This wasn't an ideal situation, but she just had to make the best of it. And Trace was probably right. If she did try to walk, she probably wouldn't let the group get very far. She would just be holding them back. So, a piggyback ride from Trace was going to have to do.

"We're close," he told her. "Carrying you is giving me a great workout too. And the smoke we're all constantly inhaling is really testing my lung capacity. I bet when we get back to Earth, I'll be able to run a marathon."

Charlie looked around them again at her surroundings. At all of the black rock. At the smoke that seemed to be getting thicker. Upon noticing it, she instantly coughed.

"Are you okay?" Trace asked immediately, pausing in his step.

"I wish I had some water," she admitted.

"So do we," Amberly called over her shoulder. Charlie felt her cheeks turning red from embarrassment. She didn't realize they could hear her. Did that mean they heard her when she woke herself up by mumbling Kire's name, too?

How embarrassing.

"Hopefully, there's some water in the castle," Kaos said as they walked. They were going up a steep incline, but Charlie could see just up ahead that the incline was suddenly cut off. Did that mean that they were about to arrive at the castle? Would Albus be inside of it?

"Rose, are you sure you're all right?" Kire asked, sounding as though he was in pain while he walked with the others.

"I..." Charlie trailed off. For some reason, it took great effort for her to get words out. She still felt confused and hazy. She thought she was okay... but maybe she wasn't.

"This isn't good," Kaos said.

"What if she drops dead on us?" Amberly asked. "Wh-what if there's only four of us, and we have more monsters to defeat? We work better as a team. We need to be a team. There's got to be some way we can get her back to normal."

"I'm fine," Charlie tried to say. But it came out as a muttered, mumbled mess. Then she got hit by another overwhelming wave of dizziness, and it pulled her under again.

THE NEXT TIME she came to, they had all stopped walking. Charlie was no longer on Trace's back. She was on the ground, leaning up against a black rock. It was hot wherever they were. As Charlie rubbed her eyes and tried to make sense of her surroundings, she quickly realized the reason why it was hot. Just to her right, where Trace, Kaos, and Amberly were standing observing something, Charlie saw a long rope bridge. It led to the entrance of the castle.

It would've been exciting, and Charlie would've felt relieved that they were finally here. But the big dilemma was what the rope bridge was draped over.

A giant fiery pit of lava.

"It's not a mountain at all," Kire said. Charlie turned her head the other way and saw that he, too, was sitting down, leaning up against a rock just a few feet away from Charlie. He was cleaning his own wounds and wincing in pain every few seconds. "It's a volcano."

"Creepy place to have a castle," Trace commented.

"Well, are you guys ready?" Kaos asked. "We have to cross this bridge. We have to get to that castle."

"It looks like it can only hold the weight of one person at a time," Amberly pointed out. "If Trace and Rose try to go together, or if you and I try to help Kire like we've been doing this whole trek up the mountain, I'm afraid it's going to collapse."

Collapse? That can't be good.

"I can get there myself," Charlie tried.

"I... I don't know about that," Trace said. "You're not in good shape, Rose."

"He's right," Kire agreed.

"Neither are you," she felt the need to spit out at Kire. She figured she was just more angry than anything that she was even in this predicament at all. She wasn't necessarily mad at Kire.

"So, what, then?" Kire asked. "Should we just wait here while you guys go into the castle?"

"No," Amberly said quickly. "We have to stay together as a team. Right, Kaos?"

"I... I don't know," Kaos said, looking uneasy. Charlie wondered if maybe Kaos had a slight fear of heights. "I do want us to stay together. But if you two can't walk on your own, and the bridge isn't strong enough to hold the weight of multiple of us... I'm not sure how to go about this."

"Here," Charlie muttered. Using her powers again, even though she knew she was weak and that she shouldn't, she focused on the tiniest weed—the probably only living plant around them for miles—and began manipulating it. She made it stretch itself long enough so that it could wrap around each teenager like a harness, with plenty of slack between each of them. Then it reinforced itself around a particularly large boulder on their side of the bridge. "Even if the bridge does collapse, we won't fall into the lava."

But even doing that little bit of magic had made her start to get dizzy again.

"Great," Kire sighed. "Rose, your nose is bleeding again."

Charlie didn't even bother to wipe it away this time. It was all over her face still from the last time it had happened. She didn't have a mirror, but she could feel it.

"Rose, you really need to stop using your gifts unless it's an absolute emergency," Kaos said. "We don't know what's happening to you. You could die. I'm not kidding. Just... chill out, okay? We want you to feel better."

Charlie couldn't even answer. For she was in fear that she was going to faint again.

Kire forced himself to his feet. He was unstable on the hurt one, but he was at least standing. "I can make it over on my own. So I say us three will go separately. Trace, you have to carry Rose. You go last; that way, the rest of us can at least get the other side first in case it doesn't hold the weight of you both. Then when you guys go, just... try to be fast."

With everybody in agreement, Amberly stepped up and crossed the bridge first. It swayed and was rickety and didn't look the least bit safe, but miraculously, she made it to the other side, unharmed, but slightly pale-looking.

Then Kaos had Kire go next, in case he collapsed on the bridge because of his injured leg and needed somebody to go rescue him and get him to the other side. Kire had to hold onto the rope railing for sturdiness and stability since he had to limp across it, and it kept making the bridge sway from side to side, which terrified Charlie, but eventually, he, too, made it to the other side.

Then Kaos went next with relative ease, not seeming at all scared of the loose wood planks of the bridge and the way it was rocking.

Now all three of them were over on the other side safely.

"You ready?" Trace asked, holding his hand out to Charlie. She took it, and he hoisted her up onto his back. Trace stepped onto the bridge. *So far, so good.*

He took a couple more steps.

Then on his fifth step, Trace's foot went straight through the wood, and a plank fell down into the lava below them. Across the bridge, everyone screamed. Trace was holding not only himself up by hanging onto the rope railings of the bridge, but Charlie as well. He grunted as he tried to get his foot out of the hole and to get them back to a stable position again as the bridge rocked back-and-forth dangerously.

Charlie couldn't even imagine the strength it was taking Trace to not only stay steady, but to support his *and* Charlie's weight.

"Be careful!" Amberly called. "If you die, Trace, I'll... I'll kill you!"

Charlie felt Trace snicker. Then they carried on, Trace stepping carefully over the hole. He moved more cautiously, checking each plank first to see if he felt like it would hold his weight before he stepped onto it.

Then thankfully, they made it over to the other side.

"I don't believe it," Kire said, looking up at the great big black castle in astonishment. "We're actually here."

"We're at the castle," Kaos echoed, looking up as well.

"It's huge," Amberly said. "I didn't look this huge from way back where we started."

"I wonder what the inside of it looks like," Trace mused.

"I bet there are old skeletons inside," Kaos said, wiggling his eyebrows. "Maybe even a dragon."

"There's not a dragon," Amberly snapped, not looking quite like she believed her own words.

"Guys..." Kire trailed off, changing the subject. "What if... What if Albus isn't here? Or what if *worse*? What if he's dead? What if he *and* his family are dead?"

"We can't think like that," Trace said. "Come on, dude. What happened to being positive?"

"I know," Kire replied. "I just... I don't want our journey over here to have been for nothing."

"It definitely wasn't for nothing," Amberly said. "There's going to be something in there that helps us with the portal, even if we don't find Albus. I just know it."

Kire nodded. "When we get inside, we need to find somewhere for Rose to rest."

"I'm fine," Charlie tried to say again. But it came out as another mutter.

"She looks like a ghost," Amberly commented.

"Shut up," Charlie tried to say, but nobody understood her.

"I'll go first," Kire said. "I'll hold Halo out in front of me as a shield in case anything comes out of nowhere."

"Do you still think we're in danger?" Amberly asked cautiously as she stayed close behind Kire as they walked, Charlie still on Trace's back.

"We could be," Kaos said. "Think about it. We've defeated so many of Yash's minions. Either we got stronger somehow, or they simply got easier to beat. Whatever the case, we got through a lot of them. Once Yash finds this out, I got a feeling he's going to come here himself. He's going to realize that his beasts are no match for us, and if he wants to have any chance of getting rid of us, he needs to come here and get rid of us on his own."

"Ugh, don't tell me that," Amberly said, slapping a hand over her face in dread.

"We just have to keep moving forward," Kire said. "We can do this, you guys. One step at a time."

54

From the moment Trace entered the castle with Charlie on his back, Charlie was in complete awe. She had never been inside of a castle, let alone inside of a castle in a different *realm*. What she was seeing was simply incredible. It was breathtaking. And she could tell based on how silent everyone else was being that they felt the exact same way.

For one, the foyer they were in had ceilings that were at least fifty feet high. Stone columns made from lava rock were every couple of feet and reached all the way up to the ceiling. The castle itself looked as if it had slowly been deteriorating over the years from lava and weather. But another thing Charlie noticed about the place was that there didn't seem to be much furniture. The castle itself didn't look to be too lived in. Still, they hadn't gotten very far into it yet.

"Albus?!" Kire called. But then Kaos slapped a hand on his back. "What are you doing?!" he asked sharply. "We need to be keeping our voices in a whisper."

"Why?" Amberly asked, whispering anyway.

"We don't know what's in here," Kaos said.

"You're right," Kire agreed, the tips of his ears turning red. "Good point."

"But this place is huge," Amberly said. "How are we possibly supposed to find Albus in here? And what if he's in hiding? That's going to make it even worse."

"We just have to search. What else can we do?" Kaos asked.

"Can you let me down?" Charlie asked Trace. She was tired of being on his back. Tired of being a burden. She wanted to be free of him. Or more so, him to be freed of her.

"I don't think that's a good idea," Kire said. But even Kire was hobbling on his own okay by now. And Charlie was seeing clearer than she had since she first fainted back after they defeated the chupacabra.

"Please," she begged. "I'll be okay."

"Just let her try," Kaos said.

Trace stopped walking and dropped Charlie carefully to the ground.

Everybody stared at her.

"How do you feel?" Amberly asked.

Charlie didn't want to admit the truth—that everything was blurry and hazy and that she was still incredibly dizzy. She wanted to walk on her own. She didn't want to be anybody's burden.

"I'm fine," she managed to get out. So then the group kept walking.

There were many forks in their paths. Many different hallways and corridors to go down, but what they did know they needed to do was stick together. They couldn't find themselves without the help of each other in case they ran into danger.

"This place just goes on and on," Trace said after a while, walking next to Amberly now that he didn't have to hold

Charlie was on his back. He draped his arm around her. To Charlie's surprise, Amberly draped her arm around him in return. Apparently, she was glad to have Trace back. Maybe she felt closer to him now that they had talked a little bit about the real Amberly.

They all continued to search. Corridor after corridor, room after room, crumbling staircase after crumbling staircase, there didn't appear to be a soul in here. Charlie was beginning to fear the worst. That not only were they not going to find Albus, but that they weren't going to find what they needed to close the portal in here, either.

"Let's pause for a moment," Kire eventually said. Everybody stopped walking and waited to see why. He flipped open Halo and grabbed another writing utensil out of one of the pockets of his backpack, which Kaos was now holding. Then he started writing something to Halo.

"What is she saying?" Amberly asked.

"What are you doing?" Charlie asked.

"I... I want to see if she can help us at all," Kire replied. He set his pen down and then waited.

"And?" Kaos asked.

Kire stared hard. "And..." He let out a sigh. "It's hopeless."

"What do you mean *hopeless*?" Trace asked.

Kire shut the book. "She's drained. She's used too much magic today. She doesn't want to help us anymore right now."

"Of *course* not!" Trace moaned.

"Now what?" Amberly asked, crossing her arms and tossing her tangled, dirty hair over her shoulder. Charlie had to admit she was surprised that she hadn't heard Amberly complaining about how badly she wanted a shower in a while.

They journeyed through the castle a little bit longer until they came across a dark, dusty room with a fireplace.

"I think we should take a break in here," Kaos announced to the group. They stepped inside of it, and even though there was no furniture to sit on, they all took a seat on the ground around the fire, but nobody wanted Trace to light it with his sword. It was already warm in here. Warm from all of the lava down below them.

Charlie was relieved that they wanted to sit. It felt amazing to not be on her feet anymore. She was still woozy, but this was better than trying to walk.

The gang sat there in silence for a while, recuperating and probably thinking about what their next course of action was going to be. Probably thinking about what they would do next if they couldn't find anything in this castle that would help them.

Then eventually, Kaos got back to his feet. "I say we keep exploring the castle. But this can be our meet-up spot. Rose and Kire, why don't you two stay here and get some extra rest? No offense, but you'll only hold us back if you come with us again."

"I agree," Trace said, laughing at them.

"Whatever," Kire said. Charlie crossed her arms and looked away from them, staring into the empty stone fireplace.

Amberly didn't look like she wanted to go help them in their journey around the castle, but she also looked like she didn't want to stay here with Kire and Charlie, either. So she got up and joined the other boys as they left the fireplace room and left Kire and Rose alone together.

Rose leaned back against another one of the beautiful lava stone columns and rested her eyes.

"I don't know what's going on with you," Kire said. "I don't know why this is happening to you."

"That makes two of us," Charlie whispered.

"We need to figure out a way to make sure that this doesn't happen to you anymore."

"How?"

"I... I don't know. But we need to think of something. I'm scared, Rose. You look really sick. We need to make you more immune to the effects of your powers. We need to figure out what we can do. Maybe when Halo is charged, we can ask her."

"Yeah. Or maybe I can just die."

"Don't," Kire said. "That's not even funny. Seriously."

"I'm sorry," she said with a sigh. She was tired. So tired.

"You really helped us out there," Kire told her. "We couldn't have done it without you. We *can't* do this without you."

"Don't worry, Kire. I'm not going anywhere."

Suddenly, Kire reached out and took her hand in his. She was so stunned that she opened her eyes and looked directly into his. They were glistening.

"I sure hope not," he said to her.

So this is happening again.

Charlie and Kire.

Holding hands.

Charlie and Kire sharing a romantic moment.

But what did it all mean? Why was this happening now? What was going to come of it later? What if they made it back to Earth after having saved here and there? Would they finally be in a relationship? Was that what Kire wanted? Was that what *Charlie* wanted?

She felt confused. Conflicted. Kire had really hurt her. But yet, she still felt crazy about him. It was a fact that she couldn't deny herself. But she was scared of getting hurt again. Terrified, really. She would take the physical pain of getting weakened from her powers over the pain that came with being hurt by Kire any day. Thinking about it made her remember why she always thought she was better off alone.

"I..." Charlie trailed off, unsure what to say to Kire. She wanted to ask him what he wanted from her. If he wanted to be with her, or if he planned on hurting her again. But she didn't know if now was the time.

"What is it?" Kire asked, leaning closer toward her.

But outside the fireplace room, somewhere in the distance, the noise of somebody yelling stopped Charlie from whatever it was she was about to say.

"Kire! Rose!" It was Kaos' voice. "Get over here! Both of you, if you can!"

"Hurry!" Trace added.

Kire jumped to his feet. Then he helped Charlie slowly get to hers. She was dizzy on the spot, but her heart was beating quickly. Adrenaline was pulsing through her making her feel as if she had a little bit more energy to keep going.

"Are you okay to go?" Kire asked, looking unsure.

"Let's just hurry," Charlie said, ignoring the question. So what if she didn't feel totally okay? She wanted to know what the others had found.

"Where are you?!" Kire called as they left the room.

"Follow our voices!" Amberly replied.

They did as they were told, and it led them inside a small room. It looked about the size of a large walk-in closet. But inside of it, there was a small cot, an old lantern, and a man. A man sitting leaned against the wall, his entire body covered in soot. From what Charlie could tell, he was bald. And he had the strangest eyes. Foggy blue ones that seemed to be staring at nothing, even though five teenagers were standing right in front of him.

This man didn't look like Albus. This was somebody else entirely.

But still, Charlie thought this was a good thing. Initially, she had assumed there was *nobody* inside this entire castle. But now, she felt hope. She felt as if maybe they had finally found somebody that would be able to help them.

Help them get to Albus and help them close the portal.

55

Charlie stared at the frail, small old man covered in soot. She wondered how long he had been there. She wondered what he was doing there. She wondered if he had been running from something. If he had been hiding from something. If he had been forced there. Maybe the door had been locked from the outside, and he had been trapped there all this time, and it was Kaos and the others who found him and freed him.

But it didn't look like this man wanted to go anywhere.

He continued sitting there on the floor, his frosted eyes not seeing them. He stared at nothing. He barely even moved.

Charlie didn't even know what to say. Part of her wondered if she was just imagining this. If she wanted somebody to be able to help them so badly that she had just conjured this man up in her imagination, and they weren't really seeing anything except the cot and the old lantern. The cot, which, by the way, was *also* covered in soot. It looked like any time the ground had been stopped on from the floor above, more charcoal and dust rained down and coated this room and everything in it with black stuff.

"Hello?" Kire tried talking to the man. He stepped closer to him as if stepping into his line of vision would help him to realize he was there.

Still, the man appeared to not see him. And still, the man said nothing.

"Who are you?" Kaos asked.

"*What* are you?" Trace added.

"Guys, don't be mean," Charlie said. But they acted as if they hadn't even heard her.

"Sir, are you all right?" Kire asked. He even knelt down on the ground in front of the man. But still, the man didn't reply.

"Look, we need your help," Kaos said, kneeling in front of him as well. Charlie kept a safe distance away. She wasn't sure why, but there was something about the man that unsettled her. Something that made her feel like she couldn't go any closer. Besides, it wasn't like she much felt like walking. And she doubted that he wanted to see *her* in his line of vision—not when she was covered in her own blood, looking like a girl from a horror movie.

Kaos continued.

"We're looking for Albus. Or... one of the Albuses. The one who has the connection to Earth. Who projects himself there to talk to the Quintets. The owners of the gifts. If you have any idea what I'm talking about, we're the new owners of the gifts. We are the new Quintets, and we're trying to save not only *our* earth, but this realm as well. We fear Yash is coming to destroy this place. And after he destroys this place, he'll destroy Earth next. So we really would appreciate it if you could answer some of our questions."

"I don't think he's going to say anything to you guys," Amberly said.

"Maybe... maybe he's hurt," Kire pointed out. "Maybe he's starving and dehydrated. Maybe we need to help him first in order to get him to talk to us."

"Help him?" Trace asked. "What can we do?"

"I don't know." Kire opened up Halo again, but it still looked as if she was being lifeless and unresponsive. Still, he tried writing something anyway. But he got no answers.

"What can you guys do?" Kire asked. "I don't want to do everything. And Halo still doesn't want to help us right now."

"Hang on a sec," Kaos said. He straightened his crown on his head and then held his fingers to his temples. He stared hard at the man and looked like he was concentrating greatly. But then he let out the long breath he had been holding in, and his shoulder sagged. "I can't even read his mind. It's as if nothing is in there at all."

"There can't be *nothing* there. He's clearly alive," Amberly said. "I can see him breathing. But it's not like I can use my kinetic powers to get him to talk to us. What you want me to do, make him *stand*?"

"No, you're right," Kire said. "Your gifts won't be any help to us."

"I have my sword," Trace said. "I could threaten to hurt him, and maybe that will get him to talk?"

"Don't do that," Charlie said, stepping forward involuntarily. As unsettled as the man made her, she didn't want any harm to come his way. He seemed helpless. Like if he *could* say words, he would.

"What about you, Rose?" Trace asked. "What can *you* do?"

"Rose shouldn't do anything," Kire said. "She's just barely getting her strength back from our battle."

Charlie didn't like the others thinking she was weak, even if weak was exactly how she felt. She stomped over to where Kaos and Kire were and stooped down to her knees before the man, as well. Then she took the leaves off the wound around her arm and manipulated them into going into the soot on the ground and sprouting anew. A whole new batch of leaves formed, and Charlie manipulated them to dust some of the soot off the man's face and hands. This may not get him to talk to them anymore, but she at least felt like she helped. And maybe helping clean him off would let him know that he could trust them.

She sprouted more leaves so that she could change her bandage. Then she sprouted more so that Kire could put some over his bleeding ankle as well.

"That was... nice of you and all," Kaos said. "But he's still not talking." Then he turned back to the man. "Please, sir. We really need your help."

Nothing.

Charlie sighed and got back to her feet. But the moment she did, she fell back down again. On her hands and knees, blood dripped from her nostrils onto the stone flooring.

"Rose, are you all right?" Kire asked quickly, turning away from the man and helping Charlie get back to her feet. "That's it. I told you not to use your powers anymore, Rose. Not right now."

"She needs rest," Trace figured. "She needs water and food. Sleep. I think that's the only way she's going to get better."

"Help me get her up," Kire said. They both helped Charlie to her feet together. "Why don't you and I go through some more of these rooms and see if we can find a place for her to lie down properly?"

"I'm fine," Charlie mumbled, but no proper words really came out.

Great.

She couldn't even do simple little things such as making leaves grow without feeling like she was going to faint?

What was happening to her?

"We'll be back," Trace said to the others. "Amberly. Be careful."

"What about *me*?" Kaos asked with a fake pout. Trace rolled his eyes, and then the three of them left the room and searched the castle some more. They went up a couple more staircases, then they searched through some more rooms, and then they realized they were finally coming across some places that still had furniture. One room had an old wardrobe in it. Another room had an armchair. They almost stopped to let Charlie rest on the armchair, but then they figured that still wouldn't be comfortable enough.

Then, at last, they entered a room with a four-poster bed. A canopy draped over it and a fluffy quilt laid on top of the mattress.

"This is perfect," Kire said, and he and Trace slowly helped Charlie make her way over to it. Charlie nearly collapsed onto the bed. It wasn't anything like her mattress at home, but to Charlie, it was the most comfortable thing she had ever felt.

"Just stay here. You'll be safe in here," Kire said. "You just need to get a little bit of rest."

Charlie forced herself to lay down. She knew they were right. She needed to rest if she was going to be able to use her powers again. And she needed to be able to use her powers again if she was going to have any chance of helping them get out of here in the end.

"We're going to go try to find you some food and water," Trace said. "And don't worry, Charlie. We know that you need your strength. I don't know about the other guys, but I don't care how long it takes. I don't want to leave here until you're in tiptop shape. So if we have to camp out here a few days, with the creepy guy who doesn't speak, while you recover, so be it."

Kire reached out and lightly grabbed Charlie's shoulder on her non-injured arm. "You're going to be okay. We're going to take care of you."

Charlie nodded, but her eyes were already drifting closed.

Yet, the second Kire and Trace left the room, and Charlie realized she was alone, her eyes snapped back open. She was all alone in here. Really all alone. And this castle was huge. If something happened to the rest of the Quintets, what if she couldn't hear it? What if, without realization, all of her friends died while she was up here sleeping? What if somebody found her here and attacked her while she was all by herself, and she didn't have the rest of the Quintets to save her?

A million scenarios played through Charlie's mind. She had every instinct to get out of bed and go back to her friends and tell them that they couldn't leave her. But something outweighed her instinct to do so. It was her weakness. And before Charlie could do anything about it, her eyes drifted closed once more.

56

Charlie Rose found herself outside of her family home.

The sun was shining outside. The weather was so perfect that she didn't even need a jacket.

As she stood on the sidewalk in front of her house, a smile formed on her lips. She raced across the front lawn to the door and found it unlocked. Inside, her family was standing there in the living room. All three of them. Her mother, her father, and her sister, Lexi.

"You guys?" Charlie asked right away. "What's wrong?"

It was strange because of the way that Charlie's family was all staring at her. The thing was... Charlie's family was *smiling* at her. They looked... *happy* to see her.

And something was *definitely* wrong with that.

"We're so glad you're home!" Charlie's mom said.

"You look beautiful, Rose," Lexi joined in. The two women walked around the couch to wrap their arms around Charlie in a tight embrace. It felt very foreign.

Charlie stood there speechless.

"You're a good kid, Rose, you know that?" Charlie's dad said from the living room while her mother and sister hugged her. He stood there with his hands on his hips, beaming at Charlie as she looked at him.

"Is this some kind of joke?" she asked.

"Why would we joke about that?" her mother asked as she pulled away after kissing the top of Charlie's head. "Are you hungry? We've ordered pizza, but we didn't want to start eating it until you got home."

"I don't get it," Charlie said. "Shouldn't you guys be at work still? And since when do you guys wait for *me* to eat?"

"Well, I'm sorry if you feel that we did that before, Rose," Charlie's dad said. "But we're always going to act this way from now on. We're going to be the perfect family you've always wanted."

"We just want you to have the perfect life," her mother joined in. "Come *on*, let's go eat!" Lexi grabbed Charlie's hand and dragged her through the dining room and into the kitchen, where three pizza boxes sat waiting for them. "By the way, you *have* to tell me where you got that skirt. It's gorgeous."

Charlie stared at all of the food, and then she turned around and smiled at each of her family members. She couldn't believe this was her new life.

Then the next thing she knew, she was no longer in her house. She was at the greenhouse. Which meant that she was at school. The sun was still shining brilliantly outside. The school grounds looked immaculate, and everything around her looked extra green.

The door to the greenhouse opened, and Kire stood just inside of it. He was no longer injured. There was no limping when he motioned for Charlie to enter the greenhouse and took a step back to let her in.

"Took you long enough," he said with a bright smile. He was dressed in clean clothes. He smelled heavenly. And his hair was styled in a way that made Charlie want to drool over him.

But she didn't get how she was suddenly here, nor did she understand what it was Kire was doing here, too.

"Sorry," she said to him, feeling confused as she entered the greenhouse. Somehow, the greenhouse had changed. There were more plants in it than she could've ever imagined. But if there were ever a special dream haven that Charlie had conjured up in her mind, this closely resembled that. Heck, this *was* that.

"Did you do this?" Charlie asked Kire breathlessly as she looked around the greenhouse before moving her eyes back to him.

"Of course, I did," he said, taking Charlie's hand. She didn't have the instinct to pull away from him when he did it. Instead, she held his hand gratefully. His hand was warm in hers. And it felt nice. Like she was *supposed* to hold his hand. Like she was *always* supposed to hold his hand.

"It's beautiful," she said.

"I just wanted to show you how much I care about you," Kire told her. Then he leaned over and kissed her on the cheek. "I want to show you what an amazing boyfriend I can be."

Kire was her boyfriend? She had an *actual* boyfriend?

Outside, she could hear people calling her name.

"Sorry we can't stay longer," Kire said. "We've got to go to lunch." Then, with his hand still in hers, he led her back outside the greenhouse. Standing out there, calling her name and waving her over, were Kaos, Trace, and Amberly. "Will you hurry up?!" Amberly complained. But she was smiling at Charlie as she did so.

Since when does Amberly look happy to see me?

"Yeah!" Trace joined in. "Before our table gets stolen!"

"Wait," Charlie said, confused. "They want to have lunch with *me*?"

"Why wouldn't they?" Kire asked. "They're your best friends."

Charlie grinned from ear to ear. She couldn't believe this was her life. Her most perfect life. She was finally living it.

But then her eyes snapped open.

She was lying in a bed in a castle.

And she was alone.

She didn't have her perfect dream life at all. She was still stuck in this reality. One where she didn't have parents who loved her. One where she wasn't certain if she should trust Kire and let him back in. One where she didn't think Trace, Kaos, and Amberly would ever want her to sit at their lunch table.

Instead of in her perfect life, Charlie was lying useless on the bed. Unable to help the others search the castle for a way to close the portal off from the bad guys. For a way to save the Albus Realm and Earth.

Charlie closed her eyes again and continued resting. But she didn't feel as if she was going to pass out anymore. And she didn't want to fall asleep, either. Instead, she found herself thinking about her life. About how quickly things had changed in what seemed like a blink of an eye. She thought about how she had minded her own business in that cave that day, working on her bioluminescence project, when the others so rudely interrupted her. She thought about when they first got their gifts. When she had chosen the Pendantix. And how she couldn't imagine having any other of the four gifts instead of it. Even though they were chosen at complete random, Charlie felt as if the Pendantix was made for her; she *was* a lover of plants, after all.

Who knew that day in the cave would be what ignited this insane, incredible journey she had gone through. To her, that day had seemed like just any other day. She had no idea then that it would be the day her life changed completely.

Suddenly, the answer to her question—*Why me?*—seemed to wash over her in an instant. It was obvious, the reason why Charlie was lying in this very spot, feeling weak.

She thought back to what Albus had told her in the woods the last time they spoke.

Be careful with your abilities. You are fragile. More fragile than you realize. If you continue to go full force with the Pendantix when you haven't opened yourself up to the idea of letting others in, the cost will be greater than you could ever imagine.

There was a reason why the others' gifts didn't affect them as terribly as they affected Charlie.

Kire was always a team player. Kire was always willing to work with others and do what it took. That's why he never had any trouble getting Halo to work for him.

Amberly had confessed to everybody all of the trouble she was going through. She had let the others in, and she also had seemed to have a resolution with Kire. They had come to the agreement that Kire was going to finally tell their father that he knew Amberly existed. And with this, Amberly must've felt less anger in her heart. It opened her up to be able to receive her gift's magic with ease.

Trace found a new outlet for all of the anger inside of him. The past couple of days, he hadn't been at school beating up innocent kids for no reason. He had been defeating monsters. Protecting all of the other Quintets. Any anger he felt inside himself, he was able to take out on others by using his sword on their enemies. And that's why his gift was responding so well to him.

And Kaos. Charlie knew Kaos was a master manipulator. He always had been. But the gifts didn't work on the other Quintets. He couldn't manipulate his way to get them to do whatever he wanted. And when he seemed to realize this, his attitude toward them changed. He treated Kire and Charlie better. He wasn't as nasty as he used to be. And realizing he couldn't always manipulate others to get what he wanted was probably what made him more able to take on the magic given to him by the crown.

Charlie hadn't done what Albus had warned her about. She hadn't let others in. She had kept herself closed off. She didn't have the perfect family. But the others didn't even know that. She had insane feelings for Kire, but he had no idea about them. She wanted the others to accept her and be her friend, but she hadn't said a word to any of them about it.

If Charlie didn't let her walls down, her gift was going to kill her.

With that realization, Charlie threw the quilt off her and got out of the bed. She was still dizzy, and everything felt faint, but she felt better than she had before. She felt rested enough to leave that bedroom and go get to her friends.

The first thing Charlie did was go back down the staircases and into the room where she had last seen the others. The room where the non-speaking, non-moving, frosted-eyed man was. When she arrived at the site, she discovered that yes, the strange man was still there, not looking at anything. But also, she realized that her friends were no longer with him.

So, Charlie kept searching around the magnificent castle until she came across a room with the double doors of it wide-open. And inside of the room was a glorious library.

She stepped inside of it, her mouth hanging open. While the place was dusty, it was the only room in the entire castle that seemed to be fully furnished. Bookshelves were stacked higher than her two-story home. Red puffy armchairs sat in front of fireplaces. Multiple wooden worktables were lined up in neat long rows with books stacked up on them. Paintings of old men in French wigs lined the walls, and Charlie immediately recognized one of them as being the Albus they had all been trying to save.

Charlie felt hopeful being in here. With this many books, Amberly was right—there had to be something in here that could help them close the portal. Maybe there was even something in here to help them figure out where Albus was.

Charlie began walking through the stacks when a voice sounded behind her.

"Rose?"

She turned around and saw Kire standing there.

She thought about the dream she had had. Where Kire had turned the greenhouse into her dream garden. Where he had kissed her on the cheek and told her he was her boyfriend. How it had made her the happiest she had ever felt.

And with this thought so fresh in her mind, she closed the distance quickly between herself and Kire and threw her arms around him. He didn't hug her back at first, but she figured it was because he was more surprised than anything. Then once he realized that she was hugging him and not choking him, he hugged her back.

They stayed like that for a long time before Charlie stepped back and looked at him, her eyes full of sincerity.

"I don't want to stay away from you anymore," she finally decided to say. She needed to lay it all out on the line. She needed to start telling people how she felt. And what better way to start than by telling Kire her honest truth?

He grinned at her, and then he threw his arms around her again.

When they pulled away this time, they both stood there smiling stupidly for a moment, neither of them seeming to know exactly what to say to each other next. Eventually, Kire cleared his throat and motioned to the books. "Uh, we've all been looking through here trying to find something to help us," he said. "Maybe there will be something to make that guy in that room talk to us."

Charlie felt better than she had in a long time. That hadn't been so hard. Kire hadn't rejected her. What had she been so afraid of?

"I'll help," she said.

"Are you sure you don't need to keep resting?"

"I'll be fine," she said. And this time, she felt that she meant it. She felt that as long as she took it easy and tried not to use her powers like the others had been saying, she would get back to her full self in no time at all.

"Okay," Kire said. "I've already searched this half." He pointed to a section of the row of books they were in. So together, they started rifling through a part that he hadn't looked through yet. Charlie was almost in a daze, not even really reading the words in these ancient books. She was too excited about her moment with Kire.

She was still daydreaming about that scene of her in her dream greenhouse becoming a reality when Kire's voice interrupted her thoughts.

"Uh, guys?!" he shouted. "I think you're going to want to come to see this!"

Quickly, Charlie put the book that she was in the middle of searching through back on the shelf and stepped over to read the book Kire was holding in his hands over his shoulder. She heard the sound of running footsteps, and then in a matter of seconds, the rest of the Quintets had reached them, and they, too, were staring over Kire's shoulder at the book, all of them crowding around it to read what was inside.

Charlie tried to focus on what it was she saw on the pages of the book, but the sound of breathing over her shoulder distracted her. How could she hear such a thing? No one was over her shoulder. They were all crowding beside her.

It sounded as if somebody was struggling to get a breath in. And she knew she wasn't the only one who heard it when everybody in the group of Unlikely Defenders turned around and saw who was behind them.

It was the man from the room. The one with the frosted eyes. He was suddenly standing behind them, his eyes staring into all of theirs. Charlie gasped. Amberly shrieked. Traced muttered, "Whoa." Kire and Kaos were silent. Charlie hadn't even known this guy could walk, let alone that he could *see*.

But then she realized he could also do something else.

His frosted eyes. They no longer looked frosty. Instead, they were glowing—they were glowing a brilliant cobalt blue.

"Sir?" Kire tried. "Are you okay?"

"When did he get here?" Kaos muttered.

The man still made noises as if he was struggling to get a breath in. And as the Quintets stared at him in fear, he muttered the first words they had ever heard him speak. They were just two words. Two *simple* words. But they had a great effect on Charlie and sent a shudder rippling all the way down her spine. The words the man muttered in a horse, almost ghost-like sounding voice, with his glowing blue eyes still staring at them intensely, were, "He's coming."

AUTHOR'S NOTE

Dear Beloved Reader,

Thank you so much for continuing the journey with The Unlikely Defenders from Charlie Rose's point of view!]I truly hope that you enjoyed The Unfavorable Heroes. If you did, I would be so grateful if you would consider leaving a review. Reviews help other readers find my work, so a review is very valuable to me.

The next book in the series will feature Amberly McHenry, and is called The Unlucky Guardians. Also feel free to check out my other books!

https://swiy.co/UnlikelyDefenders

Click here to visit my website and interact with me on social media. There's awesome merch available for each of my series. Also, make sure to sign up for my mailing list to be the first to know about new releases and special happenings such as previews and give-a-ways!

I love getting feedback from my readers, and if you'd like to stay in touch (or discuss my books), join me over at the Lily Skyy Readers' Group. I'd also love to connect with you on Instagram, TikTok, and Twitter! Feel free to reach out to me directly via email at social@lilyskyy.com.

Again, I thank you for reading, and I can't wait to join you on the next adventure!

Sincerely,

Lily Skyy